DECKER

TOREY HOPE: THE LATER YEARS

A.D. ELLIS

Decker

Torey Hope:
The Later Years

A.D. Ellis
www.facebook.com/adellisauthor

Copyright © 2015

By A.D. Ellis

Updated Cover by
A.D. Ellis 2019

A NOTE FROM THE AUTHOR

The book you are reading wasn't even an idea in my head when I started writing my first book. A Torey Hope Novel Series is my first series and the idea for Torey Hope: The Later Years came along when I was about to publish the final book in the first series.

Torey Hope is a small fictional town in Illinois. The series revolves around the main families of The Morgans, The Deckers, The Jordans, and The Martins. I'm including a family tree and short narrative to help you navigate these families if you're new to Torey Hope.

I've also included a little background on The Center+ so that you can get a feel for where it began and what it's grown into.

Also, this book has some suspenseful moments, but it wasn't written to be a mystery. As a writer, I knew the secrets going in, but I also assumed that most readers would figure out the secrets long before the characters did. So, don't be disappointed if you figure the secrets out, just enjoy the story and take the suspenseful moments for what they are.

I hope you'll take a moment to find me on social media and connect with me; I love hearing from readers. Don't forget, authors rely on reader reviews so please leave one when you finish reading.

Facebook

Amazon

Website

THANK YOU FOR READING!

A.D. Ellis

FAMILY TREE

For those who like a little narrative along with a family tree. Here are the families of Torey Hope. Meet the Morgans, the Jordans, the Deckers, and the Martins.

John and Cindy Morgan have twin boys Nate and Nicky Morgan.

Nicky Morgan married Carly Malone and had children Zachary Malone Morgan and Alyson Elizabeth Morgan.

Nate Morgan married Libby Decker and had children Abigail Emerson Morgan and twins Decker Nathaniel and Sawyer Nicholas Morgan.

Libby Decker is sister to **Audrey Decker**, both are daughters of **Captain Robert Decker** and the late **Lois Decker**. Robert later married **Janie**.

Audrey Decker married **Jeremiah Jordan**. Jeremiah had a son, **Beckett**, from a previous marriage. Jeremiah and Audrey had **Megan Elise Jordan** and **Kendrick Robert Jordan**.

Jeremiah is the son of **Jack and Judy Jordan**.

Captain Robert Decker had an estranged brother, Richard who was married to Corrine and they had a daughter named **Josie**. Josie married Jeremiah Jordan's best friend, **Kyle Martin** and they had children **Zoey Belle Martin** and **Asher Jeremiah Jordan**.

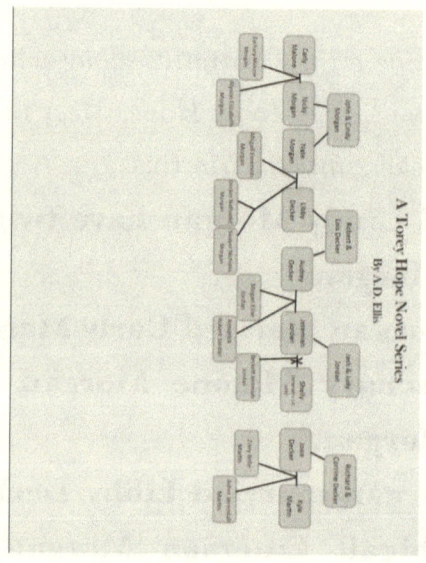

THE CENTER+

(for those of you who haven't been with The Center from the beginning)

The Center+ started out much smaller in the first Torey Hope Series (bit.ly/ToreyHopeAmazon). This was the place where Cindy Morgan worked as a receptionist and her son, Nicky, attended classes. Due to Nicky's developmental disabilities, The Center was a better fit for his needs. He took classes there instead of going to the local high school with his twin brother, Nate.

Nicky later got a job at The Center where he met Carly Malone (she was taking over the media specialist position for Libby Decker while Libby and Nate had their first child, Abigail Emerson; Nate and Libby later had Decker and Sawyer, the twins in this book). Nicky and Carly later married and had Zach and Aly.

Cindy and John Morgan were involved heavily in The Center because of Nicky. Libby later became involved and Nate naturally helped her out as needed. Over the years, other family members helped with monetary donations and time/services. When the younger generation (Nate and Libby's twins, Decker and Sawyer; Nicky and Carly's son, Zach; Jeremiah and Audrey's son, Kendrick) were growing up, and spending much of their time at The Center along with their cousins and siblings, they began to dream and envision more classes, added facilities, and bigger programs for The Center.

These four men, Decker, Sawyer, Zach, and Kendrick headed out of Torey Hope for college, but they had every intention of returning to take over The Center and making it bigger and better (and later renaming it The Center+).

The Center+ offers art classes, fitness classes, talk therapy sessions, cooking/baking courses, health/safety courses, extracurricular activities, sports teams, life skills classes, trade skills, and various other games/activities.

PROLOGUE

*F*irst day of Kindergarten

Beckett Jordan gathered his younger brother and cousins around. "You guys are starting a new adventure, and it's going to be great. You are brothers and cousins which means you'll always have best friends to turn to. Be there for each other, support each other, have fun, learn a lot, and enjoy this journey."

Always wise beyond his years, Beckett nodded sagely to the small boys staring at him intently with wide, solemn eyes. Decker Morgan nodded his head with a serious glint in his eye. His twin brother, Sawyer, took a deep breath as if to settle his nerves. Zach Morgan smiled playfully, eager for his first day of school to begin. Kendrick Jordan's eyes lit up with anticipation and his usual adventurous spirit.

These boys had spent their entire five years of life

together. They had sisters and girl cousins among them, but the four male cousins were just months apart in age and had grown up more as brothers and best friends than just cousins. They appreciated their wise, older cousin, Beckett, imparting his advice as they looked forward to this big step ahead of them.

Thirteen years later

Beckett Jordan once again gathered his younger brother and cousins around. "Well, guys, you made it through high school. It's not been an easy road for some of you, but you've stuck together just like brothers and cousins and best friends should. College is going to be a new journey and a new set of challenges. I want you all to promise me that you'll continue to stick together and support each other. I hope you all know how proud our family is of all of you. We are really going to miss you while you're gone; we'll be looking forward to seeing you on breaks. Have fun, be safe, and never forget where you came from."

The four high school graduates nodded at their cousin and clapped him on the back. High school had brought a lot of challenges to the Morgan/Jordan boys, but they had stuck with each other and supported each other through it all. Years ago the boys had decided they would attend the same college and return to Torey Hope to help expand The Center that so many of their family members were involved with. Decker Morgan, always the serious, by-the-book one, was chomping at the bit to get settled at college and get some classes under his belt; but he knew his brother and cousins wanted to enjoy their summer of freedom, so he settled for taking some online classes.

Four years later

Four years of classes, homework, studying, tests, jobs, dating, parties, and fun had finally passed and the Morgan/Jordan boys were heading back to Torey Hope: back to their roots, back to their families, back to where they felt the most at peace and planned to settle down.

1

"So, what exactly are you saying here, Decker?" Angela Ford spoke in a way that made it obvious that she was not on board with Decker Morgan's plans for their future.

"Angela, just listen. We've had three years together, but college is over and we aren't heading in the same directions with our lives. You've got big plans in the city; you are starting at one of the biggest companies around. But I've got big plans too; you know that the guys and I have planned on going back to Torey Hope and expanding The Center. This has been our plan since before our first day in college, and we've never wavered from it. I'm not saying that we don't have a future together. Actually, I'm not sure there's a girl more perfect for me; you and I are on the same wavelength most of the time. We are both motivated, in control, and driven by success. But, for now, I think we need to just go our separate ways." Decker paused a moment and felt irritated at his soon-to-be ex-girlfriend's pseudo pouty face; he wasn't impressed.

"Are you really telling me that you think you're going to have time for a long distance relationship once you step into your new job?" He cocked a dark eyebrow and waited on Angela to almost imperceptibly shake her head 'no.'

"Right, you're going to be too busy climbing the ladders and jumping hoops and impressing the shit out of your new bosses. Just like I'm going to be too busy managing the new expansion of The Center; you know I'm going to have to keep my brother and cousins in line like usual. Plus, I'll be back home with family I've missed for four years. I'm just being realistic and honest here; I know for a fact that I'm not going to have time for a relationship."

A look of anger flashed in her eyes and Decker wondered if maybe Angela Ford wasn't as perfect of a match for him as he'd once thought. They had never had heat or romance, but they had common goals and the same drive to succeed.

True, his brother and cousins thought they were a poor match. "Dude, I bet you and Angela sync your phone schedules so that you can schedule in sex." Kendrick Jordan, the "baby" of the bunch by a few months, had teased Decker just the night before. "'Oh, yeah, Decker! Give it to me baby! Harder, Decker! Faster! No, seriously, faster! We've got a meeting with a potential business partner in an hour, let's get this finished'."

Kendrick enjoyed trying to ruffle Decker's feathers and found that it was very easy to do most of the time. Decker was a straight-laced, organized, in control type of guy. There was no gray area with him, things were either black or white. Rules were made to maintain order and control. Kendrick, along with Decker's other cousin, Zach Morgan, felt that rules were made to be broken or at least bent on occasion.

Decker had rolled his eyes at Kendrick's impression of his and Angela's sex life, but deep down he realized that it stung a bit because it hit a little too close to home. It wasn't that sex wasn't good, but he couldn't say he'd felt the earth move when they were together. He'd been with a couple other girls in high school and a few in college before he started dating Angela. The sex was good; he was a guy, was any sex ever bad? But, he'd always had to force himself to concentrate on the task at hand so that his mind didn't wander to other, more pressing items on his agenda.

"So, let me get this straight. You're breaking up with me? We've spent the last three years building a solid relationship and you're going to break up with me on the night before we head back to our hometowns? Wow, Decker, we HAVE always been on the same wavelength, but you just lost me on this one. I thought we had something here; we're so good together, baby."

Decker had to fight the urge to wince at Angela's attempt to sweet talk him; her calling him "baby" was like Cruella Deville speaking baby-talk to a toddler, it just didn't work.

Taking a deep breath and trying to keep the annoyance out of his voice, Decker spoke firmly and with finality. "Angela, I've made my decision; this is what I feel I need right now. My time and energy and loyalties lie with my family, always; I need to be able to pour 100% into these next several months of building The Center to what the guys and I have always dreamed it could be. Once you and I are both a little more settled, we can revisit where things are with us. But, for now, I want us to part as friends; I have no plans on dating, but if you find yourself with the time and desire to date, go for it." He thought his words were diplomatically delivered and made complete sense.

Angela obviously didn't agree if the slap to his face was any indication. "Screw you, Decker! I didn't put three years' worth of effort into building this relationship only to have you throw it away because of some childhood dream between brothers and cousins. Go build your little 'play-scape,' but don't come crawling back to me when you realize that you need me in your life." She turned on her heel and stomped away.

Having never seen the ugly, dramatic side of Angela, Decker let out a deep breath and headed toward his bedroom in the apartment he shared with his twin, Sawyer, and his cousins, Zach and Kendrick. Thinking of the three men he considered his best friends, he wondered where the hell they had disappeared to; they had been playing video games when Angela arrived. He reached up to rub his still stinging cheek and heard a snort of laughter from behind him. Turning slowly, taking a deep breath to steel himself for the onslaught of joking that he knew was headed his way, he found them coming out from their hiding places where they had apparently witnessed the whole unexpectedly messy breakup.

From years of experience with his brother and cousins, he knew better than to interrupt their laughing and teasing; letting them get it out of their systems while they made fools of themselves was the quickest and easiest way to move on from their shenanigans.

"Bro, are you okay? She landed a solid one to your face there, man!" Sawyer, his younger brother by 2 minutes, attempted to look concerned and draped an arm around his shoulder.

"Yeah, man, I'm fine; I didn't realize she'd be so upset about the breakup." Decker rolled his eyes as Zach and Kendrick held each other and guffawed until tears ran down their cheeks.

"Dude! If that scene right there didn't just prove that you and Angela were NOT a match made in heaven, I don't know what will! That girl might as well have told you she wanted a ring on her finger before allowing us to pack up and head back to Torey Hope. We've told you before, just because she's your little business-minded equal does NOT mean that she's the girl for you. I've seen more chemistry between you and your sister than I ever saw between you and Angela. Let her go, man; good riddance I say." Kendrick sobered for a moment as he spoke. Then, eyeing the ever-reddening hand print on his cousin's cheek, he doubled over in another fit of laughter.

"Man, Kendrick's right; that girl was not the one for you. I'm not sure the type of girl who will be 'it' for you, but you need to breathe a sigh of relief that Angela is out of the picture now. We've got a lot of work ahead of us in Torey Hope, but we'll hook you up with some of the local girls. Well, the local girls who don't want us at least. Maybe you can get laid by someone who doesn't check her day planner to clear a slot for sex." Zach, ever the jokester, seemed to be genuinely concerned for his cousin.

Decker allowed the three to finish their laughter and wipe their tears before speaking. "Okay, so maybe you've all been right these last three years. I thought Angela and I were a good fit because we had the same goals and business sense. I don't plan on dating for the next several months since we've got so much work to do on the expansion, so it's probably good to make a clean break for it now. I'm glad you guys got such an entertaining show on our last night here." Decker smirked at his best friends and knew that they loved him and would support him with no questions asked, just as he would them. "Come on, let's finish packing; I want to hit the road early tomorrow."

THE NEXT MORNING, the four friends stood outside of the apartment they had called home for the last four years. There had been both good and bad times in those four years. But, a day's drive was all that stood between them and their futures; loading up the last of their belongings in the U-Haul, they piled into Zach's dark red Ford F-150 Raptor. They would each drive about three hours and planned to reach home right about dinner time. The other three vehicles had been driven home by family members after graduation the past weekend.

The young men had enjoyed their time away; they had grown and learned and spread their wings. But, deep in their hearts, home had always been and would always be Torey Hope; they smiled to each other and felt a peace within as the truck rumbled to life. "The boys" were heading home.

2

"*D*amn, how can they sleep like that? Talk about a major crick in the neck. Hey, Kendrick is drooling, hand me your phone." Silencing the phone, Sawyer turned around in his seat and snapped a quick picture of his cousin sleeping with his mouth gaping open. "Sweet revenge for when the time is right," he laughed as he handed the phone back to his brother and Decker couldn't help but chuckle a little at the thought of Kendrick's reaction to that picture.

"We'll stop in about forty-five minutes to get gas and stretch; Kendrick can take over the driving then. Man, I'm so glad we're almost there; my ass is numb and I'm starving. Part of me wants to grab a snack, but you know the grandmas will have gone all out with the taco bar for supper and I definitely want to have room for that." Decker rubbed his stomach and laughed. He worked out religiously so he knew he'd work off the big meal and he planned to take advantage of their first home cooked meal in a while.

"Nah, man, I asked Grandma Judy to have a baked potato bar for our first night home. Damn, you know how they pull out all the stops on toppings; I plan on putting so many toppings on that it will be hard to find my actual potato." Sawyer, with the same workout regimen and lucky genes as his brother, had no worries about eating a big meal; he'd burn it off within one workout tomorrow.

"You both need to shove it, Grandma Cindy asked me what I wanted for our homecoming meal and I told her it would be fun to make pizzas like we used to do when we were kids. Remember we'd all get a small pizza crust to make just the way we wanted it? She laughed when I told her and said, 'I doubt those little crusts would fill you up now, but I bet we can figure out something'. So, sorry 'bout 'cha, it's pizza night." Zach had awakened and joined in the conversation. Kendrick stirred next to him.

"What the hell are you all talking about? And why so loud? How about a little respect for a guy trying to get some beauty sleep?" Kendrick grinned, knowing that he had been blessed by both of his parents' good looks and needed no rest to improve his attractiveness. "Besides, I told the grandmas that I wanted a whole 'Surf and Turf' spread. Steak, chicken, shrimp, lobster, salmon. Damn, I can almost taste it now."

A quick stop for gas, drinks, restroom, and a little

stretching brought them to the last leg of their journey. The excitement was thick in the truck. True, the guys had spent their whole lives together and the last four years had been no different, but they were all anxious to be back with family and start their new endeavor.

To pass the time, they spoke of their plans. Decker, ever the task-master and planner, had insisted from day one at college that each of them get the best job they could get that would still allow them time to study and do their best. He didn't force the others, but he highly suggested and they grudgingly agreed, to build up their savings accounts. Over the four years, the four of them had saved a hefty sum of money. Decker had advised them in solid investments and they'd worked together to set up spending accounts. Thanks to him, they were coming back home with a good amount of money to start their new lives.

"Okay, so we'll stay with family the next couple nights. Then on the weekend we can move into the house. Monday we start work, so be ready boys. Be ready." Decker was a mixture of stern and giddy over the next step in their plans.

As young boys, they had talked endlessly of their plans to expand The Center where many of their family members worked or contributed time and/or money. Before the boys were born, the twins' mother, Libby Decker Morgan, began working at The Center as the media specialist. Later, Zach's father, Nicky Morgan, took a job at The Center where he had spent most of his youth because his mom, their Grandma Cindy Morgan, had worked there as an administrative assistant. Zach's mom, Carly, met his dad at The Center. Over the years more family became involved in the unique programs and setting of The Center and the ideas for making it even bigger and better grew in the minds of the boys.

Now, the Morgan, Jordan, Decker, and Martin families were sole owners of The Center. Some family members were more silent partners while some were more active; everyone, no matter their monetary involvement, spent many hours keeping The Center running and functioning at its best. The family had been drawing up expansion plans involving the boys for several years and it was time for those plans to come to fruition.

Decker graduated top of his class with a degree in business management. He would be the active manager of The Center. His parents were the CEOs and his Aunt Audrey and Uncle Jeremiah were the COOs; this was on paper only, but having actual positions named was helpful in any business. One of the first changes Decker had to convince them of was the name change. He had proposed that they keep The Center but add a plus sign to show the addition of more programs. The board had offered unanimous approval of The Center+. Decker's first order of business was to hire an assistant manager. He had a pile of resumes and a list of numbers to call for interviews starting Monday.

Sawyer graduated as an Art major. He had interests and talents in several types of art, including sculpting, music, dance, and graphic design. Between him and his mom's cousins, Josie and Kyle Martin, they were starting a much more extensive art program at The Center+. Sawyer had lamented the fact that The Center only had a small art program over the years and he was chomping at the bit to get the new courses set up and started.

Zach had graduated with a degree in business and marketing. The guy could sell ice to an Eskimo; he was a charmer, but the appeal of Zach was that he was genuine and honest. All of the expansions at The Center+ were possible because of their family's financial backing, Decker's sound business plan and investments, and Zach's task of advertising and bringing in new funding. Along with that undertaking, Zach had offered to help teach several fitness classes. Their cousin, Zoey Martin, had graduated early from high school and was taking classes at the local college to become a personal trainer. She was going to teach several fitness classes too, but Zach knew there would be times when her classes conflicted with teaching. Zoey and Zach weren't technically related, but they had always been super close; she was who Zach had missed the most during his four years away.

Kendrick, the all-around sport jock, had graduated with a degree in recreational sports management. He had big plans for a huge advancement of The Center+'s whole sports program. His part would probably take the longest to realize success; it would take a few years at least for him to build up the reputation of solid, quality sports programs and teams. But, Kendrick was a patient man; he would wait and slowly make his teams some of the best around. He had plans for his sports program to be a feeder for local high school and college teams.

"Alright, men, let's review the rules of our new place before we get home." Decker might as well have written a handbook; he probably would have if he didn't know the others would have tossed them in the trash within five minutes.

"Dude, how many times do we have to listen to this? We survived four years living together and eighteen years growing up together before that; I'm pretty sure we can live together peacefully now that we're back home." Kendrick rolled his eyes as Zach chuckled silently and shook his head.

"I know, I know, but I just want to move into our new place with a new slate. First, we'll continue our spending budget; if we find we need to revise it we can take a look at it. We'll stick to our once a week grocery trip; if you need something, add it to the list and then whoever goes to the store can get everything needed. Second, it makes the most sense to continue washing clothes together. We'll set up a basket system to make it easy. We all know how to do laundry, so it shouldn't be a problem. If you take a load out of the dryer, try to be respectful and at least lay shirts and pants out nicely for the person they belong to. I know none of us likes to iron.

Dishes should be done once a day, bathrooms cleaned once a week, trash taken out when it's full. We'll do vacuuming and dusting once a week. Once The Center+ is up and running maybe we can look into hiring a housekeeper, but until then it's on us to make sure our place represents us as the professionals we are. Parking shouldn't be a problem, I arranged for all four of us to get a covered spot. We'll get internet and cable set up soon. The final thing is the spare rooms; this is an older house as you know. It was actually built to be a double, but the last owner remodeled it to be a single dwelling. We'll each have our own room and there are two spare rooms along with a den and an office. The basement is perfect for Sawyer's art stuff; I think we can also set it up for some workout gear. I think Zach and I can share the office space as needed and the den can be set up for video games."

Listening to him talk about their new house had the other three looking forward to seeing it and getting moved in; however, they knew his final comment wasn't done.

"The spare rooms will be perfect for when we have people over. I don't want us to be a place for parties or for people who drink too much to crash; we're now business owners and professionals in town, we need to carry ourselves as such. I thought we'd keep the spare rooms set up for our siblings or cousins. Who knows, we may have nieces and nephews in a few years and they may want to have sleep overs with their uncles when they are old enough. I doubt Abby or Megan or Beckett will be spending the night much since they have lives of their own." Decker spoke of his own sister and Kendrick's siblings. "But Zoey will probably hang out at our place a lot since Zach is back home and we all know that if Zoey is around then Aly won't be far behind." Zoey wasn't blood related, but Aly was Zach's little sister. "I think Asher will buddy up with us now that we're back home. He's the one I feel like we know the least. He was only ten when we left, I'm looking forward to getting to know him." Asher was Zoey's younger brother. "My last word on the subject is that we all," he gave a pointed look at Kendrick, "need to remember that we are back home, this is where our futures are, and we have impressionable kids watching our every move. We have to act like grownups, we aren't college students anymore."

At his final words, Kendrick groaned and grumbled, "Do grownups at least get to have sex? Because I'm planning on having sex and a lot of it. I'll hang a sock on my door so the youth don't see something they aren't ready to see." He paused for a moment and laughed. "Can you imagine Kyle and Josie if they had to explain things to Asher if he found me, ass in the air, puttin' it to some fine chick?" He chuckled again.

Zach, good-natured as always, just smiled and shook his head, "Yes, Mother, we'll be on our best behavior. Hear that Sawyer? No girls in your bed when the youth is around." Sawyer looked uneasy, but smirked at his cousin's comment.

In a not so subtle attempt to change the subject, Sawyer

shifted in his seat. "Aw, man, look; they hung a banner out for us."

All four turned to look out the windows of the truck; the words WELCOME HOME blurred slightly in four sets of eyes as they blinked back tears.

3

The homecoming was located at John and Cindy Morgan's house. A large banner was strung between the bannisters on the front porch and every member of their family was on the porch, ready to welcome them home.

The boys didn't miss the hands over their mothers' mouths, the tears in their eyes, or the way their father's hugged their wives close to comfort them during such an emotional time. Kendrick put the truck into park and the men drew in deep breaths.

"This is what we've wanted since before we left for college; this is our dream. Beckett told us a long time ago that we were cousins, siblings and best friends and that we had to support each other. We've done that and it won't ever stop. I love you all. Now, let's go hug our mommas." Decker clapped each of them on the shoulder and they piled out of the truck.

Unable to wait any longer, Libby, Audrey, and Carly all rushed down the front steps and caught their boys up in hugs and tears. Each mother, as only mothers can do, wrapped arms around her son or sons; if coming home hadn't felt right already, it sure did in that moment.

Nate joined Libby and grabbed each son up in his arms. "Decker, Sawyer, it's good to see you back home. It's been a long four years, but knowing you were coming back made it a little easier." Abby Morgan, the twins' older sister joined them in hugs.

"Hey, twerps, it's good to see you." She smiled as she spoke and both boys ruffled her hair, knowing she hated it. She may have been a few years older, but they were now much taller and broader than her.

"Ah, Abby, it's going to be so good tormenting you again. That's one of the things we've missed the most." Sawyer laughed at his sister's crinkled nose.

"Yeah, well, it's a good thing that none of us are living at home anymore. I don't know if we'd survive." Abby gave both brothers a quick punch to the gut and laughed as they feigned pain.

Next to that scene, Audrey had not let go of Kendrick. It was unusual for her to be at a loss for words, but the tears and lump in her throat had her struggling. Jeremiah wrapped his arms around both his wife and his son. Kendrick's older brother and sister, Beckett and Megan, joined the hug and they all hung on for several moments. Kendrick's past had some dark moments and had threatened to take him from them; the five of them knew what a blessing it was to have them all back home and together.

"Hey, momma, think you'll ever be able to let go? I mean, I know you love me more than Megan and Beck, but maybe you should try to hide your favoritism of me since they are right here." Kendrick broke through the emotional moment with his exaggerated whisper and wink at his siblings. Laughter erupted and tears were dried.

Carly had stepped aside to let her husband engulf Zach in a bear hug that shook with sobbing tears. Nicky Morgan, never one to hide emotions, spoke to his son as he pulled Carly back into the embrace. "Zach, I missed you. I know you're my son, but you're also my friend and I missed having you here to talk to and hang out with. I'm really glad you're home. Now I have both of my babies back home with me." He reached out for Zach's younger sister Alyson. "Aly, I don't think you can go to college, I'm not sure I can live through you being gone that long."

Aly smiled and kissed her father's cheek, "It's okay, Daddy, I don't plan on going very far from Torey Hope. I'll be able to visit more often than Zach."

Nicky seemed satisfied with that answer for the time being. Carly hugged him to her and comforted him as he calmed from the emotional reunion.

By the time the parents and siblings had gotten their hugs done, the rest of the family couldn't be held back any longer. All three sets of grandparents, along with Josie, Kyle, Zoey, and Asher Martin, crowded around to gather the boys into their arms.

A squeal of delight escaped Zoey as she ran toward Zach. Raised as cousins, but not blood related, Zach and Zoey had always had a close relationship. He was about five-years-old when Zoey was born and he took to her right away. The boy had loved his own baby sister, but he was attached to Zoey at the hip even before she could walk. Picking her up around the waist and swinging her around, he hugged her close. "Zoey Belle, girl, I've missed you so much." She buried her head in his neck and breathed deep.

"Zach, you have no idea how much I've missed you. I'm so glad you're home, I need you here with me. We can talk about it more later, but I'm just really glad to have you here again." Zach raised a questioning eyebrow at her words, but more welcomes and hugs were being given and the subject got dropped for a while.

Grandma Cindy, Grandma Judy, and Grandma Janie clapped their hands and announced it was time for dinner. Four voices cheered all at once and raised a fist in victory, "Taco bar!" "Baked potato bar!" "Pizza!" "Steak and shrimp!" At the boys' outburst, the grandmas laughed and raised their own fists in the same motion, "Chinese!"

Their newly returned grandsons stopped short and all four grunted out, "Huh?"

"Well, boys, you all four asked for something different. It seemed crazy to fix all four meals for one dinner; we decided Chinese would allow us to visit without having to fix food or do much clean up. No worries though, we're having your requested meals over the next four dinners; make sure you're here each night because we aren't telling you which night is your meal request." Janie Decker had married their grandfather Captain Decker when Kendrick and the twins were about six-years-old, and she had adopted all four into her heart as her grandchildren immediately; Janie never even mentioned that not a single one of them was blood related to her. She smiled at them all now as she told of dinner plans.

Shrugs of acceptance were given, and the entire clan trekked up the porch steps to begin their first evening of being back together. All was right in Torey Hope.

4

The guys had spent two nights at their parents' or grandparents' homes and then the whole family helped them get moved into their new house. Zoey and Aly claimed one spare room as their own; Asher, like any hormonal teenager trying to be tough and cool, had tried his best to hide his grin when he was offered the use of the other spare bedroom anytime he wanted to stay over, as long as Kyle and Josie were okay with it.

After four nights of fabulous dinners between four separate homes, the guys had headed to their house on Sunday night to hit the sack early in preparation for their first big day at The Center+.

"Rise and shine, jackass!" Kendrick laughed and snapped a photo of Zach with massive bedhead and a drool pool. "Oh, look at how pretty you are."

"Shut the hell up, man. Damn, can't a guy wake up peacefully around here?" Zach, the ever good-natured one of the crew, wasn't a morning person.

"Come on, we need to get a workout done and get to The Center+. I'll make you some coffee, pansy. Get your ass out of bed." Kendrick yanked the blankets off the bed and laughed at the obscenities Zach let fly. It was so easy to piss Zach off in the mornings.

With a cup of piping hot coffee in his hand, nothing but boxers on, and sexy messed up hair, Kendrick was model perfect leaning against the kitchen counter. Knowing he'd already pissed one cousin off, he decided to try for two more when Decker and Sawyer stumbled into the kitchen. Of the four men, Kendrick was the most broody and dark, but in the mornings he was like a little bluebird of happiness compared to his three cousins who were pissed off toddlers until they got coffee and a shot of adrenaline from a good workout.

"Well, well, well, if it isn't BDSM. Good morning, boys." Kendrick smirked at the grumpy looks from the twins. BDSM was something Kendrick had started in college their freshman year. He'd been dating, no, dating was the wrong word, he'd been sleeping with a girl who had quite the kinky side. He'd heard of BDSM but this girl had creeped him out with all the whips and chains. Kendrick controlled everything in the bedroom, but he didn't need whips and chains and collars to do it. One day, shortly after letting the girl know it was over, he'd been doodling BDSM on a piece of paper while he waited for his cousins between classes. "**B**rothers **D**ecker & **S**awyer **M**organ" had popped into his head; BDSM, a new nickname he knew would piss them off.

"Grow up, jackass." Sawyer growled as he stalked to the coffee pot.

"What's wrong, Sawyer? Do you need to get kinky? Maybe a good solid lay would turn that frown upside down." Kendrick enjoyed his time of merriment, knowing that once the other three got some caffeine, he'd be back to being the moody one.

"That nickname is so childish, Kendrick. You better hope none of the moms or grandmas ever hears that and asks for an explanation. You want to explain BDSM to the grandmas? Maybe tell all our moms what that girl wanted you to do to her with those whips and chains?" Decker nodded smugly, satisfied when he'd seen Kendrick's face pale a bit at the thought of sharing any of the nickname joke with the older females in the family.

They headed to The Center+ with plans of getting a good solid hour and a half to work out before showering and preparing for their first day. Ninety minutes later, after they had run two miles and done a good hour of strength training, they took quick showers and dressed for their day. Zach was in dressy casual as he had meetings with potential advertisers and funding partners; he had a clean set of workout clothes for when he helped Zoey with a kickboxing class. Kendrick was in a pair of basketball shorts and simple t-shirt as he planned on working with some of the teams right off; a quick change of clothes was in his locker in case he got the chance to meet up with any of the local coaches as time allowed. Sawyer, dressed in jeans and a t-shirt, was headed to the art supply store with Josie and Kyle so that they could get the basic supplies updated and get a good start on some supplies for the new art courses; later he would meet up with Luke Hamilton who had expressed interest in teaching some martial arts classes. Decker, perfectly at home in his dark gray suit and tie, looked ever the business professional. While the other men set off for their individual plans and responsibilities, Decker headed straight to his office. His fingers itched to riffle through the resumes and start making phone calls; he was ready to get an assistant manager on board.

FOUR HOURS LATER, Decker pinched the bridge of his nose feeling an annoyed headache coming on. A couple of the resumes had looked promising, but those applicants had already taken positions elsewhere. The other phone conversations he'd had as a first round of interviews in hopes of weeding out those who were not a good match had been abysmal. Decker had planned on getting three or four solid applicants lined up that day and start the more intense interview process through the rest of the week; he wanted an assistant manager to start the following week. Decker did not handle it well when his plans didn't go as expected.

"Hey, boss man, how's it going?" It made Decker smile when his Uncle Nicky called him "boss man;" in Nicky's mind, even though Decker was his younger nephew, he was still his boss.

"Well, Uncle Nicky, it's actually not going as well as I had hoped." At Nicky's look of concern, Decker motioned him to have a seat.

"What's wrong? Do you not want to work at The Center+? Do you need to fire someone?" Nicky's genuine questions brought a little peace to Decker, and he felt his shoulders relax from the tension of the last four hours.

"No, nothing like that. I just need to get an assistant manager hired and the people who want the job just don't have the right qualifications; I need someone I can speak to easily, someone who has the same vision as me, someone I can trust. The people I've been talking to today just don't fit the bill." Decker sighed heavily; but talking about the problem had helped him put it into perspective a bit.

"Well, boss man, I know you'll get it figured out. Ever since you were a little boy you were always able to solve tough problems; you have a lot of drive and determination. Keep looking; you never know, the next one may be the absolute perfect person. I'll let you make your phone calls." Nicky stood to leave the office but stopped and turned back around. "Decker? I want you all to know just how happy we are that you're all back home; it just didn't seem like Torey Hope without you all here. We love you." Nicky and Decker smiled at each other, and Decker took a deep breath before picking up the phone to call the next applicant.

"Hello, this is Decker Morgan at The Center+. I'm calling for Ms. Katherine Turner in regards to her recent resume and job application." Decker held the phone away from his ear as he heard an earsplitting blare coming through the line.

"Oh my God! I'm so sorry! Hold on please Mr. Morgan! This is Katherine Turner....hang on just a second! Where's the damn broom?!" A cacophony came through the phone and Decker was tempted to hang up; if this was the way Ms. Turner conducted herself on the phone she was obviously not the one for the job.

"Shut up, damn it! Just shut up!" Her words were barely distinguishable over the shrill alarm-like noise. "There! I'm so sorry, Mr. Morgan. Mr. Morgan? Sir? Are you there? Please accept my apologies. I was helping my grandma bake cookies. I didn't realize that Grandma had accidentally turned the oven up to 500 and the timer to thirty-one minutes rather than thirteen minutes. Needless to say, our little cookies are now burnt offerings. On the bright side, we know her smoke detectors work." Katherine Turner spoke in an airy, breathless way that had Decker picturing her in a smoky kitchen, hair askew, with a broomstick to turn off the offending smoke detector.

"Well, Ms. Turner, you're the first applicant I've called who has provided so much entertainment in such a short amount of time. I trust that there's no danger to you or your grandmother?" Decker really couldn't explain why he felt the need to continue with this phone interview; the girl obviously wasn't management material, but he wanted to hear her answers to his questions because she had him feeling something he hadn't felt in a long time. Intrigued.

Forty-five minutes later, Decker hung up from the most enjoyable phone interview he'd ever conducted. Katherine Turner was not the typical uptight management applicant that he'd been speaking to; this woman was genuine, whip-smart, well-spoken, and on the same path as him. It amazed him just how much they had in common both personally and professionally. Before ending the call with her, Decker had done something he'd never planned on doing; he offered her the job over the phone, sight unseen, no further interview. She had accepted, and he was pumped to meet her in person the next day and get the paperwork filled out so that she could get to work right away.

Looking at the clock, he realized that it was late enough he could call it a day. There was really nothing else he needed to do right then. He texted his brother to see if Sawyer wanted to play some basketball before they headed home. As it turned out, Sawyer's meeting with the potential martial arts instructor had run over so he wasn't available; Zach, Kendrick, and Decker played a little game before their dads and uncle showed up. Nate Morgan, Jeremiah Jordan, and Kyle Martin had been playing ball together for years and gave the younger men a run for their money. In the end, all six men were sweaty but laughing. Decker paused as he left The Center+ on his way home. Yeah, it was good to be back.

"Unknown caller" flashed on his phone screen as he worked on some paperwork for Katherine Turner. Absent-mindedly he picked up the phone, "Decker Morgan."

"Hello, Mr. Morgan. I'm really sorry to call you at home in the evening, but you gave me your number and said I could call if I had any questions. I have to apologize, I think the whole cookie burning had me flustered today; I don't normally accept a job sight-unseen and without meeting my boss in person. I still plan on coming in tomorrow, but I was hoping to discuss the position with you a little more now that the smoke has cleared from both my head and my grandma's kitchen. That is, if you have a moment to speak to me." He admired her straightforwardness and knew she was just as knocked off-kilter as he was after their whirlwind phone interview earlier that day.

"I have time, Ms. Turner. Please, ask anything you'd like." Decker waved to Sawyer as his brother popped his head in the office to say hello. Plopping down on the couch, Decker stretched his 6'2" frame out and got comfortable.

"Well, I've been doing some research on The Center+, but I'd like to hear your description of it. Please." Katherine had a smile in her voice as she added the *please* to her request.

"The Center+ has been a part of my family's life since long before I was born. My Uncle Nicky attended school there and my Grandma Cindy worked there as an administrative assistant for several years. Uncle Nicky had finished schooling, but he attended several recreational programs even after high school and he met the new librarian, Libby Decker who later married my dad. Not long after, my Uncle Nicky met my Aunt Carly while they were both working there. When my brother and cousins and I were younger, we spent almost every spare second at The Center+, although it was just The Center in those days. We enjoyed all of the programs available and took full advantage of the recreational sports. We used to always talk about growing up, going to college, and coming back to Torey Hope to expand the programs; make The Center+ bigger and better than ever. That brings us to today; we are adding two new wings, several new programs, revamping and improving the sports program, and enlarging the arts program by leaps and bounds. My family owns The Center+ now, so we have the ability to grow the business as we've always dreamed." Decker paused in his description; on the other end of the phone Katherine was touched at the sense of pride the man had in his family's business.

Several minutes later, Katherine had asked as many questions as she could come up with and their conversation turned to more personal information. Decker learned that she had also recently graduated and returned to Torey Hope, her childhood home. She and her mother lived across town and her elderly grandmother lived with them. She had always planned to leave Torey Hope for college and thought she would move to the big city, but when her mom divorced and her grandmother moved in she took inventory of her life and her plans for her future and realized that Torey Hope was her heart, and she didn't want to leave.

Decker found himself lulled by the melodic lilt of her voice and nodded in agreement with her that finding a business management job in a small town was a definite challenge. He smiled when she shared her excitement over the potentially perfect job opportunity he had presented her with.

Through their conversation, Decker felt a definite connection to this girl; she shared his vision for success, she was a hard worker, she was self-motivated, she was a people person, she knew how to get a job done. She was perfect. Damn, the first girl he'd ever felt truly drawn to was going to be his assistant manager which meant that the connection he felt to her couldn't go anywhere. One of his hard and fast rules was that business and pleasure never mixed. Never.

"Well, Mr. Morgan, thanks for answering my questions. I feel a little bit more at ease over my spur-of-the-moment acceptance of this job. I just want to say one thing, please remember how perfect I am for the job when you meet me again tomorrow." Katherine had a smile in her voice as she spoke. "Goodnight, Mr. Morgan."

Meet her again? What the hell did that mean?

5

ecker's sleek, black Chevy Camaro pulled into his parking spot at The Center+ early the next morning. He'd wanted to get to work early to get his workout done so he had time to prepare for Ms. Turner's arrival. Decker felt a nervous buzz of energy throughout his body; he didn't do nervous.

He was surprised thirty minutes into his workout to see Sawyer walk into the room. He and his twin had always had a strong connection, and he immediately felt and saw tension in Sawyer.

"Mornin'. What's up, man?" Decker stopped the treadmill and waited for this brother to speak. The way Sawyer ran his hands through his hair and closed his eyes told Decker that his brother definitely had something on his mind.

"Let's do some weights, man." Sawyer spoke nothing else and headed to the weights.

Knowing he'd have to let Sawyer talk about whatever was bothering him on his own time, Decker followed. He felt a strong pull to his brother. Placing a hand on the other man's shoulder, he spoke, "Hey, you know you can talk to me or any of the guys, even Dad or our uncles or grandpas. We've always had the luxury of having a multitude of people to talk to. I want you to talk to me, but if you can't then talk to someone."

Decker was taken by surprise when Sawyer turned to him and embraced him. A shudder traveled through Sawyer's body and he held tight to his brother. Decker's heart plummeted at the thought of what could be bothering him. Sawyer had always been the more emotional and sensitive of the two; Decker kept his emotions closed up and controlled, Sawyer was more emotionally demonstrative and reacted more overtly to bothersome situations.

"Man, I just miss when things were simple. I miss the days when our biggest problems were if we were going to kiss our girlfriends or try to get to second base with them. Sometimes this grown-up thing just sucks; I'm not sure I'm ready for it." Sawyer stopped speaking and drew in a deep breath, "I just wish...." He stopped again. "Never mind. Spot me."

Decker allowed Sawyer to let the subject drop for the time being, knowing he'd talk about it when he was ready. His mind drifted. Sawyer speaking about kissing was sort of peculiar, he hadn't had many girlfriends. He had one serious girl-friend during high school and he'd dated a couple girls off and on through college. The breakup in high school had hit him hard, but he'd recovered fairly quickly. Sawyer never seemed interested in the girls he dated in college, more like he was just friends with them; Decker always felt like his twin was dating just to keep up appearances. Appearances of what? He wasn't sure.

Workout finished, mind slightly preoccupied with his brother, Decker finished his shower and dressed in a dark suit with a red tie. He had a penchant for unique ties; nothing gaudy, just different colors and patterns.

Walking past some of the construction for the new wing at The Center+, Decker acknowledged the early morning crew and continued to check his email. Head down, focused on his phone, he literally slammed into a body in front of him.

As his phone clattered to the ground, he immediately grabbed for the body in front of him, and he swallowed hard at the initial contact as his hands filled with smooth, soft, warm skin.

"Miss, I'm so sorry. Are you okay? I was in my own little world and didn't even pay attention to what I was doing." He spoke as he steadied her. His body reacted to her scent, her softness, her nearness. Breathing deeply to calm his heartbeat and clear his head of the thoughts he was having about the complete stranger he'd just run down in the hallway, he waited for the woman in front of him to gather herself and turn around. When she did, he lost his breath. Thick, gorgeous, dark brunette hair hung in shiny waves around a strikingly beautiful face; grayish green eyes behind long dark lashes stared at him and a pair of soft pink lips spoke as recognition slammed down around him. "Yes, Decker, I'm fine. No worries." The girl laughed and Decker grabbed her up in a hug. His body still reacted in ways it hadn't in, well, in ever, but now he stamped those feelings down permanently. This girl was off limits.

"Katie Smith? God, girl, I haven't seen you in years. Are you here to see Sawyer?" The beauty in front of him was the girl Sawyer dated for a while in high school; they didn't last, as most high school relationships don't, but Sawyer had been distraught when they broke up. He'd later admitted that they were better off as just friends. Decker knew the conflicted Sawyer would be happy to see his old friend.

Without letting Katie speak, he led her around the corner to Sawyer's studio. Finding that his brother wasn't there, Decker turned to her, "I'm sure he'll be right back. He'll be thrilled to see you." Looking at his watch, he realized his meeting was quickly approaching. "Listen, I have to get to a meeting. Set something up with Sawyer so we can all get together." Leaning in to kiss her cheek he ignored the increase in his already quickened pulse. She smelled like warm sunshine and his gut tightened.

Katie smiled and looked at her watch. "Actually, Decker, I have a meeting soon too. We'll all definitely have to get caught up soon. It was great seeing you. Please tell Sawyer I said hello."

Decker watched her walk away, berating himself for admiring the curves of the woman his brother had dated all those years ago. Just like his hard and fast rule of no relationships with workplace colleagues, he had a similar rule of no dating any girl his brother or cousins had dated first. He shook his head to clear it; sometimes rules were a pain in the ass, Katie Smith was a sight for sore eyes. If Sawyer and Katie rekindled something, Decker would need to get the thoughts of her backside out of his mind and quickly.

DECKER CHECKED through the paperwork he needed to go over with Katherine Turner and glanced at his watch. Ten minutes; he really hoped Ms. Turner wouldn't be late. Tardiness on her first day wouldn't set a good first impression, no matter how impressed he'd been with her over the phone.

A knock on his door brought him out of his thoughts. When The Center+ was running at full capacity, Decker would hire a secretary, but for now clients had to find his office and announce their arrival on their own.

He walked to the door and pulled it open. His mind filled with a strange and unfamiliar mixture of confusion, frustration, and lust. Katie Smith stood in front of him. Sticking her hand out, she spoke as she shook his hand; he attempted to decipher her words through the roar in his ears as he fought the heated feeling her hand in his brought to his body.

"Good morning, Mr. Morgan. Katherine Turner. Nice to meet you." She spoke professionally, but the glint of humor flickered across her face.

"Ms. Turner, it's a pleasure, but I'm sure you can understand my confusion." Decker attempted to keep it light, but he was feeling extremely aggravated at feeling duped. He didn't like feelings of confusion or being out of the loop.

"Mr. Morgan, may I speak freely?" At the nod of his head, she continued, "I knew that the position I was applying for was to be your assistant manager. I didn't reveal to you who I was because I wanted to be hired based on my skills and qualifications, not because I used to date your brother. Also, I feared you would possibly not hire me if you knew who I was; I know how you are with rules, and I figured you'd see this as some form of rule breaking." She spoke matter-of-factly. "My name is Turner now, I took my mom's maiden name after she divorced my father. I still go by Katie, but Katherine is more professional sounding for interviews and job applications. Remember when I asked you to keep in mind how perfect I am for the job? I hope you'll do that, Mr. Morgan."

Having this beautiful, well-spoken, intriguing girl call him Mr. Morgan was doing weird things in his mind; things that he'd never thought about before were now playing out in an overly active imagination he never knew he had.

"Please, Ms. Turner, call me Decker." They were going to be colleagues and, he hoped, business partners in this undertaking with The Center+ so he needed her to be comfortable with him.

"Fine, Decker, I'll call you by your first name if you promise to call me by mine. Katherine is acceptable, but I prefer Kate or Katie. Shall we try this again?" She smiled and stuck out her hand, and he felt his heart all but stop. What had he gotten himself into?

"Good morning, Decker." The jolt of awareness that traveled up his arm as her skin touched his was unnerving.

He pushed the unwanted feelings away and smirked at her, "Good morning, Kate. I'm glad to have you here. Come on in, we've got a lot to get done and then we'll get the day started. Do you want coffee?" His words came out just as he realized she held a coffee cup in her hand.

Katie smiled, "I'm tough in business, but my weakness is frou-frou coffee drinks. The stronger and sweeter the better." She tipped her cup at him before taking a drink.

He laughed and poured himself a cup of coffee, and they settled in to get the necessary paperwork done.

6

*A*fter a week of working with Kate, Decker knew a couple things. One, he had absolutely made the right decision in hiring her. She was a force to be reckoned with when it came to business; together they already made the perfect team, growing and perfecting The Center+.

Two, he had resigned himself to cold showers and gritted teeth. Never in his life had he felt such a strong physical attraction to a woman. He was drawn to her brilliant mind, her sparkling sense of humor, and bright personality; but his body ached with wanting her on a purely physical level as well.

The problem with admitting this little bit of knowledge was two-fold. First, he had a hard and fast rule that didn't allow for dating in the workplace. He knew dating could get messy and he didn't have room for messy in his business life.

Nothing would be worse than losing a girl he cared about who was also his kick-ass assistant manager. But he was really struggling with that rule after his time with Kate.

Second, Katie and Sawyer had dated in high school and he had another rule about not dating girls who had been involved with his cousins or brother. He was pretty sure that Sawyer and Katie hadn't gone very far physically, he and his brother had shared a lot of details on this subject and nothing had been mentioned about more than making out with Katie. It wasn't so much about not wanting "sloppy seconds," although, if he were honest, that *would* sort of turn him off if he thought the two had gone that far; it was more loyalty and respect for his brother and cousins.

As much as he hungered for this woman, he couldn't make a move on her. Could he? No....no. Well, at least not until he knew where Sawyer stood on things with Katie. But, even if Sawyer didn't have feelings left for her, that wouldn't change the fact that they worked together. Maybe that was a hurdle he could jump if it ever got to that point. He shook his head at the fact he was already questioning his rules; Kate made him think about things in a totally different way.

But he couldn't just ask Sawyer, "Hey man, remember when you were heartbroken over Katie Smith in high school? Well, I was wondering if you'd care if I made a move and asked her out." Yeah, that wasn't really a conversation he wanted to have.

Maybe he could get the two of them together and gauge

his brother's feelings toward Katie. Picking up his phone, he texted Sawyer.

Decker: *Hey, man. If I can get Kate to agree to it, would you like to meet up with us for drinks later? Old times' sake and all that.*

Decker shook his head; when had he become such a pussy? He and Sawyer had always had an open relationship, no secrets between them.

"Fuck this. I'm not going to hide this from him." Decker jerked his office door open and started towards the new art wing, knowing he'd find his brother there. Before he reached his destination, his phone binged with a new text.

Sawyer: *Sure, sounds good. I miss that girl; it would be great to hang out.*

"Fuck." Decker quickly changed his direction and headed back toward his office. He'd wait to see how drinks played out before he approached Sawyer. Even if Sawyer didn't have an interest in Katie, Decker didn't know if he could break his rule about no dating in the workplace.

"Hey, Kate, I was just talking to Sawyer. Want to meet up with us after work for some drinks? He's been wanting to get together and tonight seemed like the perfect time." Decker poked his head through their adjoining office door. He knew when he helped draw up the plans for the new addition that the adjoining offices for manager and assistant manager was a good idea; they worked together so much that it was perfect to have access to her office without having to walk down the hall.

"That sounds great. I wanted to get a quick workout in before leaving, but I can shower and change here and meet you wherever you're going." She smiled brightly at him as he tried to block out the image of her body sweaty from a workout climbing naked into a steam-filled shower. She gave a little foot tapping squeal as she spun around in her desk chair, "Decker! This will be so much fun! I haven't really been out much since returning to Torey Hope. You guys can be my first. Now, I better get this report finished if I'm going to work out and meet you guys on time. Just text me the time and location."

She turned back to her work as his brain continued to short circuit over her words. "Be my first" kept floating through his head; he knew the chances of her being a virgin were few and far between, but the thought of it filled him with a carnal lust that he'd never experienced before. He shook his head and retreated into his office, closing the door, before she saw just how much her words had affected his body.

Whether the girl was a virgin or not, he wanted her. Badly. But, with the excitement Sawyer had shown about their get together, he needed to prepare for the fact that his brother wasn't over her. Decker knew he'd have to step back and let the two of them rekindle their romance if push came to shove. Maybe he should also consider that Katie didn't feel the same about him as he'd been feeling about her.

"Damn it! This right here is the exact reason why dating and business don't mix." He shook his head, disgusted with himself that he'd let his lust for a beautiful woman break into his perfectly regimented business life.

7

Katie tried to calm her nerves and excitement as she parked in front of the bar where she was meeting the Morgan/Jordan boys. *Men* was the more accurate term. She'd grown up with them as boys, but she'd seen them all around The Center+ and they were most definitely *men* now. She gathered from Decker's text a bit ago that the planned get together between the three of them had expanded to include Zach and Kendrick as well. Katie was glad they'd all be there; she hadn't lied when she told Decker she hadn't been out much since returning to Torey Hope. She'd had friends when she was growing up, but most of them had moved away for college and had no plans on returning; knowing she'd have the Morgan/Jordan crew to pal around with gave her a warm feeling and made her heart go pitter-patter.

That pitter-patter feeling was one she'd have to temper and fast. She'd been in "puppy love" with Sawyer Morgan back in high school, but soon realized that they could only be the best of friends. Zach Morgan was a cutie and a lot of fun, while Kendrick Jordan was devastatingly handsome with that bad boy vibe, but neither of the three men caused her heartbeat to speed up. No, that position went to one Mr. Decker Morgan. Of course it did, because he was her boss and wasn't that just lovely. She'd never really dated a lot; she'd preferred hanging out with large groups of people. The guys she hung out with always seemed to think she was unapproachable and regarded her as just "one of the guys." That was great for always having friends to hang with, but it didn't do much for her romantic experiences.

Once she got to college, she was so busy juggling classes, studying, and working that she barely had time to date. She'd gone on dates here and there, but never really felt that any of the guys were worth more than a date or two. During her sophomore year, after watching girlfriend after girlfriend go through pregnancy scares and the heartache of sleeping with a guy only to find out he was a jerk, she made a pledge to herself. She'd hold on to her virginity at least until she found a guy who made her heart beat faster. And once she found the guy, she wouldn't just hand it over on a silver platter; he'd have to earn it and deserve it. From that point on, she dated with the goal of finding "the one," but it just didn't happen. Maybe she was too business minded, too driven, too serious?

She shook her head. "Stop it, Turner. You are fun and know how to have a good time. There's nothing wrong with the fact that you've not slept around. You'll find the right guy someday. Until then, enjoy hanging out with these guys as friends." She pushed away the nagging thought in her head that whispered, *"Decker Morgan makes your heart beat faster. He makes your palms sweat and your body feels warm in all the right places whenever he's around."* Decker Morgan was her boss, he couldn't ever be "the one" no matter how much he made her heart feel all fluttery. Decker was a rule follower and she knew the handbook at The Center+ clearly stated that dating relationships at work were frowned upon.

Walking into the bar, Katie smoothed her skirt and gazed around trying to spot the guys. She saw Decker raise his arm to signal her. Calming her heartbeat, she waved back and wondered what it would be like to be meeting him for a real date. "Never gonna happen, Turner, so get it out of your mind."

Decker took a deep breath and forced his lusty thoughts to take a back seat as he watched Kate walk toward their table. He very much wished that she was walking toward just him and not to a night of drinks with his brother and cousins. "Not gonna happen, Morgan, so get it out of your mind."

Kendrick looked at him with a raised eyebrow, "Did you say something, Deck?" At the abrupt shake of Decker's head, Kendrick glanced briefly toward Katie and back at his cousin. A smirk of dawning comprehension formed on his face and Decker felt the urge to punch him right then and there.

Gritting his teeth, Decker growled, "Let it go, man. It's nothing." His gaze was direct and fiery. Kendrick gave a curt nod, but Decker knew he wasn't going to drop it completely.

"Katie Smith, as I live and breathe!" Zach, ever the charmer, stood and pulled her into a hug. She assumed there were many women who would envy her position in Zach's arms, however, she felt nothing for Zach.

Smiling, she returned his embrace, "It's so good to see you. And it's Katie Turner now. I took my mom's maiden name after my dad left." Turning to the rest of the men she found Kendrick Jordan on her right; he stood and pulled her into his chest. If she'd been anyone else, she may have responded to the way his hand traveled up and down her back and lingered just a little longer than necessary, but she just shook her head and wondered at the death glare Decker directed toward Kendrick.

She wanted Decker to pull her into a hug, but he just nodded in her direction. "Kate, glad you could make it." She pushed down the feeling of disappointment and turned to find Sawyer waiting on her with open arms.

Tears filled her eyes and she walked into his warmth. "Sawyer, it's so good to see you. I hate that we lost touch after graduation. I've missed you so much." She was surprised at her reaction to seeing Sawyer again after all this time. For the short time they dated during high school, she had fancied herself in love with him, but she realized shortly after their relationship began that he didn't feel the same for her. After they broke up they formed a very close friendship and were practically inseparable for the rest of high school.

"Katie, it's so good to have you back home with us. I've missed you, girl." He rubbed her back and tucked her head under his chin. She breathed him in and knew again, for the millionth time since moving back to Torey Hope, *this* was where she belonged; she was truly home in this place.

Hearing Decker clear his throat, she backed away from Sawyer's touch. She had been wrapped in the arms of three extremely attractive, sexy men and yet her heartbeat didn't double until she looked across the table at Decker. It would be so much easier if she was attracted to one of the other men, or none of them at all. Having feelings for Decker was just really bad timing, and she couldn't risk messing things up at work. Maybe she should talk to him about it, just lay it all out there and let him know how she felt. She could tell him the truth about her feelings, but let him know that she understood they were unreciprocated and she wouldn't let the feelings cause any trouble at work. Decker was a straightforward type of guy; he'd probably appreciate her openness. Taking a deep breath, she decided she'd speak to him at the next available opportunity.

DECKER TOOK his one hundredth deep breath since she'd walked in the door and felt his jaw clenching as she moved from Zach to Kendrick to Sawyer. He knew Zach was just being his usual charming self, Kendrick was purposely trying to piss him off letting his hands linger like that, and Sawyer... well, his brother looked like he'd reunited with his long lost love. He had known this was a very real possibility. Hell, he'd done everything he could to prepare his heart and mind for Sawyer and Katie to rekindle something, but seeing her in his brother's arms was a little too real for him and the spark of feelings he'd had for her took a crashing nosedive straight to his gut. Taking another deep breath, he chastised his mind, *"This is for the best. Nothing could have come from it since you work together. If they are happy together, just be happy for them."* While his mind tried to adjust to being happy for his brother, he decided maybe he should just be upfront with Kate and let her know his feelings. She was an upfront type person, maybe letting her know about these feelings would be helpful; he could assure her that his feelings would not interfere with her and Sawyer or with their work relationship. Cementing the plan in his brain, he decided he'd talk to her at the next opportunity. Just to clear the air.

THE NIGHT HAD BEEN FILLED with laughter and memories and rebuilding friendships, but the five of them knew they had work in the morning so they finished their drinks and prepared to leave.

"We should definitely do this again, maybe make it a weekly thing? What do you guys think?" Zach had a sparkle in his eyes and dimples to die for, who could say no to the man?

"I'm up for it! I don't have much going on outside of work and spending time with my mom and grandma." Katie raised her eyebrows expectantly at the other men, hoping they'd want to make this a regular thing.

"That and burning cookies, huh?" Decker spoke with a wink and Katie groaned at the memory.

"Mmm, that sounds like a story for next time. Be ready, Katie, I think Decker has a good tale to share from the looks of that smirk on his face." Sawyer put his arm around her as he teased her.

"I think a group thing once a week is a great idea, let's make it happen. But, what about you two? Are you two going to rekindle that romance from high school?" Kendrick asked innocently enough, but Decker saw the gleam in his cousin's eyes as he threw a glance his way; Kendrick was purposely trying to rattle him.

Sawyer shuffled his feet and mumbled a bit as he grasped at an answer. "Um, yeah, that sounds great. What do you say, Katie-girl? Want to set up a date?" The other men either missed or chose to ignore the strange look she gave to Sawyer and the sheepish, desperate look he returned to her.

With an understanding and comforting hand on his arm, Katie replied, "Yeah, Sawyer, that sounds great. How about you call me and we'll set something up."

As they paid their bills and left the bar, hugs were given all around with promises to see each other next week.

Decker gave her an awkward hug and then glanced between her and his brother as they stood together on the sidewalk. "Well, I'll let you two have some privacy. Really good to have you back home, Kate. I'll see you first thing in the morning. Get your coffee good and strong in the morning and come to my office first thing. We've got some things to go over." He'd break it down for her tomorrow, first thing, so they could move past this, and he could get his head on straight again.

Sawyer and Katie watched Decker walk to his sleek, black car. He waved as he drove away and Katie turned expectant, worried eyes toward the man who had been her best friend all those years ago.

Hanging his head, Sawyer sighed deeply. "Don't Katie, just don't. It's not that easy; please don't give me that look."

"How do they not know, Sawyer? Surely I'm not the only one who knows?" Katie's words implored and she felt tears rise again as she realized what her best friend had been living with for so many years. Reaching for him, she pulled him into a hug and rubbed his back. "Sawyer Morgan, you're lucky your best friend is back in town. We'll get you through this; there may be some storm clouds ahead, but a cleansing rain may be just what you need so you can face brighter days." They chuckled together and she held his hand as they walked to her car. He kissed her cheek as she climbed in and he watched her back out of the parking space before he headed to his Honda S2000. A movement to his right caught his eye; if he didn't know better he'd swear Decker was circling the parking lot. Why would his brother have come back here?

HE SHOULD HAVE JUST DRIVEN home but he was obviously a glutton for punishment. The tiny bit of hope he'd felt when he sensed Sawyer's awkwardness over the suggestion of a date with Katie was dashed as he watched her pull Sawyer into a hug and rub his back. The kiss at her car had been the final nail in the coffin of his hope. Katie and Sawyer had something between them and he'd respect it. Tomorrow, he'd lay it all out so there was no awkwardness, and they'd move on as colleagues. He'd also talk to Sawyer just so there were no secrets between them.

8

The next morning, Katie grabbed her coffee before heading to the office. As an impromptu peace-offering, she grabbed a black coffee for Decker knowing he'd be there working out before he started his day; he and the other guys, along with the employees, always did their work-outs before classes/programs started for the day or after hours. Facing the conversation she had planned, she was nervous, but felt strongly that clearing the air was the best thing for keeping their working relationship positive.

Arriving at The Center+, she caught a glimpse of Decker in the gym as she walked past toward her office. The man was pure perfection; tall, dark, and handsome was an accurate label for him. He and Sawyer both had their father's athletic build and their mother's dark hair. With a crooked little smile and breathtaking golden brown eyes, they were absolutely devastating. But, when she saw Sawyer in the weights section, she didn't feel her breath catch. Watching Decker on the treadmill sent her heart beating into overdrive. Pushing the feelings down, she thought back to high school when her girl-friends had been gaga over both of the Morgan boys. She recalled how the girls always talked about having trouble telling them apart, but Katie had never had that problem. From the first moment she met them, she saw a softer, more vulnerable part of Sawyer; Decker had a harder glint about him, physically, emotionally, socially. Caught staring, she blushed as both men waved at her and then hurried toward her office.

Stopping his run at two miles, Decker stepped off the treadmill and headed toward the weights. Clearing his throat, he started to speak at the exact moment as Sawyer. They both abruptly clipped out, "So, um, I need to talk to you..." Chuckling nervously, Sawyer nodded toward his brother, "Go ahead. Floor is yours."

Decker thought lifting weights while he talked would be helpful, but he found he needed his wits about him; placing the barbell back on the rack, he sat up on the weight bench. Clearing his throat yet again he closed his eyes and took a deep breath before speaking. "Listen, man, this is rough, but I know you and I don't have secrets between us, so I'm just going to put it out there. If it pisses you off, we can go a couple rounds in the ring if you want to." Sawyer raised an eyebrow and waited expectantly for his brother to continue.

"Yeah, so, here's the deal. I like Kate. As in *like* her. But, I saw how things were between you guys last night and I can tell there's still something there, so I'm just letting you know that I promise not to interfere with whatever you guys have. In the long run, it's for the best since I don't date colleagues and dating my assistant manager would most likely spell disaster. But, I just wanted to clear the air so there were no secrets between us. She's a great girl and I wish you both nothing but the absolute best." Decker spoke in a rush and then turned pleading eyes toward his brother, begging him to accept the admission and allow them to move on.

Sawyer took a deep breath and closed his eyes tightly, slight tears squeezing from the sides. A shuddering breath and a sarcastic chuckle escaped him before he whispered, "Secrets....yeah, no secrets."

Decker frowned at his brother's response. "Man, please tell me that this isn't going to cause issues between us. I didn't tell you to cause problems, I just couldn't walk around with these feelings without letting you know. I figured laying it all out there would help me get rid of the feelings; I didn't mean to upset you."

He reached for his brother's shoulder, "Hey, man, you okay?" Decker got the feeling that his admission wasn't what Sawyer was upset about. Wondering if this reaction had anything to do with what Sawyer was so upset about a week ago, he waited for his brother to speak.

"Deck, we need to talk. Not about Katie, but there's a lot

to talk about. Work isn't the place to do it. Thanks for letting me know about Katie. I love that girl with everything I have. But...well, let's talk soon, just you and me, okay?" Sawyer let out a deep breath and headed toward the showers, leaving Decker confused and concerned. He didn't like the thought of Sawyer being upset; something was definitely bothering him.

"Good morning, Decker. I got you some coffee. Um, I know we have a lot to go over today, but I was wondering if I could have five minutes of your time?" Katie spoke directly but nervously, which brought Decker an extra dose of confusion. First his brother was acting strange and then Katie acting nervous; the strong woman in front of him didn't seem to do nervous often.

"Sure, Kate, what's up?" Decker leaned back on his desk, stretching his long legs out in front of him. Katie imagined walking close to him and positioning herself between his legs.

Closing her eyes, she took a deep breath and spoke quickly, "Decker, I have feelings for you. I know nothing can happen between us because of work and the fact that you probably don't feel the same. I feel silly even telling you this, but I felt the need to be honest and upfront about it in hopes of just moving on." Finishing her speech, she dared a glance at him and winced at the look on his face.

"Un-fucking-believable..." Decker sighed out the word. "Well, Kate, I might as well present you with the main thing I wanted to discuss with you this morning."

At the look of confusion on her face, he continued, "You see, the main thing I wanted us to go over this morning was the fact that I have these crazy feelings for you. I honestly have never been so drawn to a woman before. But, there are a couple issues. One, we work together and I don't want to mess that up. Two, Sawyer." When Katie cocked her head at him as if needing more explanation, he huffed out, "You guys dated; last night it was evident there's still something between you; he just admitted to me that he loves you. No matter what the two of us feel, I will never disrespect my brother by stepping in on what is his. I hope we can just push these feelings aside and continue with our work relationship without there being any problems. If you don't have feelings for Sawyer, that's going to have to be something you two discuss, but I can't be the reason you're not with him. My loyalties will always lie with him, with my family." Katie noticed the hard set of his jaw and knew his words came with a strong conviction and dedication to his family. She respected that, and it made her feel even more for him in that moment.

"Decker, I respect that, I truly do. First, I'd like to point out that I'm a person and I don't belong to anyone so I'm not 'his,' but I think you and Sawyer need to have a serious talk and soon. I won't go any further into it....let's just say that there's nothing between Sawyer and me anymore aside from being very close friends." Katie wanted to wrap her arms around Decker and hold him as she watched the confusion and unsureness dance across his face; she could tell that he didn't like feeling unsettled like this.

"So, where does this leave us, Decker?" She wanted him to throw the rules out the window, but she knew he still had major reservations about her and Sawyer. Rules could be discussed, but nothing was going to change until he and Sawyer had an honest, heart-to-heart conversation.

"You are the best thing to have happened to me, Kate. Hiring you and having you working by my side is exactly what I needed. I wish I could say we could expand to something more, but there are too many hurdles to overcome. I hope we can continue our positive work relationship and push the rest of this to the back of our minds. Are you okay with that?" Decker spoke professionally, no emotion, no indication of the feelings swirling inside; he wanted to pull her into his arms and kiss her until neither of them could catch their breath. Damn his rules.

Sadly, but with complete understanding, Katie smiled at him, "Yeah, Decker, I understand, and I think that's probably for the best. I'm glad we spoke and got it all out there. We can't work well together if there are secrets between us. But, seriously, promise me that you'll talk to Sawyer. Soon."

The sparks between them as their gazes met across the room belied their little agreement, but they continued about their day, pouring over reports and plans. Both of their brains insisted to their hearts that they could handle whatever was between them just fine; a working relationship was what had started first and it was all they could have. End of story.

"SAWYER NICHOLAS MORGAN! You need to talk to your brother NOW!" Katie smacked his shoulder as she spoke to him, and he hung his head. "First, I can't believe he doesn't know. Second, I can't believe you've kept this from them. Third, surely they all have an inkling. Fourth, you have one of the best families in the history of families, they will love you no matter what. Fifth, Decker has feelings for me, and I have feelings for him, but he won't disrespect you by asking me out. Oh, and the convenient little fact that we work together isn't helping matters either." She took a deep breath after releasing her faux fury on her best friend.

Smiling at her, Sawyer focused on the last part of her speech, since it was easier to face. "Does my best friend have feelings for my brother? Do you want to kiss him and love him and have his babies?" Seeing her feelings written clearly on her pretty face, he sobered a bit. "So, you really like Decker, huh? Wrong brother all those years ago? I have to be honest with you, Katie-girl, even if you remove me from the equation, I don't see Decker breaking his rules. You'll still be his assistant manager, and I don't think he'll pursue you." He watched as his best friend raised her eyebrows, obviously waiting on him to address the other issue that stood like a huge white elephant in the room.

"I know, I know, I've wanted to talk to them all so many times over the years. Honestly, I wish someone would have just straight-up asked me about it because I can't ever figure out a good time to bring it up. I truly think they will all eventually be okay with it; I just don't want to cause any stress or problems for them with their friends or people in town. What if it causes problems at The Center+? It's like this huge weight on my chest, but I don't want to put the weight on them; it's my issue, I should be the one who has to shoulder it. Right?" He hung his head, partially out of shame for being so much of a pansy that he couldn't speak to his family and tell them the truth, partially out of fatigue, exhausted from carrying around a secret for so many years.

"No, Sawyer. They are your family, they love you. They've supported each other through a lot of ups and downs. I've heard the love stories of your grandparents, your aunts and uncles, your parents, none of those times was easy. But, they loved each other and supported each other and made it through to a happier time on the other side. Share with them, let them support you. Even if some of them balk at first, I truly do think each and every one of them will eventually come around. But, you have to start with Decker; he's your brother, your twin, your other half. He deserves to know and to hear it from you." Katie hugged her friend tightly.

"He's going to be so pissed. He was just talking today

about how we don't have secrets between us. And now I need to tell him something that is the mother of all secrets." Sawyer knew Decker would be mad, but he thought he'd probably be hurt more than anything. They'd always shared everything, but Sawyer had been keeping something from him for many years.

"Yes, he's going to be pissed. Decker doesn't like secrets. But, I think he'll be more pissed at himself for not realizing it sooner. You'll throw him off-kilter for a while, and he doesn't like the feeling of not being in control. But, he's your brother, your biggest supporter, he'll come around." A kiss to his cheek and Katie turned to leave Sawyer with his thoughts. At the door she stopped, "Sawyer?"

"Yeah?" Sawyer was sitting on the floor, against the wall of the studio, looking like a lost little boy.

"Talk to him soon. I know he and I have some huge obstacles to get past, but I don't need his loyalty to you being one of the hurdles I have to jump." She spoke with a smile and a wink before leaving the studio.

With a deep breath, Sawyer steeled himself. It was time, past time, to talk to his brother. He promised himself he'd do it before a week was out. First Decker then the rest of his family. He'd never felt so anxious, excited, and sick to his stomach about something before, but Katie was right, he had to tell them.

9

"Man, we've got a problem. Possibly a big problem." Zach spoke from the doorway of Decker's office.

Not one to get ruffled unnecessarily, Decker waved his cousin in. "Okay, let's hear it, and we'll get it worked out."

"Well, one of our biggest backers just called me and said he'd received some confidential information detailing some 'unsavory labor practices' at one of our suppliers. He's put a freeze on his contributions until we can prove that the supplier isn't involved in anything illegal or corrupt or unsavory. Without his money coming in, the supplies for the new wing can't be bought which means the construction has to stop for now. I'm sure I don't have to explain that we're still under contract to pay the construction crew even while we are losing days to this." Zach delivered the news and Decker's stomach plummeted.

"Damn, this is bad. Which supplier is supposedly bad? And where the hell did this confidential information come from?" Decker was pissed.

Zach rattled off the name of the supplier, but had no leads on where the confidential info had come from.

"Fuck!" Decker held his head in his hands. Taking a deep breath, he calmed himself. "Okay, I will call the backer and let him know that I have the utmost faith in this supplier. I'll pay a surprise visit to the supplier and take pictures and video of the day-to-day procedures so that I can reassure myself and the backer. There's no way the supplier is involved in anything wrong." Pacing his office, he knew he could solve this problem easily within a few phone calls and a day or two out of the office. "Sit down with the crews and come up with lists of things they can continue working on the next couple days while we get this taken care of."

His biggest concern was who was messing with the expansion. Someone had to have it out for him or The Center+ to go to this amount of trouble to pause construction. "Who the hell would take the time to mess with The Center+? It's a place for learning and growing and having fun; who could oppose that?"

"I don't know man; maybe it doesn't have anything to do with The Center+. Maybe someone has a beef with the supplier? Or someone is hoping for our backer to pull his monetary support from us and put it somewhere else? Just get on the phone with the backer and make your plans to pay a visit to the supplier." Zach stopped before leaving Decker's office. "Maybe take someone with you? Kendrick and I can't go, we've got meetings scheduled. I'm pretty sure Sawyer is booked with introducing new programs to the community. Maybe Katie could go? Having another witness to prove there's nothing corrupt would probably be helpful." As Zach retreated, Decker acknowledged the wisdom behind his cousin's suggestion; but he questioned his own wisdom in considering Kate as his partner for the trip. This was going to be an overnight trip; could he ignore what was between them? Did he want to continue ignoring it?

On a strangled whisper he spoke to the empty room. "Shit, what am I talking about? There's no question about it. She's my assistant manager so of course she's the one I should take. There's nothing to ignore. She's my colleague and my brother loves her, no matter what she says." Decker nodded his head at his own little pep talk. Walking to the adjoining door, he knocked and popped his head in.

"Hey, Kate, got a minute? We've got a problem I'm going to need your help with." The smile she turned on him did funny things in his gut. This was going to be a long trip.

AN HOUR LATER, Decker had explained the problem to Katie

and called the backer with assurances and an explanation of his plan. Katie had pulled a history, all clean of course, of the supplier in question including a BBB report, tax filings, and statements of satisfaction from former and current employees.

"Okay, we need to leave in about an hour. I'll head home to pack. Can you pick me up at my place? We'll get there tonight, grab a bite to eat, find a hotel, and then go check the supplier out tomorrow." Katie was excited about the trip; she wanted to prove to the backer that The Center+ wasn't involved with anything unsavory. Her excitement had nothing to do with an overnight trip with Decker. Nothing at all.

"Yeah, I'll run home and pack too. I need to let Sawyer know I'll be gone. I'll have to let my dad and Uncle Jeremiah know what's going on as well since they'll act as decision makers while I'm away. I'll pick you up in an hour. Hopefully this will be a quick fix." Decker nodded at her as they went their separate ways. The anticipation in his chest had nothing to do with spending time with Kate. Nope, it was all about solving this problem quickly and efficiently. That's all.

KATIE REPRESSED the excited squeal she longed to let loose when she saw Decker's black Chevy Camaro pull in the driveway. Since they weren't doing any business that day, she had dressed more casually in a pair of denim slacks and a fitted shirt with large chunky jewelry. Rubbing her hands down her pants, she picked up her overnight bag and headed to the front door. She stopped short when she saw her mother, grandmother, and Decker sitting around the living room. She shot a questioning look at Decker who just smiled and shrugged his shoulders.

"Now, young man, what exactly are your intentions with our Kate? I'm sure I don't have to tell you just how inappropriate it looks for her to be traveling out of town for an overnight trip with a man. I should hope that you have no plans to soil her virtue." Katie's elderly grandmother was a trip, and she was holding nothing back with Decker.

"Grandma! Decker is my *boss* and we're going on a *business trip*. Nothing inappropriate is planned." Patting her grandmother on the shoulder, she threw quick glance at Decker and mouthed *I'm sorry*. He just winked and smiled.

"Is that what you young folks are calling it today? *Business?* Well, I remember just what kind of unplanned *business* your grandfather and I used to have. Young man, I hope you're packing some protection in those pretty pockets of yours. My precious Kate better not come back from your supposed *business trip* with a baby or any other problem in her *business*." Grandma nodded her head sagely, and Katie shot a desperate look at her mother.

"Mom, we need to head out. Maybe you could get Grandma settled in for her tea?" Katie's eyes implored her mother to help with the mortifying situation. Her mother discreetly covered her smile and led her mother out of the room.

"I'm so sorry; Grandma is quite the character and has no filter at all as I'm sure you could tell." Katie felt her cheeks flush as Decker stood to join her at the door.

"Not a problem, she's a hoot. I almost expected her to pat me down in search of protection." With a wink he assured her that he wasn't offended and took her arm and steered her toward the door. Just as quickly as he'd grasped her arm, he let go and looked at her guiltily. "Sorry about that."

As they settled into his car, Katie spoke. "Decker, we've got to stop tiptoeing around and apologizing. We find each other attractive. End of story. We're not dating, we're not getting married, we're not falling into bed together. We're grownups, I'm sure we can handle an inadvertent touch here and there without going crazy with lust." She ended on a questioning note. She didn't truly feel the words she was speaking; she wanted him to disagree with her.

Clearing his throat, he nodded and agreed. "You're right. We can surely handle things like adults. No more apologizing."

The long drive was pleasant from that point on. They spoke of high school memories, mutual friends, ideas for The Center+, and their families.

"I can't believe you don't remember that ice cream place in town!" Katie spoke incredulously. "It was *the* hangout for all the cool kids and had the best ice cream; I hated to see it close down. How do you not remember it? I know you were one of the *cool* kids because your brother and cousins were as well."

Sheepishly, Decker shrugged his shoulders, "I was probably too busy studying or writing up mock business plans or proposals; I was in the *in* crowd, but mainly by association, I didn't spend a lot of time with anyone but the guys. I dated occasionally, but never seriously; I always felt like dating wasted my time when I could have been working on school stuff and getting ready to take over The Center."

"That's sort of sad, Decker. I always remember thinking you were so very serious all of the time; Sawyer was the emotional one, Zach the funny one, Kendrick the broody one, you the serious one. You seemed so unapproachable back then. I wish we had known each other; I'm glad our mutual love of business has brought us together now." Katie took the conversation to an easy place.

"Ah, yes, our *mutual love of business*, that sounds so exciting. Surely we've got something more in common than love of business?" Decker smiled at her.

"Well, I guess we'll find out as we get to know each other a little better. I love Torey Hope and Sawyer; we've got that in common. I love my parents and grandma, and you adore your whole family; there's another thing in common. Music? What do you like? I'm pretty diverse, if it's got a good rhythm or great lyrics, I probably like it." Katie was rattling off facts about herself and Decker let her voice just float over his ears; he liked hearing her talk and being close to her.

"I like a lot of different music as well. Old stuff, new stuff, hard rock, pop, some country, a little rap, new indie work, I like it all. We'll have to compare music playlists someday." He liked the idea of sitting around, sharing some of his favorite songs with her. Once again he was bombarded with frustration over this situation; dating a colleague wasn't a good idea, but trying to tell his heart and brain that was proving difficult.

"Pizza? You like pizza right?" Katie looked at him expectantly.

"Of course, who doesn't like pizza? But, the real question comes down to toppings. I want a little bit of everything on my pizza. What about you?" Decker narrowed his eyes as if her answer was of terrible importance.

Wrinkling her nose, Katie shook her head, "Nope, sorry, I want only cheese; sometimes I like pepperoni. If we ever get pizza, we can do half/half or I can pick off all your nasty toppings; I don't like onions or olives or peppers crunching in my teeth when I'm trying to enjoy pizza." She laughed at his faux horrified face.

"I obviously didn't screen you well during the application process; how can you call all those delicious veggies and meats *nasty*?" Decker pretended to be disappointed. "I guess you'll have to be with Aly and Zoey on pizza days at The Center+ when they get their plain cheese pizzas. It's a real shame there's something so wrong with you." He laughed as she swatted at his arm.

"I'm almost afraid to ask, what's your crust preference? Please tell me you're not the type who wants that cracker thin crust." Decker glanced at her and waited for her response.

"No way! I like traditional crust the best, although I can eat a deep dish every now and then." She smiled as he pretended to be relieved.

"Whew, okay, at least you saved yourself with that answer. Now, what about drinks?" Decker hadn't talked this much to a girl about random, useless information in his entire life.

"Like soda or tea? I prefer unsweet tea with lemon most of the time; especially freshly brewed tea. As far as soda, I'm a little weird I guess. I like Pepsi from a soda fountain or can, but I want Coke at McDs; there's nothing like their coke or their unsweet tea." Smiling like a little kid over something as simple as drink preferences, Katie lit up the entire car.

"Well, I'm in total agreement with you on your drink choices, but I like my tea sweet; my grandmas made sweet tea while I was growing up and I just can't break myself from it." He handed her his phone to check the map, and tried to ignore the electricity that flowed between their hands when they accidentally brushed against each other.

By the time they reached their destination, they knew each other a lot better and most of the awkwardness of their situation had passed. While Decker would never admit it because he knew he could never act upon it because of work and his brother, he finally understood what his mom was always telling him, "When you find *the one* you'll just know, you'll feel it in your heart and soul." Wasn't it just a damn fucking shame that his *one* was the only one he couldn't have? Wonder what his momma would say about that?

Katie on the other hand, being privy to the fact that there was absolutely zero romantic relationship between Sawyer and her, decided something on the drive. Years of dating, wondering if each man was *the one* had brought her to this point; she'd never felt this way about any other guy. She knew they'd have to work through the working together part, but she felt it deep in her heart and without a doubt that Decker Morgan was her *one,* and she wasn't going to give that up easily.

10

"What do you mean you only have one room?" Decker spoke professionally, but Katie knew he was gritting his teeth.

"Sorry, man, we are the only hotel in town, and there's some antique show going on this week. You're lucky I've got this one room; up until a cancellation an hour ago, we were booked solid. So, do you want the room or not?" The young man behind the counter didn't seem to understand the dilemma that Decker faced.

Turning to Kate, Decker raised his eyebrows. "Kate? You okay with sharing a room with me?" His mind was a jumbled mess of feelings; *please share a room with me* battled with *please don't agree to this* and his heart beat full force waiting on her answer.

"Decker, I know you'll be nothing but a gentleman. Of

course I'll share a room with you." As Decker slid his card over to pay for the room, he swallowed thickly, and his eyes shot to her when she leaned in and whispered, "Too bad I can't promise that I'll follow the rules." She smirked at him and winked, but her mind scoffed at her, *What the hell was that? You want to flirt a little, not come across like some brazen hussy.*

Decker forced a smile. She had been joking, right? He could understand if she wasn't totally on board with him denying their relationship over the work issue, but if she couldn't respect his decision to step back out of loyalty to his brother then maybe she wasn't the woman he thought she was.

As they walked to the room to drop off their bags and freshen up for dinner, Decker spoke a little harsher than he meant to. "Kate, listen, I can see that you may not agree with my no dating a colleague rule, but it's really disappointing that you would hurt Sawyer and disrespect my decision to step back when he obviously still has feelings for you."

"Well, thank you for that proper chastising Mr. Morgan." She rolled her eyes at him which earned her a look that mixed shock, anger, and a little lust; he clearly wasn't used to attitude or eye rolling from his employees. "Decker, I know you won't believe me until you've spoken to Sawyer, and I won't interfere with that. But, please trust me when I say there is absolutely nothing between Sawyer and me; there hasn't been anything since high school and even then it was just some experimental making out." She reached for his hand as he unlocked the door, "As for the work thing, let's just see where this thing goes and see if it's worth dealing with repercussions at work, okay?" Leaning in, she kissed his cheek.

He took a ragged breath and fought the urge to toss her on the bed. She took the same ragged breath and tried to convince herself that she hadn't just stepped in way over her head.

"So, yeah, let's get ready for dinner. You can have the restroom first. I'll look up some places we can eat; you have a preference?" Decker tried to sound calm, but the warmth of her lips on his cheek still stung. He wanted to call Sawyer right that minute and demand to know what his brother felt for Kate. But, no, he had more control than that. He wouldn't go off half-cocked like some horny teenager. He could share dinner and a hotel room with a woman without letting things get out of hand. He was always in control; of course he could keep the situation under control.

"Nope, I'm up for anything. I'll just wash my face and brush my teeth and we can head out." Katie grabbed her bag and headed to the restroom.

Five minutes later she emerged and his gut tightened when he saw her. Her hair cascaded down her back, her eyes sparkled and her lips shimmered. She smelled like fresh sunshine and warm citrus mixed with brown sugar. She had changed into a skirt that hit her about mid-thigh and his eyes traveled up her legs for miles. A simple tank and blouse finished her outfit, but she might as well have walked out in a bikini; he could see every curve of her beautiful body and his own body was reacting in appreciation.

"Fuck." He whispered to himself and took a deep breath.

"What was that, Decker?" Katie smiled at him good-naturedly. "Did you say something?"

"Damn it, Kate, are you *trying* to make this harder on me? I thought we had an agreement?" He was slightly annoyed with her, but he was more annoyed with himself for not being able to control his reaction to her.

"Decker, I'm wearing the same outfit I'd wear if I was with all four of you guys. I'm not purposely trying to make anything *harder*." With a smirk and a wink, she continued, "We're attracted to each other, no matter what we do, that's not going to change. Once you realize that Sawyer isn't an obstacle, maybe you'll be more willing to see where this could be headed."

A shrill ringing broke into their conversation. Seeing it was a blocked number, he ignored the call and headed to the restroom to get ready for dinner.

When he was out of sight, Katie sat down on the bed with a sigh. She had never been the flirty type; she hoped her plan to show Decker they could be good together didn't backfire on her.

She noticed his concerned look when he walked out of the restroom. "What's wrong?"

"Nothing that I know of, but I just got a text from a

blocked number, I'd assume it's the same blocked number that called me a minute ago." Decker was trying to decipher the text.

"What did it say?" Katie didn't like to see Decker worried.

"It said, '*Too bad your plans aren't working out the way you thought they would.*'" Decker assumed the text was in reference to the work issue they were dealing with.

"Save the message. Maybe it's unrelated, but we may need it later. Come on, I'm starving, let's go eat." Katie convinced him to forget about the text for a while.

They walked into the restaurant and Katie groaned. "This is the third place we've tried and they've all got lines out the ass. I'm hungry, Decker." She tried very hard to hide the whine in her voice, but she was seriously hungry.

Decker spoke to the hostess. "We're in luck, this place has open seating in the bar. Come on, I'll get you fed, Katie-did." She felt warm inside at his use of the nickname. She had to laugh that her new nickname with him was in reference to an insect, but she basked in the warmth of him speaking to her in a more intimate, informal manner.

"Katie-did? Really? A bug?" She spoke in a teasing tone and bumped his shoulder.

He smiled sheepishly and shrugged. "Well, I heard Sawyer use 'Katie-girl' so I figured I'd need to be original. I guess a nickname derived from an insect isn't all that sweet or romantic, huh? Not that I'm trying to be romantic or sweet. It just sort of came out. Sorry, I won't do it again." Decker finished speaking as she took her seat, but before she could respond, he slid into the booth beside her and pinned her into the corner with his arms.

"You know what, fuck that. I'm not sorry. I want to have a nickname for you. It's the first thing that popped into my mind, and I find it endearing. So, I take back my apology. I'd like to call you Katie-did. And, so help me God, I have no clue what you're doing to me woman." He leaned close to her, almost burying his nose in her neck; with a deep growl in his chest, he backed away and took his seat across from her. Katie just raised her eyebrows and smiled at him.

"I have no complaints about the nickname, Decker. I like it. You're welcome to sit next to me if you'd like." She offered him a genuine smile. That was what was killing him; she was so real and so genuine. Kate wasn't a fake, she wasn't ditzy and flirty; he sensed the flirting she was doing with him tonight was foreign to her. What would it be like to just take her on a date, to get drinks, to invite her to his place? His mind drifted to his mouth on hers, her dark hair spread out on his pillow, waking up beside her in the morning. Damn it all to hell, this wasn't him; he didn't get ruffled by a woman like this. Taking a deep breath, he smiled at her and let his words come tumbling out.

"I think we're both safer if I'm on my side, and you're on your side. I started today thinking we could keep these feelings covered up and just go about business as usual, but after spending more time with you, I'm pretty sure I'm going to have to admit that I was wrong. I don't know how things are going to play out, and I'm not willing to let anything happen until I've spoken to Sawyer, but I'm pretty sure this thing between us isn't going to be forgotten about. The more I try to cover up my feelings for you, the more they fight their way to the surface. Let me talk to Sawyer and then we'll figure out what to do about things at work." In the one minute it took for him to speak those words, he felt the weight of fighting his feelings lift and he relaxed for the first time in over a week. He'd had no plans on revealing all of that to her, but his words just came spilling out and it felt good to just let them loose.

Smiling at his words, she sipped her amaretto sour, turned to the waitress and placed her order for a big juicy burger and fries. Decker followed suit with a steak and baked potato. "Hey, Decker, when you talk to Sawyer, be patient with him. He's got a lot to talk to you about, and I'm afraid you're going to get frustrated with him for not talking to you before now. Just remember that he had his reasons for not talking to you sooner. He's your brother, your other half, your closest friend, and he's going to need you on his side."

He frowned at her words, "Kate, I don't like where this is

going. You're talking like there's some huge secret between us; Sawyer and I don't keep secrets from each other. Even if something were to happen between you and me tonight, I'd have to tell him about it because I can't keep things from him. What could he have possibly kept from me?"

Katie shook her head, "It's not for me to share, Decker, just remember that you love him no matter what."

Decker huffed out a breath, "You know, I'm starting to get a little pissed that you seem to know this secret, and I don't. Why do you know more than his twin brother?"

Katie smiled sadly, "I just happened to be in the wrong place at the wrong time. Now, no more plying me with drinks and getting information from me. This is all I'm drinking tonight, and I'm done talking about Sawyer." She was saved by their order arriving. Glancing at Decker over the food, she could tell he wasn't completely satisfied, but he'd taken the distraction.

Halfway through her burger and fries Katie glanced at Decker and caught him staring at her. "What? Do I have something on my face? Why are you staring at me?" She blushed as he smiled at her.

Shaking his head, he just continued to smile. "Nothing's wrong. You're just...I don't even know how to explain it... you're just *you*, and I can't stop looking at you. I love that you're eating a real meal and not acting like a salad and water is filling. I love that you ordered what you wanted and didn't wait to see what I'd get. I love that you're drinking an amaretto sour. I love that you're acting the same way with just me as you'd act if my brother and cousins were here." He reached for her hand across the table, but after a gentle, warm squeeze he let it go, she knew he was still tempering things because of Sawyer. She had half a mind to call Sawyer and tell him to text Decker the all-clear so they could see where things went tonight, but that wasn't the purpose of their trip, so she wouldn't call.

"Well, Mr. Morgan you're *really* going to love me when I order dessert and take you on the dance floor." She smiled at him and perused the dessert menu. "Perfect! We can share apple crisp with ice cream. Yum." After ordering the dessert, she turned to him, "Want to dance now or after dessert?"

He shook his head. "Nope, that's where I draw the line. Dessert, yes; dancing, no. I don't dance. As in, I don't know how. Never have, never will."

Feigning shock, Katie put a hand to her chest. "Why, Mr. Morgan, I'm shocked at you! Don't you know that dancing is like foreplay with clothes on?" She was pretty sure she'd read that fact in a magazine somewhere; she definitely didn't know it from first-hand experience.

Groaning, he leaned in toward her, "For the love of God, please don't talk about foreplay." He was saved by their dessert arriving. Although, watching her eat was almost as bad as talking about foreplay. Oh, how he longed to be her spoon.

"Come on, Decker, let's dance." She squinted her eyes at

him as he shook his head, "Fine, you party-pooper. I'll go dance by myself. See ya later, chump." She poked at his chest and sauntered toward the dance floor. "Wings" by Little Mix came on as she reached the dance floor. She found the beat and fell into step with a couple other women and three guys. After shaking her ass and doing some fancy steps, she turned her gaze toward Decker. His hooded eyes took in every move she made, knowing she was dancing just for him. His teeth and fists were clenched by the end of the song as he had to watch the men taking turns dancing up behind her. Maybe he should rethink his stance on dancing.

Katie rejoined him at the table when the song ended and slurped down her water. "Whew! I haven't danced like that forever, since high school probably. I'm spent; are you ready to head out?"

Decker paid the bill and they walked out into the night. "Want to walk a bit before driving back? You worked off the dessert with your ass-shaking, but I need to walk off that meal." He smiled at her and offered his hand.

Glancing down at his hand, she smiled and let her own slide into his. She'd never really held hands with a guy. Sure, in grade school and high school, but not since being an adult; the dates she went on never usually went past one or two times and she never felt comfortable enough to hold hands with those men. Having her hand in Decker's felt like fitting the last piece of a puzzle together. His hand was warm and strong and seemed made just for her. The electric jolt of awareness that traveled through their bodies when their hands met was strong enough to cause goose bumps. "*Ass-shaking?* That was dancing, not just ass-shaking. One day, I'll get you to shake your ass with me." She smiled at his vehement refusal as he shook his head.

"Negative, there will be no dancing." He winked at her; teasing her felt natural even though he was pretty sure he'd never teased a girl in his entire life. Maybe he'd teased his sister, Abby, or his cousins Aly or Zoey, but teasing a woman he had romantic feelings for had never happened. Probably because he couldn't remember a time when he'd had romantic feelings toward a woman. Angela had been convenient, she didn't take him away from his business pursuits, she was there when he needed a physical release, but she didn't demand his time. Looking down at his hand holding Kate's, he thought he'd like nothing more than for her to demand some of his time.

As they neared a small picnic area, Decker veered off the sidewalk, pulling her with him. He walked to the backside of a large, old oak and gently pushed her against the tree. "Kate, this thing between us was never in my plans. I never thought I'd have the time or the desire for romance and relationships. I figured I'd never marry, or I'd marry someone to benefit my business pursuits. That woman and I would be equals like you and I are, but I didn't expect desire and feelings. Then you came into my life and all I've ever known was tipped upside down. I may have to apologize to my brother for this later, but if I don't get my mouth on you soon I might go insane." Without waiting for permission, but seeing heated agreement in her eyes, Decker let his hands roam up her arms until he was cupping the sides of her face. As their eyes met, his voice husked out, "Know that there has never been a woman in my arms that I wanted to kiss as badly as I want to kiss you; I ache for you, my brain short-circuits around you, I lose all control. I don't lose control for anyone, but then you waltzed in...." Without finishing, his face inched closer. Kate felt the warmth of his breath on her face; the beer he'd had with dinner mingled with a mint he'd popped at some point on their walk. Just when she thought his mouth would claim hers, he pressed his forehead against hers. "Give me a second, Katie-did. I'm afraid I won't stop once I get a taste of you; I need to get control of this."

Katie tilted her head until their mouths were only a whisper apart, "Decker, shut up and kiss me."

Her words jolted his brain into action and his mouth met hers, lips whisper soft, testing, caressing. The moan that slipped from her zinged straight to his cock and all bets were off. Pinning her hips against the tree he ground his length into her and his tongue demanded entry at her lips.

The kiss was more than she had ever experienced; heat from his body engulfed her and her core ached with a molten fire. When Decker moved a thigh between her legs, she groaned as it connected with her center. The need to rub herself against him was almost more than she could handle. A mewling sounded around them and penetrated the fog surrounding her brain as she realized it was her making the noise; breaking the kiss she pushed him away slightly.

"Wow, that was....wow. Um, in order to keep our clothes on, maybe we should keep that walk going?" He smiled at Katie's words and obvious shaken reaction to their kiss. Truthfully, he'd never felt his body react like that to a kiss. Even as a horny teenager, he'd enjoyed making out, but his body had never been as on fire as it was when he kissed her.

Holding his hand out to her again, they resumed their walk.

"I feel guilty; if I find out my brother still has feelings for you, I'm going to need my ass kicked. This isn't me, I don't make moves on the girl my brother likes." Caressing her thumb with his, he whispered, "You make me crazy, Katie-did." He pulled her into his body and they approached his car looking very much like a couple in love, enjoying a stroll.

Once settled, she turned to him, "Decker, you know that if I thought Sawyer felt anything for me, I'd never have let you kiss me like that, right?" She didn't want him to think she would betray his brother that way.

"*Let me* kiss you? I'm pretty sure you demanded I kiss you." He flashed her that perfect lopsided smile and grabbed her hand; bringing it to his mouth he brushed a kiss along the sensitive skin on the inside of her wrist.

"Semantics; you were going to kiss me either way, I just

nudged you along in your decision." She shivered at the warmth of his mouth on her skin.

A short drive later, they pulled into the hotel parking lot. Brief panic skittered through her; she needed to let Decker know that she wasn't all that experienced.

"Hey, Decker, after I shower, I need to tell you something." She quickly grabbed her bag from the bed and locked herself in the bathroom.

"What is it with everyone needing to tell me something?" Decker sighed deeply and laid down on the bed. With the vision of a naked Kate sliding soaped up hands along her body in his head, he reached down to rub the ache in his cock. After a moment of sweet relief, he sat up and rubbed his hands across his face. "Damn it, Morgan, get it together. You can't have her walking out here to find you stroking yourself." Walking to the bathroom door he knocked and smiled at her yelp of surprise. "Hey, I'm going to go get some ice, okay?" He hoped a walk to the ice machine would cool down all parts of his body.

She had dried her hair until it was just damp when he returned. Her tank and flannel pants were modest, but did nothing to deter his desire for her. Quickly grabbing his bag he groaned silently as he walked into the steamy bathroom for his own shower. Climbing into the steamy jets of water he knew he needed to take care of his *problem* before he went back out there to share a bed with Kate.

With the scent of her body wash and shampoo

surrounding him, he soaped up his hand and gripped his shaft firmly before he began a strong, slow pumping action. Closing his eyes, he breathed deeply and recalled the touch of her lips on his. His release came quickly and he fought to contain his groan. Turning the water as cold as he could stand it, he finished his shower and tried to keep his mind from straying to her.

Usually the type to sleep in just his boxer-briefs or nothing at all, Decker donned a pair of basketball shorts out of respect for Kate and survival for himself. The more layers between them tonight the better.

She was laying on the left side of the bed, Kindle in hand, looking sexy as hell. His mind flashed to them, married, sharing a bed, and the nightly activities they could take part in. *Yeah, best keep those thoughts on the back burner, Morgan. Just get through tonight.*

He sat on the edge of the bed and contemplated sleeping on the floor. Deciding against it, he climbed under the blankets and turned to face her. "So, Katie-did, what did you want to talk to me about?"

Her pretty cheeks blushed pink and she laid her Kindle down on the nightstand. Taking a deep breath, she fumbled her words, "Um, I've never, I mean, I've done some things, but I've never been with a guy." Her words weren't registering with him and he waited for her to continue. "I've kissed quite a few guys and made out with some, but, um...."

As dawning filled his expression, his voice, like fiery hot gravel, gruffed out, "What are you saying, Kate?"

"Sex! Sex, Decker. I've never had sex." She didn't hang her head, she wasn't ashamed; she stood strong in her conviction of waiting for the right guy. But getting the words out was still difficult.

"I'm going to need another fucking cold shower..." Rolling to his back, rubbing his hands over his face, he blew out a deep breath. "I'm not sure if that bit of information makes sharing a bed with you tonight easier or harder."

"I'm not going to apologize for being a virgin, Decker." She felt a bit irritated at what she read as annoyance from him. She slid down in the bed and turned to face him, propping her head on her hand.

Rolling back to his side to face her, he sighed, "I'd never expect you to apologize for that. I'm not mad or frustrated. I'm not sure I can even explain what I'm feeling because I'm not sure I even understand it." His eyes pleaded with her to just let it go.

"Can you try? I feel like you're mad at me right now." Katie frowned a bit at him.

"I feel out of control here. I don't like that feeling. I'm sharing kisses and a bed with a woman I consider a friend and partner while not being 100% certain that my brother is over her. I'm jacking off in the shower to control the need to spread your legs and bury myself in you. These things aren't me, I don't react this way to women. Then you tell me that you've never done any of what I want to do to you, and any control I thought I had on this situation flies out the window. I'm glad you're a virgin. It means that I get to show you a whole new world; it also means that nothing will happen tonight because I'm most definitely not taking you for the first time in a cheap hotel room. Plus, I'm sort of scared of your grandma." He ended a serious conversation on a humorous note and leaned in to kiss her nose.

She laughed out loud and his heart swelled with feelings for her. Sobering a bit, she spoke shyly yet directly, "I'm grateful that you're willing to protect my virtue tonight, but could you give me a little preview of what's to come?"

He wasted no time rolling her onto her back, settling himself between her legs. "I'd be happy to give you a bit of a sneak peek." Leaning in, his mouth captured hers; her sigh warmed him and threatened to send all rational thought straight to his cock.

He let his mouth travel down her neck as his hand slid up her torso and filled with her breast. The caress of his thumb over her nipple sent warmth flooding her body and she arched against him.

Decker pulled her to a sitting position and removed her tank, his breath whooshing out when he realized she wore no bra. Pulling her up farther so she was on her knees, he slid his hands under her waistband and cupped her perfect ass in his hands. Pushing her pants down, he sat back on his knees to take her in; chest heaving, nipples pebbled and begging for attention, proof of her desire soaking the fabric hiding her center, he'd never seen anything more beautiful. Raising himself up on his knees, "You are the most beautiful woman I've ever seen," he whispered reverently as he cupped the back her head and kissed her thoroughly. His lips and tongue traced a path down her chest until he reached her nipples; taking one in his mouth and another between his thumb and finger, he pushed at her gently until she lay back against the pillows.

"Oh, God, Decker, that feels so good." Her words panted out as she writhed under him.

Determined to keep things fairly tame, he let his hand travel down her stomach; teasing at the top of the lace, he tested her willingness as he slid a finger under the band. When her hips thrust upwards, he allowed his hand to slip the rest of the way under the patch of lace until he found her warm, wet center. His mouth longed to follow his fingers, but he knew he needed to take things slowly. Circling her most sensitive part, he captured her moan with his lips against her mouth as he slid one long, thick finger inside. Feeling her stretch for him, he added a second finger and drew them in and out in a slow, strong motion.

"Decker! Oh, God, please don't stop." Her fists clutched the sheets and he watched, enraptured, as his fingers entered her body over and over. Flicking a thumb over the bundle of nerves, he felt her body begin to clench around him.

"Let it go, baby, come for me." He whispered in her ear

and increased the speed of his fingers and the pressure of his thumb.

With an arch of her back, she moaned deeply as her body contracted around him.

As she rode out her release, he thanked his lucky stars that he'd taken care of business in the shower earlier. He reached down to adjust himself; her hand joined alongside his.

"Let me play, Decker. I'm not ready for anything else, but I want to touch if that's okay." Katie spoke with a look of relaxed bliss on her face.

As her hand gripped him, she whispered in his ear. "Someday, soon, I'm going to let you spread my legs and slide into me." His cock jerked in her hands and he knew he wouldn't last long if she kept talking like that. "I'll be tight around you and I'll cry out as you slam into me over and over."

"Fuck, Kate!" He growled as his release rushed from him. Less than two minutes and she had him going off like a gangly, pimply teenager getting his first hand job.

"Damn, Katie-did, where did you learn to talk like that?" For someone with no experience, she knew the exact right words to say to him.

She held her hands to her flushed cheeks. "Decker, I've *never* spoken like that to anyone. It was just what I felt. Was I too dirty?"

"Baby, you can talk dirty to me anytime." With a kiss to

her nose he slid from bed to clean himself up. Returning, he knew it would be better to keep to his side of the bed, but he wanted to hold her. Gathering her in his arms, he whispered in her ear. "Katie-did, if Sawyer says he still has feelings for you, I'm going to be shredded; I don't know if I can let you go after tonight." They both drew in deep breaths and sighed contentedly as they drifted into a peaceful sleep.

11

"What the fuck, Decker? The one girl I have real feelings for and you steal her from me right under my nose?" Sawyer spoke with unbridled anger.

"Sawyer, no, it's not like that. I never meant to fall in love with her, it just happened. I didn't steal her from you. We can fix this man. Please." Decker pleaded with his brother for forgiveness.

"Decker, you made out with her, you slept in the same bed with her, you've fallen in love with her. There's no way to fix this. You aren't the man I thought you were. I no longer have a brother." Sawyer's eyes filled with tears as he turned and walked away.

Decker fell to his knees, head in hands, tears pouring down his face. The nightmare of it all was that he had lost his brother, *but his heart still beat for the one girl he wasn't supposed to love.*

"Decker? Decker! Wake up! Damn, Deck, you must have been having one heck of a dream." Katie elbowed him in the gut and unwrapped his arms from around her. "Decker? Are you awake now? What the hell were you dreaming about?" His moaning had awakened her; he'd sounded like he was being tortured.

He sat up, breathing heavily, rubbing his hands over his face. He used to think his worst nightmare was something going wrong with his business endeavors; he now knew that he very possibly was living his worst nightmare. He was falling for the one girl he should have stayed far away from; she should have been off-limits because of work and Sawyer. But turning his head to look at her beautiful mussed hair and sleepy face, he knew he could no more stay away from her than he could stop the sun from rising each day.

She reached out and smoothed her palm across his cheek. "You okay?" At his weak nod, she cocked her head as if she wasn't convinced. "Want to talk about it?"

"No." He just wanted to get the problem with the supplier taken care of and get home to talk to Sawyer. "Let's just get today started so we can get back to Torey Hope." Distracted by the vivid dream and the conflicted feelings jumbled inside, he slid from bed and hit the shower.

Katie drew her knees up to her chin and watched him disappear into the bathroom. She knew the gist of the dream;

he'd been talking to Sawyer about her. Her heart longed to ease his pain and guilt, but Sawyer's secret was not hers to tell.

Later, as she finished her makeup in the bathroom, she heard Decker return to the room. "I've got coffee and breakfast, Bug." He came around the corner smiling; she glanced at him in the mirror as she finished the last coat of mascara. Putting her makeup back in her bag, she walked to him with an unbelieving smirk and narrowed eyes pinned on him.

"Did you just call me *Bug*? As in an insect, a creepy-crawly, a BUG?" She spoke with laughter in her voice, her heart warming at the ridiculous nickname.

"Well, Kate interchanges with Katie which became Katie-did. Since a katydid is an insect, I thought *Bug* was sort of fitting." He twerked her nose and smacked her on the ass before handing her a large coffee from her favorite coffee shop. "Strong and sweet, just like my girl." He leaned in and kissed her softly. "Sorry about this morning. That dream rattled me; Sawyer and I may have some serious words, but I'm in too deep, I can't give you up." He kissed her again.

"I wish I could ease your worry, Decker. I also find it a bit irritating that you think I have no choice in this. Even *if* Sawyer had feelings for me, I'm a big girl, I think I'm capable of choosing the man I want to spend my time with." She huffed out the last part and took a fortifying drink of her coffee. "Ahhh, sweet bliss for my tongue." She winked at him when she caught him staring.

"I have many plans involving bliss and tongues, Katie-did, but let's get this taken care of and get back home." He pulled her into his side and kissed her cheek.

Two hours later, they walked out of the supplier's office. Their financial backer had paid a surprise visit and met with them when they arrive that morning. Everything checked out, as Decker had known it would, and the backer was very pleased with the supplier's set up, employees, and procedures.

"Decker, sorry you had to waste time getting proof for me. I should have believed the reports you provided and trusted you to use only legit suppliers; that information I got about unsavory practices must have just been a ruse to slow things down or mess with someone. You? The Center+? Me? I don't know, but I'll think twice before I believe something like that again. You two drive safe and have a good rest of your day. My contribution to The Center+ will continue." The man climbed into his expensive car and drove off, satisfied.

"Well, that went very well, but I'm still pissed at the amount of time we lost. Oh well, it's over and done now, let's head home." Decker held her hand until they reached the car. Opening her door for her, he gave her a soft kiss. "There's one thing I'm not upset about."

"What's that?" She smiled and tipped her face up to his just slightly.

"This trip gave us last night and I wouldn't trade that for the world. I had a really good time with you, Kate. I don't know if I've ever just hung out, had fun, and relaxed on a trip, at least not since I was a kid. You do that to me." Kissing her nose and leaning his forehead against hers, he spoke softly, "Thank you for last night and for being you."

12

"We're doing *what?*" Decker looked at Sawyer as if he'd grown a second head.

"You heard me, we are going camping. Today is Friday, Katie said she could handle stuff at work. You, me, the great outdoors. Go pack." Sawyer tried to talk tough, but Decker could tell he feared Decker's rejection.

"Okay, man, you and me and the great outdoors. Sounds great. I'll go pack." He smiled slightly at Sawyer's obvious relief. What in the world could his brother need to talk to him about that was so huge he needed to remove him from civilization to do it? Camping was something they'd done as kids, but Sawyer was the one who enjoyed it more than Decker. Camping brought a lot of down time, Decker usually tried to keep his mind busy.

Sawyer entered the room as Decker was packing his

laptop. "No way, it's CAMPING; there is no internet, no electricity, no WORK. Just us. I need to know I've got your 100% attention." His brother swiped the laptop and laid it back on the bed. "Meet me outside in fifteen minutes. Zach is letting us borrow his truck; I've got it loaded." Sawyer nodded and left the room. Decker picked up the nervous energy from his brother. Something big was brewing.

Kate: *I'm glad you two are getting away to talk. Just remember that you love him more than anything and that you've always been loyal to your family. He needs your support and loyalty. Please don't get mad at me; if it was my place to tell you, I would have already. Don't worry about work; come back when you two are all talked out.*

Smiling at her words, but feeling apprehensive, he grabbed his car charger just in case he'd be able to get any reception wherever Sawyer was taking them.

"Alright, brother, let's get this show on the road." Decker walked down the steps and threw his bag in the back of Zach's truck. Texting Zach, he let him know the keys to his car were on the hook in case he needed them. He glanced at Sawyer; his brother was reading a text on his phone and a grin filled his face.

"Who's got you all smiley and flushed over there?" He joked with his brother. It felt good to see him smile like that. It had been a long time since he'd felt his brother was truly happy.

"Just a friend." Sawyer chuckled as he put his phone away, but his continued smile belied that statement.

"A friend, huh? Maybe a friend you'd like to turn into something more?" Decker laughed at his brother's face.

"Yeah, I think I would, Deck. I really think I would." Sawyer seemed surprised by his answer, but he also seemed to relax with his admission.

An hour and a half later they pulled into a clearing; Decker recognized the area as a place where his dad and uncles Nicky and Jeremiah had brought them all when they were younger. There was a decent little rustic cabin to keep them safe from the rain that threatened. A short hike brought them to the cabin and they threw their bags inside.

By silent agreement, they began gathering wood for a fire. A piece of sheet metal served as an overhang from the cabin and a fire pit was located under it. They could build their fire and keep everything protected from the rain.

Never Boy Scouts, Sawyer pulled out a newspaper and lighter fluid while Decker rummaged around for a lighter.

They laughed when they realized they weren't exactly "roughin' it."

"I'm starvin', please tell me you brought food." Decker always forgot how being out in nature and doing something as simple as gathering wood for a fire could make a person so hungry.

"I had the grandmas pack us something. Let's see what they sent us." Sawyer opened a basket and began producing all the fixings for a tried and true wiener roast. Hot dogs, buns, condiments, chips, napkins, plates. In the cooler they found ice-cold pop, potato salad, and pasta salad. "Mmmm, the grandmas never disappoint." Sawyer grinned like a kid and began to set the food out on the table. "I think Zach said he's got roastin' sticks in the back of the truck, could you check? If not, we better go cut some before it starts raining."

After three hot dogs each along with all the extras their grandmothers had included, the men were full. "I think it's time for some beer. I know the grandmas didn't pack any, but please tell me you've got some hidden under that pop." Decker nodded his head with appreciation as his brother pulled out two beers from under the frosty ice.

After a long pull on the bottle, Sawyer leaned back in the chair and rested his hands on his knees. He took a deep breath and began to speak, but grabbed his words back and sat silently.

"Sawyer, I've been going over this in my head for days. You're my brother, my twin, my other half. Aside from telling me your murdered someone in cold blood, I can't think of a single thing you could tell me that would make me feel any different about you. If it's something bad, we'll talk it out, but just spit it out and put me out of my misery already." Decker was irritated, but he also wanted his brother to understand he wasn't going to stop loving him. Ever.

Sawyer nodded and took another long swig of beer.

"I'm gay, Decker."

THEY SAT in silence for several minutes. Sawyer watched as his best friend played the information over and over in his mind. He felt it was best to give Decker a chance to process before speaking.

Decker heard the words over and over in his head. *I'm gay, Decker.*

He sat still, trying to organize his thoughts. Those three simple words changed so much, yet nothing changed. Those three words explained so much, yet he had so many questions.

"I need a moment to think. I'm going to take a walk. I'll be back shortly." Decker stood and grabbed another beer as he walked off into the night.

Gay.

My brother is gay.

I have a gay brother.

My brother.

He weighed the words in his mind and in his heart. Did he feel any differently? No, Sawyer was still his best friend and his brother. Nothing would change that.

My brother is gay.

He needs my support.

He's going to face hard times.

I'll be there for him. Always.

The sky broke open and he was caught in a deluge; within seconds his clothes stuck to him like a second skin. He finished his beer and walked back to the cabin.

Breaking through the underbrush, he found Sawyer sitting by the fire, head in hands.

"Sawyer?" Decker stood in front of his brother and motioned for his to stand up. When the men were face-to-face, Decker spoke. "You're my brother, always have been, always will be. I wish you could have told me sooner, but nothing has changed between us. I'll be there in any and every way that I can." He grabbed Sawyer and pulled him into a deep embrace; communicating his love and acceptance through his touch.

Breaking apart, Decker felt a little sad at the evident relief on Sawyer's face. It hurt that Sawyer hadn't been sure his brother would always have his back. "Man, I'm going to get some dry clothes on then we can talk."

Several minutes later, they sat by the fire. "So, is this a

free-for-all? No limits?" Decker had a lot of questions, but didn't want to put his brother on the spot.

"Wide open, man. Ask anything." Sawyer felt like a different person; he'd confided in his closest friend and Decker had reacted in the way Sawyer had always hoped, deep down, that he would. No more hiding, no more secrets. He wanted to answer his brother's questions.

"Who else knows, aside from Kate and me?" Decker knew deep in his heart that Kate couldn't have shared Sawyer's secret, and he respected that. He was just hurt that she knew before he did.

"You two are the only ones who know for sure. I think others have their suspicions, but have never asked." Sawyer wasn't completely ready just yet, but he knew the time would come soon when he told the rest of his family. Knowing he had Decker and Katie on his side meant the world to him.

"How long have you known?" Decker was having trouble wrapping his head around some things. All those late night discussions about making out and rounding bases with a girl, his brother had been fantasizing about guys?

"I think I started suspecting when I was about twelve. I remember seeing some guys at The Center who had taken their shirts off to play basketball and I thought they were absolutely beautiful. I'd seen girls and women in swimsuits and felt nothing, but an attractive guy with his shirt off made my heart beat faster. Then, in high school, poor Katie. I tried my best with her; we made out, but there was absolutely nothing there. I probably wouldn't have told her, but she walked in on me and a 'friend' one day. It's sort of hard to explain to your high school girlfriend why you've got another guy's dick in your hand; we both cried, but it felt good to tell someone, she's been my friend and support ever since. Losing her after high school was hard; I'm so glad she's back home." Sawyer stared into the night as he spoke.

"Dating? When? How? Who?" Decker had a hard time putting his musings into words, but he knew his brother would understand what he was asking.

"Yeah, I 'dated' some girls in college; had to keep up appearances I guess. I don't think I'd completely found peace with it yet. But, then I met Adam and I slowly began to meet other gay students on campus and they'd show me places to meet guys." Decker nodded in understanding when Sawyer mentioned his obviously gay friend, Adam; looking back, he wondered how he'd not put two-and-two together. He was pulled from his musings as Sawyer continued to speak.

"You'd probably be surprised at the number of dating apps out there just for the gay community. Some of them are for finding hook-ups, some for dates, some for relationship seekers. I had some hook-ups in college." He paused and rolled his eyes. "Don't look so shocked, it's no different than Kendrick bringing a new girl back to the apartment every weekend. I dated some too. I liked most of the guys, they were fun to hang out with, they knew what I was feeling and going through; I just never felt serious about any of them..." The way Sawyer let his sentence trail off, Decker got the feeling that maybe there was someone he *could* picture being serious with now.

"Does the text that had you smiling earlier have anything to do with a certain guy you may consider getting serious with?" It was strange to think of his strong, muscular, athletic brother being physically attracted to and intimate with other men, but he saw the twinkle in Sawyer's eyes when he spoke. *This* was the real Sawyer, he shouldn't have to hide who he really was. He deserved to be happy. Decker knew others questioned, and if he was being honest, he had questioned it himself at one point, *Is someone born gay or do they make the choice to be gay?*

He thought of the nervousness and apprehension that had come from Sawyer just wanting to talk to him about his sexuality. Coming out to the rest of his family and friends wasn't going to be easy, and those were people who already loved him. He could only imagine the pain, heartache, and turmoil his brother had endured over the years and it would probably increase ten-fold once more people knew; Torey Hope wasn't a big town, people would talk, and that talk wouldn't always be kind. Why would anyone *choose* that for themselves? The answer was clear in his mind, this was the way Sawyer was born. He could no more change his feelings than he could change the path of an approaching rainstorm.

"So, um, maybe sometime we can talk about things in a little more detail. I'm weirdly curious about sex between guys, but I think I've asked enough questions and taken in enough information for now." They laughed; it felt good to just share with his brother.

"Let me know if you need or want my help when it's time to talk to others. I'll be there every step of the way; Kate will too." Decker cleared his throat and chuckled at the mention of her name. "Um, speaking of Kate." He threw his head back and laughed, "She kept telling me there was nothing to worry about." When Sawyer gave him a questioning *go on* look, he calmed his laughter and shook his head.

"From the day I talked to Kate on the phone, not knowing it was our old friend, I've been pulled to her. But, I hired her and she's kick-ass at what she does. Strike one for anything between us since we work together. Then there's the issue that she used to date you. Strike two for anything between us. Or so I thought." Decker paused and shook his head again as he thought about his dark-haired beauty.

"I'm really relieved to hear you like guys because I may have gotten pretty close to Kate on our trip, and I was feeling all kinds of guilty that I'd made a move on the girl you may have still had feelings for." The brothers laughed and Sawyer clapped him on the back.

"She's a gorgeous girl; she's almost perfect, but she's not packin' anything I'm interested in. Although, despite our brotherly loyalty, if you every hurt her, I'll have to kick your ass." Sawyer smiled at his brother through the seriousness of his statement.

"She's got feelings for you too, man. She told me. In fact, she's the one that insisted on this little talk; if not for her, who knows how long I would have kept hiding. She was shocked to find out I hadn't told my family. She encouraged me to talk to you so you'd know it was okay to have feelings for her." Sawyer sobered, "What are you going to do about working with her? You're such a rule follower, is she your one 'freebie,' your one 'exception?' You know that Zach and Kendrick live by the motto, 'There's always some wiggle-room' when it comes to rules." Sawyer watched in amazement as his straight-laced, by-the-books brother got a soft, dreamy look in his eyes.

"Decker Morgan, as I live and breathe, do you love her?" Sawyer tried to make light of this realization, but he was truly shocked; it was like entering an alternate universe to see Decker so seemingly out of his element.

"I...I don't know if I love her, man. I've never loved a girl. I know what I feel with her is the exact opposite of anything I've ever felt with any other girl I've been with." Decker wasn't ready to label what he felt for Kate, but he knew that she was a game-changer.

He shuddered as he thought of his time with her, their lips and tongues and bodies entangled. Deciding it would be best to keep his thoughts from wandering there, he changed the subject.

"So, do I get to meet the guy who was texting you?"

Decker was trying to picture the type of guy Sawyer would be attracted to.

"Maybe. Not now, it's too new. But someday. If things go further with him, you'll be the first person I want him to meet." Sawyer's entire face lit up when he spoke of this mystery man.

"Okay, so on another topic, when are you going to tell Zach and Kendrick? You should tell them soon, get more people on your support team." Decker thought his cousins would be okay with Sawyer's sexual preferences, but he thought the sooner they found out the better.

"Should I call and have them come up tonight?" Sawyer knew Decker was right, he needed to tell his cousins. "Camping trip with the four of us, just like old times?"

"Give 'em a call, tell them to get their asses up here. But make sure they pack their own sleeping bags and bring more food. I'm not sharing my sleeping bag with either of them." Decker laughed as Sawyer set off down the road to get reception on his cell.

13

"What's up, BDSM?" Kendrick ambled through the underbrush and announced his arrival. "What the hell? Did you bring us up here to sing Kumbaya or what?" Tossing his bag through the cabin door, he grabbed a beer from the cooler he and Zach had brought with them.

"Ahhh, beer, friends, the great outdoors...the only thing missing is a nice piece of ass." Laughing, he turned towards his cousins. "No, really, what's the occasion?"

Rolling his eyes at his boisterous cousin, Zach grabbed a beer and pulled a chair up to the fire. "Who needs an occasion, man? Just pull up a chair, drink your beer, and enjoy."

The four men sat around and shot the shit for about thirty minutes. Decker sensed that Sawyer was trying to work up the nerve to tell the others, so he spoke first.

"So, listen, I wanted you both to know that I'm going to pursue something with Kate. I know she works with me which is against my usual rules, but I have feelings for her and she does for me too. I'm not sure where it's going to go, but I can't let her go without giving it a shot. So, yeah, there it is." Decker smiled as he finished, feeling awkward at sharing that with his cousins at that moment.

"You know what we always say", Kendrick started and Zach joined in, "*There's always some wiggle-room!*" They jumped up and wiggled their backsides against each other and fell back down into their chairs laughing. Decker rolled his eyes; would his cousins ever grow up?

The four men grew silent and enjoyed their beers as they waited. Decker knew the ball was in Sawyer's court. Zach and Kendrick knew something was up, they just weren't sure what. Sawyer was anxious and excited, but part of him feared losing his cousins if they couldn't accept him.

"So, I called you guys up here to spend some time like we used to do, but I also wanted to talk to you both about something." Sawyer began nervously, but he sat up straight, prepared to deliver the words he knew could change everything. His cousins waited.

"I'm gay." Two words that held such power. Would they laugh? Would they walk away in disgust? Would they be angry?

"I think I've known that for a long time, man, but thanks for telling me." Speaking quietly, Zach smiled and nodded.

"Wait, you knew? Why didn't you ever say something? Why did you joke with me about girls?" Sawyer's confusion was clear.

"I don't know, I guess I figured you'd tell me when you were ready. I didn't want to bring it up if I was wrong and it offended you. I think I joked about girls thinking it would give you the opportunity to bring it up if you wanted to." Zach stood and walked to his cousin, reaching a hand down, he pulled the other man into a hug. "Nothing changes, I've got your back, man."

Kendrick sat with his hand rubbing his chin. Would he be the one who couldn't accept it?

Eyes twinkling and a shit-eatin' grin on his face, he finally spoke. "What's it like to suck cock?" The other three burst out laughing.

"Come on, I'm serious. Maybe I'm 'bi-curious,' who knows. I know I like burying myself deep in a girl, the tighter the better; I'm assuming being deep in a guy's ass has to feel pretty much like Heaven on Earth, right?" Sawyer attempted to shake off his utter shock and awe at the words his cousin was speaking.

"Um, yeah, it's pretty close to Heaven." He felt like he was having an out-of-body experience.

"See, I've always thought guys would probably suck cock better than girls; just like a girl could probably eat pussy better than most guys. Why? Well, as a guy, I know exactly what feels good, just like a girl knows exactly what feels good.

I don't know if I'd ever actually do it, but I'd likely consider doing a guy; I don't know if I could let a guy fuck me though."

Kendrick paused in his musings and glanced at his cousins' open-mouthed expressions. "What? It's just stuff I've thought about before. Don't get me wrong, I love women, but being with a guy intrigues me a bit." And with that, all the worries Sawyer had about telling his cousins he was gay floated off into the night air.

"So, really, what's it like?" They had spread their sleeping bags out on the cabin floor. Many beers had been consumed and words were perhaps slightly slurred.

"What? Sex with a guy?" Sawyer smiled as he spoke, finding it amusing that his brother and cousins were so interested.

"Yeah, man. I don't see myself or Zach ever sleeping with a guy; Kendrick, maybe. But, what's it like? How's it work?" At the snorts of laughter, Decker huffed, "I know *how* it works, I just wonder if it's that different from being with a girl."

"For me, it's different because it feels right. Being with girls felt wrong, awkward, strange. Being with a guy makes my heart flutter, my skin tingle, and my body grow warm." Sawyer began to get lost in thought, but he pulled himself back to the group.

"Kissing. Kissing is awesome. Soft lips, slick tongue, roaming hands, a little hair pulling, kissing is perfect." He closed his eyes and pictured the soft lips of a man who made his heart flutter.

"What about sex?" Kendrick had rolled to his back and propped his head on his bent elbows behind his head.

"Depends on the person you're with and what you're both comfortable with. Oral, anal, jacking each other off, like I said, it just depends." Sawyer didn't expect this level of questions from his brother and cousins, but he appreciated them; it meant the other men were open to him being himself and were trying to learn and educate themselves. He didn't expect these types of questions from other family members; he'd answer them the best he could, but he thought it would probably be pretty awkward if he had to explain gay sex to his grandmas. Uncle Nicky was the only one who would probably ask direct questions.

"Are you the one on top or the one on bottom?" Kendrick's question brought him out of his thoughts.

"Again, it depends. Some guys will only do top, some will only do bottom, some like to take turns. Some couples don't do anal, only oral and mutual masturbation. It's very much like sex with a woman, you have preferences; guys just have different options."

"Does it feel good? Top or bottom, does it feel good either way?" Zach cocked his head to the side and waited.

"If the guy is big, it can hurt at first; if he's rougher, it can be painful. As far as being the top, it's like sex with a virgin only better because it's so tight." At Decker's choking sound, they all looked at him.

"Sorry, got something stuck in my throat." He closed his eyes tight to force himself to stop thinking about Kate being a virgin.

"Alright, enough gay sex talk tonight, boys. I'm beat." Kendrick laughed at his own words. "Can you imagine the earful someone would have gotten if they'd been outside the windows tonight?"

They all chuckled. "Guys, thanks so much for being okay with this. Your reactions wouldn't have changed who I am, but it's good to know that I have your support and acceptance."

"Dude, you told us you like dick; it's not like you told us you wanted to fuck a female cousin!" Kendrick's words were crude and crass, like him. The other men laughed. No one caught the look of pure panic on Zach's face.

14

Monday morning, after a relaxing weekend camping with his cousins, Decker walked into work whistling. A smile played on his lips as he thought about grabbing lunch with Kate today. He'd missed her this weekend and that caught him off guard; Decker Morgan had never missed a woman before.

He knew that most of the new programs were starting up soon, even as they waited on the new wings to be finished. Sawyer was excited and proud of the additions to the art program, especially the sculpting, pottery, and music classes. His brother had coordinated with the Zach and Zoey and got several dance classes and martial arts classes set up. Decker had yet to meet the new martial arts teacher, Luke Hamilton, but Sawyer spoke very highly of him.

After a full-force workout with the guys, Decker show-

ered and headed to his office. Within an hour, his calm, happy morning was blown to smithereens.

A knock sounded at his door; he looked up to see the construction foreman, Mike. "Morning, Mike, what can I do for you?" Decker liked the man, he was precise and friendly, always keeping things running smoothly on the job.

"Well, this is downright embarrassing, Mr. Morgan, but we've got a big problem." Mike's face showed true worry.

Popping his neck from side-to-side, breathing deep, Decker spoke calmly while inside he was thinking, *What the fuck now?* "Go ahead, Mike. What's the problem?"

"Every updated copy of the blueprints for both wings are missing." Decker knew the sacred importance of the blueprints; his face showed he understood just how huge this problem was.

"The embarrassing part, the part that makes me look like a total ass, is that we used the old blueprints all day Friday. So, we've got about a day of fixing that screw up, plus we need to get the correct blueprints back." Mike was pissed off at the whole situation.

"No offense, Mike, but how the hell did you lose every copy of the blueprints?" Decker was trying to remain calm, but with the incident last week and now this fiasco, his patience was worn through.

"None taken, Mr. Morgan. It looks like someone switched out the updated blueprints with the old ones on every single crew. I'm not going to go as far as to say it's someone on my crew just yet, but it's definitely someone who had unfettered access and wouldn't have been noticed or could have come in after hours." Mike was chomping at the bit to fix the mistakes, but he also had a hankering to figure out who was screwing with this teams.

"How much needs fixed from this mess?" Decker pinched the bridge of his nose.

"Some wiring needs redone, and two walls need knocked out and replaced at a different angle. Definitely an all-day job, but we'll stay late until it's done. We'll only lose today, Boss. I've already got someone going to get more copies of the updated prints, he'll be back in just over an hour; we can get started on some of it before he's even back." Mike looked at Decker, seeking permission to get the job underway.

"Go ahead, Mike. Get it started." He watched Mike's back as he retreated. "Mike?"

"Yeah, Boss?"

"Keep an eye on the workers, let me know if anyone seems off."

"You got it, Boss. And, please accept my apologies; this type of stuff just doesn't happen on my teams. I'll make it right, you've got my word on that." He nodded at Decker and walked away placing his yellow hardhat back on his head.

Sitting down hard in his chair, Decker leaned forward, elbows on knees. "Fuck!"

"Morning, Decker. I see you're already having a shitty one, but I think I've got something that's going to make it worse. Might as well go all in, huh?" Kate offered a sympathetic smile.

"The blueprints have been replaced with old plans so we're losing a whole day to fixing mistakes because the crews were following the wrong plans all day Friday. Do I want to know what you've got to add to the fray?" Decker was angry, but his heart softened marginally when he took in the beauty before him.

"You know what, don't tell me." He closed his eyes, sighed, and held up a halting hand. "Not yet. Come here, Bug." He stamped down his frustration and irritation at the blueprint catastrophe and felt his body heat as she walked toward him. He met her in front of his desk; he leaned back, opening his stance so she could fit herself perfectly where he wanted her. He shook off the uneasiness of being so open with her at work; he wasn't usually a rule breaker, but Kate had him breaking his own rules left and right with very little thought as to the outcome. In any other situation, with any other woman? Not a chance he'd risk everything he'd worked so hard for, but with Kate it was different.

"Good morning, beautiful girl." Leaning in he kissed her nose and let his lips trail across her jawline, down her neck and then back up the other side until he stopped at her mouth.

Whisper soft, Katie smiled and replied, "Good morning, Mr. Morgan." His mouth feathered kisses on hers, teasing, tasting. The slight sound from the back of her throat was what did him in. Reaching behind her, he tilted her head until he could devour her. She tasted of sweet caramel and coffee and her hips pressed against his.

"As much as I'd like to continue this, you need to read this text," she backed away, feathering her fingers over her lips and smiling at him as she produced her phone.

"It's a blocked number; it came in about thirty minutes ago. It didn't make sense until I heard you and Mike talking." She winced slightly as he read the message.

"Mother fucker..." He breathed the epithet out between gritted teeth. "Doesn't it suck when plans don't go your way? Maybe you should just give up."

"Why was it sent to you? Does this person have something against you, me, both of us? Or The Center+ specifically?" Drawing hands down his face, Decker struggled to contain his anger and concern.

"Okay, keep that message. At this point, we have to assume it's from the same person who called and texted me. I'm going to go down to the police station and see if there's anything I can do; I doubt there's much to be done since nothing illegal has been done, but maybe they can give me some suggestions." He leaned in and kissed her cheek. "While I'm gone, can you pull the profiles on each crew member? Maybe there's something in that information that can help. This would be easier and make more sense if it was a disgruntled crew member, but I feel like it's more personal against one or both of us."

AFTER A TRIP to the police station, Decker had no more answers than when he left. As expected, blocked calls and texts weren't illegal. There was no hard evidence that the prints had been switched out, at that point they could have just been misplaced; Decker knew that wasn't the case, but the police needed evidence of something illegal. He'd graduated with the police chief's son; the chief promised to have one of his patrol cars swing by The Center+ more often, especially at night.

Sitting down with Kate, they combed through each and every crew member's profile. There were some who had criminal backgrounds, that wasn't unusual on crews like the one working on The Center+; he couldn't just go accusing a man with a past of a crime without proof. He'd already spoken to Mike; the foreman would be watching everyone like a hawk.

By 5:00 p.m. he was ready to call it a day; he checked in with Mike and the man assured him that they'd be done working by nightfall and back on schedule the next day.

He stuck his head in Kate's office. "Hey, I'm going to go run a couple miles. Do you want to go out for drinks with the guys? I'm in need of a drink and some distraction after today. You game?" His heart faltered at the mega-watt smile she turned on him.

"Sounds good! I'll finish this report and come run with

you if you don't mind." He nodded his head in agreement and took a seat in her office to wait on her.

He watched as her fingers flew over the keyboard, manipulating the cells of a spreadsheet like a master. She was very efficient and detail-oriented; he was amazed every day at how perfect she fit into his business. She would have been perfect and greatly appreciated even if he hadn't found himself drawn to her like a moth to a flame, that part was just a bonus. He chuckled to himself, lost in thought. He glanced up to see her standing above him, waiting.

"Just what are you thinking about, Mr. Morgan?" She spoke in a sweet and sexy voice and he was positive a two-mile run wasn't the way he wanted to burn off stress.

AFTER CHANGING into his workout clothes, he sauntered to the treadmills as he waited for her to emerge from the dressing rooms. When she did, he had trouble catching his breath. Kate was the type of woman who could throw on a simple tank and running shorts and look like a model; she wasn't trying to be sexy, it was just a pink tank and black shorts, but he found himself growing hard just looking at the way her body curved in all the right places.

"Two miles, right? Let's get this done, I want a drink." They climbed on the machines and started them up. "Beware, I don't really like to run and I'm not all that graceful with it; I need to listen to music and focus or I won't get through it, so no talking." She winked at him as she donned her earbuds.

Twenty minutes later, they were headed for the showers. He grabbed her hand and twirled her around, pressing her into the alcove of the dressing room. In mere moments, he'd go left and she'd go right, but at that time, he wanted to hold her close. "Decker, I'm gross and sweaty." He leaned in and licked her neck in the most erotic gesture she'd ever experienced.

"One day, you'll be all sweaty because of hours of sex with me. You're not gross, you're beautiful and I want to taste every square inch of your body, sweat or no sweat. If we weren't in a building that still has people in it, I'd whisk you into the shower with me. But, for now, I'll let you go clean yourself." With a kiss to her lips, he leaned in to whisper in her ear, "Someday...you, me, soap, shower. Count on it." He laughed at her heated look and headed into the men's locker room.

SITTING WITH THE MORGAN/JORDAN boys made Katie realize two things. One, she was lucky to have them as friends. Two, she was the envy of several Torey Hope females and some of the males, too.

Sawyer seemed brighter and lighter since he'd shared his secret with his brother and cousins. She knew he still faced telling the rest of his family, but she sensed he was more at peace with all of it since his best friends were supporting him. She wasn't sure if, or when, he'd ever be ready to invite a date or significant other out with them. She hadn't spoken to him, but she had a feeling there was someone he was very interested in if the looks and smiles and body language she'd seen at The Center+ were any indication.

Zach Morgan was such an all-around great guy. Sporty, genuine, boy-next door, and charming, he was just fun to be around. He was never too serious and always knew how to have fun. She hadn't seen him showing much interest in dating since they'd all come back to Torey Hope. She knew he was busy with advertising and marketing The Center+ along with teaching several fitness classes with Zoey. In fact, the only time she saw Zach lately was on these nights when the five of them went out or in his office or with Zoey; she was pretty sure he hadn't been on a date since they all started working together.

Kendrick Jordan was quite possibly the crudest and most crass man she'd ever met, but he said things in such a way that it was funny, not offensive. He seemed to be a perfect combination of his parents, he spoke his mind and didn't care too much what others thought. The thing about Kendrick that broke her heart was that he'd been hurt in the past, so now he hid his feelings behind is wise-cracks and smartass comments. She knew he was loyal to his family and friends. Katie had a feeling that once he found the right one to give his heart to, it would be a love until death; she would be one lucky girl, whoever she was.

Decker had told her all about Kendrick's curiosity over Sawyer's sexuality. Watching him across the table, she found herself picturing him with that lucky girl and another guy; it was quite the image in her mind and she felt both the future girl *and* the possible guy were both very lucky if Kendrick chose them to be a part of his life.

All of this had traipsed through her mind while the three men talked and Decker went to the bar to refill their drinks. He returned with her fourth amaretto sour and she knew this would have to be the last one; her lips were beginning to feel a little numb which was always her sign that she needed to call it quits. Feeling the liquor and enjoying her time with friends, she was in a silly mood.

"Watch what I can do." She grabbed one of the cherries from her drink and popped the stem off. Waving it around, she showed the stem to the men in a Vanna White fashion. They laughed at her antics. Placing the stem on her tongue, she winked at Decker as his gaze heated up. Working the stem around with her tongue, she produced a perfectly tied knot in the cherry stem. She smiled as the other men clapped, and laughed when she saw the primal look of lust on Decker's face.

Feeling confident and safe as his hooded eyes bore holes in her soul, she plucked the other piece of fruit from her drink. "Hey, Decker, do you want my cherry?" She purposely made herself bat her eyelashes and look as innocent as possible.

The other men howled with laughter as Decker peered at her from molten-hot eyes with an intensity so fierce she thought her underwear would possibly catch on fire.

"Man, your girl just tied a cherry stem in a knot with her tongue and offered you her cherry; she's a keeper if I've ever seen one!" Kendrick guffawed and patted Katie on the back from his position beside her. "I know the S isn't interested, but if the D of BDSM doesn't know the perfect gift he's got right in front of him, come find me, pretty girl; I know plenty of ways to put that tongue to use." Rolling her eyes at him, Katie elbowed him in the stomach, but her eyes were 100% focused on Decker.

"You ready to head out, Bug?" Decker didn't take his eyes off her and Katie felt her body heat to dangerous levels. She wasn't sure if tonight was the night, but she definitely wanted to spend some time alone with him.

"Yeah, let me just head to the restroom. I'll be right back." On her way to the restroom, a smile played at her lips and she detoured to the jukebox. Making her selection, she grinned like a loon and headed to the restroom.

Right as she was washing her hands, she heard her song come blaring through the speakers. She waited about thirty seconds, hoping Decker had picked up on the song. She had trouble keeping a straight face as she walked back to the table and saw the other three guys laughing hysterically. Decker's jaw was ticking, but his eyes were smiling. Raising her eyebrows, masking her face perfectly, she address the four men. "What are you all laughing at?"

The other three just kept laughing and shook their heads; Decker leaned in and whispered hotly against her ear, "'Cherry Pie? Really, Bug? You're bad, so very bad." Knowing her gig was up, she just laughed and shuddered against his mouth on her ear.

Goodbyes were said, hugs were shared, and the group dispersed. Decker knew exactly where he wanted his night to end.

15

"So, if we're communicating through songs, I have one for you." Decker spoke gruffly, but he smiled at her as he thumbed through his phone for the song he wanted.

"Trouble Maker" by Olly Murs and Flo Rida came on and Katie couldn't help but throw her head back in laughter.

When they came up to an intersection, Decker hesitated. Right would take them to her place, left would take them to his. "Kate, I really want to go to my place, but I don't want to rush things. We've got work tomorrow; I want our first night together to be one where we have all night and all day because I don't plan on us getting much sleep. So, I'm going to take my *Trouble Maker* home for tonight and go home to my hand and a cold shower." They laughed as he turned to the right.

Sitting in her driveway, Katie saw her grandma at the window. They laughed at the older woman's antics. Kate knew her mother saved them the embarrassment of Grandma beating on the car window by leading her to the kitchen for hot tea and a game of cards.

"I don't want to be presumptuous and if you were just playing around tonight, that's fine, but were you telling me you're ready for something a little more with me, Kate?" His strained whisper warmed her heart; she felt his need, but knew that he would stop if she asked him to slow things down.

"Yeah, it was my attempt at being funny, but I know you're the one I want to be with. I've never felt this way about *any* guy. So, not tonight, but sometime. We don't have to plan it, that feels a little too much like Prom Night or something. But, I want it to happen and I want it to be with you. No pressure, just when the time is right." She leaned in to kiss him and sighed as his mouth took hold of hers. He pulled her to sit across him and pushed her up against the window to deepen the kiss.

"Soon, sounds good. Maybe I should exercise my tongue with some cherry stems so I can keep up with you. I know the exact place I'll be performing tongue tricks as soon as I have you naked." His hands grazed over her heat sending shivers through her with his words.

Knock, knock, knock

Kate jumped, banging her head against the ceiling of the

car. A yelp of shock and pain escaped as she scrambled over to her side of the car.

Lowering the window, Decker smothered a smile when he saw her diminutive grandmother standing beside his car with her hands on her hips.

"Is this the type of *business* you conduct young man? I better not see that hand of yours anywhere near my Katie's virtue again. You may have a nice package and a lot of potential, but I need to know you're not just here to dip your *business* a couple times and then take off." Kate groaned with mortification and Decker bit his tongue to keep from laughing out loud.

"No, ma'am, no business dipping going on here. Kate's virtue is safe." He spoke teasingly, but then sobered. "Grandma, I have real feelings for your Kate, and I'll be good to her, promise." Grandma seemed satisfied with Decker's response.

"Well, you seem like a nice young man, but there's no need to rush things. Katie, head on inside, you can see your man tomorrow." She waited until her granddaughter opened the car door and stepped out before turning and shuffling away. As she retreated, Decker heard her mumble, "There better not be any dilly-dallying at work; talk about 'on-the-job benefits'." Throwing his head back in laughter, he raised the window and waved at Kate as she smiled and walked up the steps with her grandmother.

AFTER A SHOWER, he settled into bed. He realized that in the past he would have worried about the delay at work all day, but spending time with Kate had shown him there were some things more important. His worrying would have done nothing to speed things up; he was glad he's spent the evening with her and the guys.

He smiled as he texted her.

Decker: *So, Grandma thinks I've got a nice package.*

He chuckled as he pictured Kate's cheek flaming.

Kate: *Shut up! I DO NOT need to think about the fact that my grandmother a) has checked out and spoken of your "package" or b) that she spoke of "dipping your business."*

He laid back on his bed, laughing. Grandma made him laugh. Thinking of his *package* and *dipping his business* as spoken by Grandma probably should have been a turn off; but when it came to Kate, nothing turned him off.

Decker: *Goodnight, Bug. See you tomorrow. Just us this weekend, okay?*

Kate: *Sounds good. I'll bring my tongue and cherry.*

And with that, Decker rolled over in an attempt to sleep.

16

The rest of the week had gone fairly smoothly; the construction was back on schedule and the programs at The Center+ were setting up nicely. Decker confirmed with Kate that she was up for spending the whole weekend with him. He didn't assume they'd take the next step, but he wanted to be in the right place if it did come to that.

On Thursday, knowing Kate would be coming over after work on Friday, he stopped by his parents' house on his way home.

"Decker! I'm so glad you're here! Can you stay for dinner?" His mom, Libby, met him in the kitchen as he rattled around in the fridge for something to eat.

"Yeah, I can stay, Momma. Call Sawyer and see if he

wants to come by." He polished off a piece of cold pizza, knowing his mom would be fixing supper soon.

"Well, if the twins are here, I'm calling Kendrick and Zach to see if they are available; I want to see my baby boy too." Audrey patted her nephew on the cheek as she entered the kitchen. "Hello handsome nephew of mine." Chuckling, Decker hugged his aunt.

An hour later, after Kendrick and Zach had declined the invitation due to prior engagements, the twins and their parents and Audrey gathered in the kitchen.

"Hey, Momma, can you give me your recipe for cherry pie?" Decker tried to act nonchalant, but Sawyer's snort gave him away.

His father, Nate, raised an eyebrow and squinted his eyes suspiciously.

Libby frowned from her position at the sink as she rinsed a cup, "I can make one for you. Why do you need the recipe? And why cherry? You've never really liked cherry pie."

"Oh, he likes it just fine now." Sawyer couldn't help but snicker at his brother's discomfort. Humming he mumbled some words under his breath, *"She's my cherry pie...."*

If looks could kill, his twin would be six feet under.

Nate shook his head and stood. Walking to his wife's side by the sink, he leaned down and whispered in her ear. Chuckling, he poured a cup of coffee and leaned against the counter to watch the show.

Blushing, Libby spoke, "Decker Morgan, you better not

be being anything less than a respectful gentleman. I better not find out you're pressuring a girl into something she's not ready for."

"Momma, it's not like that. Kate and I have been dating for a bit, and it's sort of a joke between us. I thought it would make her smile if I made her a pie." Decker regretted bringing this up in front of everyone.

"Awww, Libby, I think it's sweet. Your baby boy wants to trade cherries with his girl." Audrey chuckled and headed out the backdoor. "Later, all. Love you. Boys, tell that son of mine to visit his mother more often." She left with a smile and a wave.

Sawyer cleared his throat catching Decker's attention. When Decker looked at him, Sawyer nodded slightly and Decker realized that his brother was going to tell his parents his secret.

Libby finished writing the recipe and handed it to him.

"Momma, Dad, can we talk?" Sawyer's voice was shaky; Decker was glad to be here for him. He pulled a chair out and sat down next to his brother.

A look passed between Nate and Libby. He reached for his wife's hand and they sat across the table from their boys.

"First, I'm sorry it's taken me this long. I need to tell you something important; I've waited because I don't want to cause problems for you or anyone in the family." Sawyer hesitated as he watched his mom's eyes sparkle with tears and his dad place an arm around her shoulders.

"Go ahead, son. There's nothing you can tell us that would change anything." Nate nodded at his son.

"I'm gay." Each time he said the words, it seemed to get easier. He wasn't ready to tell the rest of the family yet, but he couldn't go any longer without sharing with his parents.

Libby dried her tears and smiled at him.

"Momma, why don't you look shocked? Dad, why aren't you surprised?" Sawyer had expected more of a reaction from them.

"Oh, baby boy, we've known for a while. Well, I wouldn't say we've *known*, but we've suspected for about 10-12 years now." Libby's smile was shaky, but she didn't appear devastated.

"Why didn't you say anything?" Sawyer questioned.

"Your mom brought it up to me several years ago. I think in the beginning we both hoped she was wrong, we didn't want you to have to suffer through the emotions and reactions. Then, when we were more sure about it, we talked and decided it was something you needed to come to on your own and all we could do was be here loving you until you were ready to talk to us." Nate stood and walked to his son. "I love you no matter what. I don't like the idea of you being hurt or ridiculed, but nothing will ever change the fact that you're my son and I love you."

Libby sniffled and hugged Sawyer into her arms. "You'll always be my baby boy and I will support you until my dying breath. I hate that not everyone in your life and in this town will be as open about your sexuality, but you've got us on your side, no matter what."

Nate reached out and pulled Decker into their group hug.

Knowing they had to get to work early tomorrow, the four of them said their goodbyes. Nate walked his boys to the door. "I have to tell you boys, I'm getting too old for this shit. I just wanted a quiet evening with your mom, maybe a little bedroom action..." When the boys winced, Nate gave them a look, "Really? You can't stand the thought of your mom and I having sex? Well, I just learned that one son is gay and the other son plans on popping some girl's cherry. I think we're about even." Nate threw his head back and laughed at his boys' discomfort as the twins chuckled nervously. No matter the age, offspring never want to hear about their parents' bedroom activities.

17

*F*riday afternoon droned on forever as Decker thought ahead to Kate being at his place all weekend. He didn't know if things would progress any further than they already had, but he was looking forward to just spending time with her. He had never just hung out with a woman before; he always needed a plan, an itinerary, but he had a feeling he and Kate could fill their hours just fine.

"Hey, Bug, I'm going to go run and then cut out so I can make sure the house is decent for you to come over. The guys are supposed to help keep it neat, but you never know with them. If you're still up for spending the whole weekend, pack a bag and come over any time after 6:00 p.m." He spoke as he ambled into her office, straight over to her, and pulled her out of her seat. By the time he finished speaking, she was in his arms and he was leaning in to kiss her.

His heart beat faster as her lips danced with his. The tiny whimper in the back of her throat got him every time. Sliding his tongue across her bottom lip, he palmed her backside with his hands and pulled her front side flush against him. He knew she could feel how much he wanted her by the way she ground herself against him and moaned into his mouth.

"Mmm, mmm, mmm, if this is what this half of BDSM is doing, I'd love to see what the other half is up to! Damn, Deck, I didn't know we'd added cinematography to our programs, but if you'll give me a camera I'll get your porno flick made for you. Don't worry, Katie, I'll make sure it's tasteful." Kendrick laughed as he sauntered through the adjoining door from Decker's office. "Since the 'no dating colleagues' rule just got rewritten to 'fuck your colleagues every chance you get', I think I better go see which of the employees would most like a hook up with me."

Smiling against her lips, but never breaking the kiss, Decker raised his middle finger at his cousin while he angled Kate's head so he could kiss her deeper.

"Damn lucky bastard," Kendrick chuckled as he walked out. "See you lovebirds at home. We can pop some corn, crack open some beers, and cuddle on the couch."

As Kendrick left, Decker ended their kiss. "One thing about living with those guys, there may be an issue getting some privacy this weekend. It wasn't something that occurred to me before because I wasn't bringing girls home, but those assholes will purposely hang out and bug us the whole time."

He smirked as he spoke, but Katie could tell that he wasn't too angry; he loved his brother and cousins with all that he had.

Leaning into him for one last kiss, she whispered, "Your door locks, right? We have all weekend; we can hang with the guys and retreat to your room for privacy as needed. Now, go run and I'll be there at 6:00 p.m."

Decker smiled and winked, thinking ahead to all he needed to do at home, as he kissed her cheek. "I'll see you soon."

AFTER A TWO-MILE RUN, a shower, and a quick stop at the grocery store, Decker was home and elbow deep in his first foray into the baking world. While it had seemed like a cute, funny, romantic gesture at first, he was feeling unsure of himself yet he was determined to make a damn cherry pie.

He was cleaning up the kitchen, enjoying the scent of cherry pie filling the room, when a knock sounded at the door. Checking the timer to be sure the pie wouldn't burn, he ran to answer it. Pulling open the door, he found his girl looking beautiful and a bit unsure of herself. He smiled and gestured for her to enter.

"Hi, Bug. I'm glad you could make it." A kiss to her mouth and then he took her bag, setting it on the stairs. "We'll put your bag somewhere later; I want you in my room, my bed, but if you're more comfortable in the guestroom, that's okay too."

"Thank you, Decker. I want this weekend with you more than anything, but I've never spent a night with a guy, let alone a whole weekend. I know I'm a consenting adult, but I'm nervous. I'm also a little worried that it will look bad for you at work." She spoke with concern, somewhat for herself, but mostly for him.

"Kate, the rules at work for no dating colleagues were basically 'strongly suggested' in the staff handbook, although no one ever got fired for it. The rules were self-imposed on myself because I didn't want the distraction or the hassle. But, Katie-did, if I didn't have the chance to talk to you and see you every day, or if I had to hide my feelings for you at work, I think I'd go insane. No one is going to care that we are dating, as long as we do our jobs, and you and I both know we do a kick-ass job of that. I am still a rule follower and strict in other areas, but when it comes to you, I can't help but bend a bit." He started to kiss her, but the shrill beep of the timer interrupted him. "Stay here, look around, I'll be right back."

Rushing to the kitchen, he grabbed his oven mitts and pulled the pie out of the oven. It looked perfect; golden brown crust, dark red filling, bubbly edges. "Damn straight it's perfect, I don't settle for less than the best." He laughed at his own arrogant comment, but, he couldn't help it. He was damn proud of making this pie all by himself.

"What smells so good in here?" Katie had reached the kitchen.

"Nope, out. It's a surprise for later." He sat the pie to cool on the counter; later, when they came in to get something to eat, he'd have to move it so she wouldn't see it.

At the very last moment, a thought crossed his mind. Grabbing his phone he texted his cousins and brother.

Decker: *I made a cherry pie for Kate. DO NOT EAT IT. I'm serious, fuckers. DON'T TOUCH!*

There, that should keep them from breaking out forks and sitting around the table eating his masterpiece. Although, if he were honest, he fondly recalled many late nights in high school sitting with the three of them devouring pies his mom or grandmas had baked.

Zach: *Mmm, pie. Fine, I'll stay out of it tonight, but maybe you could make me one soon, Betty Crocker.*

Kendrick: *Oh, I love eating PIE. Maybe you could leave some for us while you spend your night eating her pie. Enjoy that cherry, bud.*

Sawyer: *Yeah, not much of a PIE eater these days. The pie is safe with me.*

Decker couldn't help but laugh at the comments that flooded his phone in response to his text. He should have known they'd turn it to a sexual-innuendo-laced joke.

Sawyer: *Just FYI, the guys and I will be around tonight, but we're making ourselves scarce tomorrow day and night.*

I'm not sure where the guys are going, but I'll be staying with a friend.

Decker smiled at his brother; not only were they giving him some privacy, his brother was probably spending the night with the guy he was interested in. His heart swelled; his brother was happy, he was spending the weekend with his girl, and the work on The Center+ was back on track. Life was good.

Walking into the living room, he found Kate cuddled on the couch looking through a photo album. "I remember so many of these pictures and events. What a fun walk down memory lane." She smiled up at him as she closed the book.

"Are you hungry?" He asked her, referring to a meal, but the darkening of her eyes and the shy smile she gave him told him that her mind went somewhere else entirely. Laughing he shook his head, "You naughty girl. I was talking about getting something to eat."

"I know, I know. I just can't help myself around you sometimes." She grinned and kissed him. "I'm starving; my slave-driver boss had me working so hard today that I barely had time to scarf down a yogurt." She winked and wrapped her arms around his waist.

"Mmm, I'll show you a boss who *drives you hard*." He kissed her roughly and groaned as his phone chirped.

After reading the text, he chuckled and ran a hand over his face. "Looks like our dinner options just broadened. Seems the other guys are at my grandparents' house for Taco

Night. So, we can go out, fix something here, order in, or go to Taco Night."

"Will you be upset if I choose Taco Night?" She had a giddy expression on her face.

"No, Bug, I won't be upset. You're a fan of tacos, huh?" He had to laugh at her excitement.

"I'm a fan of your grandmas' Taco Night for sure! Sawyer and I had broken up, but we were still friends; he'd had a really crappy day. Some guy he'd thought was gay and liked him had started dating the head cheerleader and Sawyer was crushed. He asked me to come over to cheer him up; he really needed a shoulder to cry on. Anyway, he took me to Taco Night at Grandma Cindy's house and It. Was. Awesome! She had every single topping imaginable. I had so much fun building my own tacos. I think I made five of them because it was so much fun, but I could only eat two of them. I was embarrassed for wasting so much food; I think Kendrick, Sawyer and Zach all ate my extras." Her eyes sparkled as she recalled the evening from long ago.

Decker's face had fallen a bit. She reached out and cupped his cheek, "Hey, baby, what's wrong?" So many thoughts went through his head. I've never liked pet names and now I'm feeling warm and tingly over my girl calling me baby. I want to spend the night with her in my arms, but I'm excited to take her to my family's Taco Night. What in the hell have I gotten myself into?

Instead of speaking those thoughts, he sighed, "I don't

know. I guess I'm feeling sad that Sawyer didn't think he could cry on my shoulder over his crappy day. I'm also sad that I don't remember that night; my brother and cousins got to know you and spend time with you, and I was probably at the library studying or writing business plans."

"Decker, I don't think either of us would have liked each other much back then. You were gorgeous, but so serious and unapproachable. I wasn't the ditzy type, but I definitely hadn't grown into my self-confidence; I don't think I would have had the nerve to be myself and try to break you down. We were doing what we needed to be doing back then; things happen for a reason." She leaned in and kissed him, snaking her tongue out to taste his lips while her hand roamed south to palm him. "The present is what matters now. You and Sawyer are good. You and I are good; we are in the right place for *us*. Let's not focus on what we may have missed out on, let's focus on what we've got the chance to experience now." Kissing him deeper, she giggled as he growled deep in his throat and walked her backwards until she met with the wall.

With a last tease of his tongue and final sound kiss on her lips he spoke gruffly, "Come on, Bug, let's get you some tacos."

He replied to the text to let them know they should set two extra places.

18

Having never brought a girl home to meet his family, Decker grabbed Katie's hand nervously as they walked up the steps. "Why am I more nervous than you?"

"Your family knows me, I'm pretty sure they like me, we've been dating for a bit, there's nothing to be nervous about. You're just worried because this is new to you; I bet you never brought a girl home, huh?" She looked at him a bit sadly.

"No, my parents met Angela one time at dinner when they came to see me at school, but that is the extent of my experience with introducing a girl to my parents." He looked sheepish.

"No worries, Deck, we've got this. Lucky for you, I'm no

shrinking violet, I can hold my own, and I have a history with most of these people. Just be my sexy, supportive man and promise to take me home for a steamy night later." She laughed as he closed his eyes and groaned.

"Seriously, Bug? Giving me a hard-on before my Grandma opens the door? Not. Cool." He smacked her ass just as Cindy Morgan opened the door.

"Decker Morgan, you know better than to knock on the door at this house. Katie is going to think we are uppity folks and that's the furthest thing from the truth." Cindy pulled Katie into a warm embrace and then grabbed Decker as well. "Come in, come in! It's almost time to eat!"

Decker did a quick re-introduction between his family and Katie. She smiled and hugged everyone as they all got reacquainted. Being a people person and good at cataloging information, she gathered several details in her brain to store for later use.

Abby Morgan was madly in love with her long-time boyfriend and Katie suspected a proposal was imminent. Beckett Jordan was just two weeks away from saying *I do* to his beautiful, sweet fiancé, Kenja. Megan Jordan was very pregnant and happily planning her wedding to the baby's daddy. Katie was pleased that no one seemed offended that the baby had come before the nuptials; the family's acceptance of this situation led her to believe they'd be fairly accepting of Sawyer's sexuality when he finally told them all.

Zach's younger sister, Aly, was in the beginning stages of a crush on one of her classmates at the local community college. Asher Martin, the boys' pseudo cousin, was a gangly hormonal teen with a bad attitude, but Kate suspected he'd one day be a complete knock-out.

After all of the hugs and reacquainting was taken care of, Kate turned to see Sawyer breeze through the door with a smile a mile wide and a twinkle in his eyes. Walking towards him to stop him near the entrance and away from the others, she gathered him in a hug. "You smell like men's cologne and not the type you usually wear. You look like you're glowing. Tell me, Sawyer, does this have anything to do with a certain hottie at The Center+?" She kissed his cheek as he just grinned like the Cheshire cat and tweaked her nose. "Maybe, maybe not. Good to see you here, Katie-girl. It's like old times."

Kendrick and Zach came up to them, prompting Decker to join in their little group. Laughing, Kendrick spoke first. "Hmmm, Decker, I didn't expect to see you guys here. I thought you'd be having your own *taco* night in your bedroom." Decker reddened and Kendrick howled with laughter. "Taco and pie, mmm, mmm, mmm." He winked at Katie who could only laugh at Kendrick's crass comments.

"Damn it, Kendrick, do you have to be so crude?" Decker had to defend her, but she could tell he was having a good time with the ribbing his cousin was giving them.

"And, our dear Sawyer, why do you look like you just came from your own version of a hot dog bar? Did you fill your bun and squirt on all the toppings?" Kendrick was on a roll, but it was all in fun; the five of them roared with laughter and Sawyer just winked and blushed a little.

"Alright you guys, come join the rest of us, and Kendrick, knock it off with the sexual innuendos in front of this sweet girl, or all of us parents are going to start talking about our *intimate moments*." Audrey cackled at the blanched looks on her son and nephews' faces. Jeremiah came up behind her as she laughed; wrapping his arms around her, he smiled and winked at Kendrick, "What's this about intimate moments, angel?" With a kiss to her temple, he spoke to the group in front of him, "Did you all want some pointers? I could explain some of our favorite positions."

"Stop! Just stop!" Kendrick pleaded as he jammed his fingers in his ears. "Fine, no more talk of tacos or pie unless it's about the actual food, I promise." Stalking off he muttered, "Just having a good time and then the old folk have to kill the buzz with sex talk. I need to be disinfected with bleach." He pretended to shudder and everyone laughed.

Katie had grown up with loving parents; even after her dad left she saw him regularly, albeit away from her mother. Her mom was fun and sweet and loving; her grandma, crazy and outspoken, loved her dearly. Having a loving family wasn't a new experience for her. But, as she sat around the huge table with this large group, she couldn't help but smile and feel blessed to know these people.

Forcing herself to keep her taco building to a minimum, knowing she wouldn't be able to eat as many as she wanted to build, Katie made two soft tacos and one crunchy. Choosing fillings of chicken, steak, and shrimp for each taco, she loaded on the lettuce, tomatoes, cheese, and sour cream. Skipping the onions, she glanced at Decker; he smiled and winked at her and bypassed the onions as well.

Three tacos, a margarita, and hours of laughs later, Decker held her hand as they sat on the couch. Kate watched in amazement at the love still so very evident between the parents of her four best guy friends. The secret looks, the sweet kisses, the purposeful touches; so many years later, they were so very much in love. It may have been hard for the guys to watch it, but as an onlooker, it was truly a sight to behold. Even the oldest generation still had a passion about them.

As she watched the couples, she took in a couple of other things. Kendrick seemed to have a sad air about him; he'd never admit it, she was sure, but he wanted the love, comfort, and security he was surrounded by; he wanted that in his personal life, but he'd lost the chance a long time ago and Katie wasn't sure if he'd ever open himself up to it again.

The strangest observation she made throughout the evening was between Zach and Zoey. Growing up as cousins, the whole town knew that Zach and Zoey were joined at the hip. Zach's sister, Aly was Zoey's best girlfriend, but Zach and Zoey were about as close as two people could get. Katie caught several heated looks pass between them, followed quickly by flushed looks of guilt and tension. She smiled inwardly; Zach and Zoey were interesting, very interesting.

The group spent a fun-filled evening just chatting and laughing. Katie was pretty sure that some of the parents spent extra time doing *something* in other areas of the house throughout the night. Libby's face was flushed when she and Nate returned to the group within a minute of each other. Audrey was glowing and just laughed when Jeremiah smacked her ass after they returned from *checking something out upstairs*. Nicky Morgan was about the sweetest, most attentive husband she'd ever seen; he had a look of total adoration on his face for Carly. No matter what she said or did, Nicky's face spoke of his love for her. Kyle and Josie Martin were possibly the most in-sync couple she'd ever witnessed; it was obvious they knew what the other was thinking, the looks on their faces gave away the love and slightly naughty thoughts that passed between them all night. What would it be like, twenty some years later, to have a love so strong and still so right? Katie had never been in love; was she in love with Decker? She thought she was, even if she felt it was too soon to feel that way. All she knew was she had very little trouble picturing their relationship twenty years in the future. That fact thrilled her and scared her at the same time.

Since they had spent the entire evening with his brother and cousins, Decker didn't feel bad about sweeping Kate to his room. He snuck into the kitchen and grabbed the cherry pie, smiling as he thought about what her reaction would be.

"You can have the bathroom first, Bug." Decker swept his arm out dramatically, making her laugh at his gesture.

"Why, thank you, kind sir." She grabbed her bag and headed to the bathroom. A quick shower later, she dressed in her softest flannel pants, a tank, and her hair pulled up in a messy bun. She wasn't worried about impressing Decker; she knew he found her attractive physically, but it was more than just that. In the past, she'd never felt 100% comfortable with the men she went on dates with; was the skirt too short and suggesting too much, did her V-neck shirt reveal too much, did her hair make her seem severe if it was pulled back tightly or like a slacker if it was in a messy bun? With Decker, there were none of those thoughts; he liked her for her, not for her clothes or hair or body.

"You okay in there?" Decker knocked on the door lightly; breaking out of her musings, Kate chuckled and opened the door.

"Sorry, I was lost in thought. The bathroom is all yours." She kissed him. Not because she needed to prove anything to him, just because she wanted to feel his lips on hers.

Decker showered and pulled on a pair of pajama pants and an old t-shirt hoping he wouldn't be wearing it long. As he walked into his room, he realized he'd left the pie in plain sight.

"Did you bake this? For me?" She asked incredulously, eyes wide and a slightly unbelieving smile on her face.

He blushed, but pulled her close to him. "Yeah, it's supposed to be funny and romantic." He could tell she wasn't making the connection.

"It's a *cherry* pie...," he let the words hang for a bit and couldn't help but feel relieved when realization dawned on her; it would have lost some of its cute romantic notions if he'd had to explain it to her.

"Oh my God, Decker, are you trading cherries with me? That's the sweetest, cutest, goofiest thing anyone has ever done for me." She laughed, open-mouthed, against his lips as he pulled her in closer for a kiss.

"Yeah, after your cherry stem trick and your shenanigans with the song, I thought I'd get in on the game play too." Kissing her nose, he walked to his dresser. "I brought plates and forks, you want a piece?"

Blushing, she bit her lip nervously. "Um, I want a piece, but can we eat it later? I'd rather have a piece of something else right now."

Within seconds of the words escaping her lips, he was flush against her front. Their faces were mere centimeters apart; breath mingling, hearts pounding, lips longing to taste.

Leaning in just a fraction, Decker's lips brushed hers. "If at any point this gets to be too much, just tell me to stop. You got that? You have the reigns here."

At her silent nod, he brought his lips against hers more forcefully. She sighed and parted her lips slightly, allowing him entry. She would never tire of the unique taste of this man; their tongues caressed gently, and he nipped at her lip with his teeth bringing a groan from her.

Kate let her hands roam under his shirt, up his torso and then down his back, trying to take him all in. His skin was smooth and hot, muscles rippled under her hands and his breath caught when she moved her hands cautiously to his chest to rub across his nipples.

Her hands grabbed the bottom of his shirt and pulled; knowing she wanted it off, he reached behind his neck and pulled the cloth over his head.

Kate felt her pulse increase as her eyes took in the beautiful perfection in front of her. Sure that she was going to hyperventilate, she let her head fall to the side as his arms wrapped around her and his mouth trailed kisses along her jaw until he reached her neck. A shiver of desire traveled through her; just as his lips met the sensitive skin on her neck, his hard length nudged against her and she felt her senses on overload.

His strong hands roamed under her shirt and around to her back; with purpose he slid down to her waist and snuck his fingers under the band of her pants. A growl emanated from deep in his chest as his hands moved lower to cup her ass; realizing she'd skipped panties under those silky soft pants sent so much blood to his cock he was surprised he didn't pass out.

"I love the way your ass feels in my hands." Pushing her pants the rest of the way down, he maneuvered her to the bed and pushed her down so he could remove the material. Stepping back, he took in the vision before him; bare from the waist down, breathing quickly, dark hooded eyes watching his every move. "I don't know what I did to deserve you, Bug. So fucking gorgeous." He spoke as he let his hands travel from her naked thighs up to her hips. Pulling her with force to the edge of the bed, he lowered himself to his knees and moved her legs over his shoulders. "Open for me; just relax." His mouth found her center and he chuckled against her as she rocketed her hips off the mattress. "Easy, Bug." He placed his forearm across her hips and let his tongue travel, tease, and taste. Her breathy moans spurred him on; tracing a finger along her folds, he allowed himself to enter slowly. As her moans became louder and he had a harder time pinning her hips down, he added another finger and found a rhythm with his hand and tongue.

His moans vibrated against her and reached her very soul; letting herself go, she moaned his name and clutched her body around his finger and tongue.

Moving her farther up onto the bed so he could join her, he pulled her close to him. "Decker, that was incredible; I don't know if I'll be good for anything after that."

From behind her, he laughed and kissed the crook of her neck. "If you're willing to go further, I assure you you'll be good for what I've got in mind." He took her shiver as a promising sign.

Rolling so that he had to position himself on top of her, between her legs, she let herself enjoy the heavy completeness his weight brought. She felt his cock pressing against her center and realized that she was getting turned on again. "Looks like I was wrong; I guess I'm more than good for Round 2."

Knowing he needed to keep his pants on until later, he made short work of her tank and closed his eyes, sighing, when the tank's built-in bra disappeared and reveal her naked breasts. Perfect, she was fucking perfect. He brought his hands up to fill them with her smooth, creamy skin; the perfect handful, he brushed his thumbs across her rosy nipples and felt a tremor move through her body. Letting his mouth fill with her, he teased with his tongue until she was writhing beneath him and he felt like he was about to lose the one shred of control he still had left.

"We can stop if you're not sure." He knew it would probably kill him if she wanted to stop, but he didn't want to force her into something if she wasn't ready.

"No, Decker, I want you. I want *this* with you." She rolled her hips against him. "This is probably something we should have discussed earlier; have you been tested? Have you ever had sex without protection?" His *Yeah, right* look reminded her that she was talking to the king of control; she also realized that he'd never put her in danger if he wasn't 100% clean.

"Okay, so I should have known that you'd take all the precautions necessary." She smiled at him and he winked as he surged his length against her center.

"Since I'm obviously clean and I'm on the pill, I want to suggest we do this with no condom." At the look of surprise on his face, she cupped his cheeks and kissed him deeply. "I don't want to get too serious here, but I don't plan on doing this with anyone else any time soon, if ever."

His possessive growl heated her insides even more.

"So, I want this first experience with you, with anyone, to be skin-on-skin; I want to feel you completely inside me. If you're okay with it." Kate had never felt so sure of something. This man was the only one she'd ever trust to take her without protection; she would never want someone the way her body longed for his. Without over analyzing, she knew she loved him with all of her heart; she wanted to declare her love for him, but she knew she'd feel a bit melodramatic if she said it then as he took her for the first time.

"Kate, if you're sure, I can assure you that I'm clean; I was just at the doctor before we left school and I've not been with anyone since then. Plus, I'd never put you in danger if I wasn't sure I was clean." He leaned in and devoured her mouth; they'd been talking for a few minutes but his dick hadn't stopped throbbing, in fact, it was possibly even harder than it had been.

"Baby, I want to be inside you so badly, but I'm so scared of hurting you. I've never been with a virgin, but I know it's not going to be comfortable." He let his mouth trail kisses across her breasts and up her neck until he reached her mouth. Standing quickly, he removed his pants and boxers; he felt a heady surge of pride as his beautiful girl's breath caught at the sight of him.

Crawling back onto the bed and taking his position back between her legs, he felt her heat and wetness against his cock. He wasn't going to be able to prolong it for much longer; she whimpered as he rubbed himself against her tight bundle of nerves.

"Decker, I need you inside me now. I've never had sex with a guy, but I've used toys occasionally." She giggled at his helpless growl. "I'm sure I'll be tight, but..."

He grabbed her by the hair and tilted her head so her eyes were looking directly into his. "Later, you and I will talk more about these *toys*, but for now I'm going to need you to stop speaking of them unless you want me to blow my load before I'm even inside." He kissed her again and let his cock rub against her, gathering her wetness and increasing the friction.

Propping himself up on his elbows and pulling his hips back slightly, he aligned himself and began to push in inch by inch. Clenching his teeth, sweat breaking out on his body, he forced himself to go slowly. When he was almost fully inside, Kate wrapped her legs around his body, "I want you to fuck me, Decker." Any control he'd thought he had flew out the window, and he sunk himself the rest of the way into her.

She tensed slightly, and he stopped completely.

"I'm okay, it doesn't hurt, I just feel so full." She panted as she rocked her hips against him.

"Mmmm, never. Never has it felt like this." He pushed up on his arms and looked down to where they were joined. "Look at your body taking mine; we look so fucking good together." Lowering himself back down, he wrapped his arms around so that they met behind her back.

"This isn't going to last long, let's make it good." He kissed her sexy chuckle away and increased the speed of his thrusts. The sensations running through his body were nothing that he'd ever experienced; physically it was more than he'd ever dreamed sex could be; emotionally he felt his heart constrict as he looked into her eyes. He would never be able to live without this girl in his life.

"Oh, God, Decker." She felt her body begin to tighten around him. "I'm so close, baby. Please."

He slowed his speed, but increased the strength of his thrusts, and within seconds her body was shattering around him. The clenching of her heat around his cock was more than he could stand, and he felt himself spill into her. Moments later, they lay breathing hard, completely spent.

"That was freaking amazing." He kissed her temple and felt shock as he registered himself hardening inside her again. Before her, sex had been a one-and-done and back to work type event. He felt like he could do this forever with her.

"Yes, yes it was." She smiled and stretched her body against his as he took in the rosy flush of her satisfied body. "Mmm, I think I'm up for that cherry trade-off now. Get your girl some pie." She was laughing, but sobered quickly as he surged into her one more time.

"We'll have some pie and rest, but we will definitely be doing this again. And again, and again." He winced as he pulled himself out of her.

Feeling empty, she sighed as she watched his perfect form walk to the bathroom. Hearing the water running, she decided to join him to get cleaned up. They both quickly cleaned up and washed their hands. The whole scene seemed surreal to her; she'd just had sex for the first time with the man she loved, and they were now in the bathroom together, performing normal, everyday type things; she was pretty sure that she'd figure out something annoying about him at some point, but for now she could completely picture them sharing a bathroom, a room, a home, a life.

They piled onto his bed, each with a plate of pie, and dug in.

"Decker, this is seriously good pie." She spoke while trying to keep a bite from escaping her mouth.

He laughed at her and leaned in to kiss a spot of cherry filling off of her lips. "Well, if Kendrick were here, he'd have some crass comment about how seriously good *your* pie is." They both laughed, knowing it was true.

"But, all kidding aside, what just happened between us was amazing. I've never had that with anyone. Sex was a release, but it also distracted me. With you, my mind lost all ability to function; I didn't want to be anywhere but with you." He took her empty plate and laid it with his on the floor. Laying back on the pillow, he pulled her close to him.

"So, there's something I wanted to tell you earlier, but I was afraid the timing would make it seem less heartfelt." She spoke as her head lay comfortably on his chest. He rubbed her arm in a sign to continue. "I love you, Decker. I've never said that to a guy. I always wondered how I'd know it was truly love, but you and this thing between us has shown me that love is easy to recognize when it's with the right one."

She waited a few seconds for him to speak. When he didn't, she looked up at him. His eyes were shiny and the expression on his face was hard to read.

"It's okay if you don't feel the same. I know we've not been together very long. I just wanted you to know how I'm feeling." She meant what she said, but had to push back her disappointment. Maybe she had read things wrong? She had thought he was feeling the same things as she was.

"Just give me a second." He took a breath and seemed to be weighing his words. After a moment he took a final breath and sat up. Sitting cross-legged, facing her, he held her hands.

"Katie, I've never told anyone I love them, outside of my family. I'm a man of my word; if I tell someone something, I'm true to it. In my business, my word is my reputation. I've believed that since I was old enough to understand it. So, even when the girls I occasionally dated in high school and college would tell me they loved me, I couldn't ever bring myself to say it back to them. I usually enjoyed spending time with them, but to use such a big emotion as *love* to describe what I felt seemed like not being true to myself." He paused for a second and stared at their entwined hands. "You changed me, changed things I didn't even know needed changed. You're helping me loosen up, while at the same time you're on-board and in-sync with me businesswise in a way no one has ever been. I've had more fun with you in the time we've been together than I can ever remember having with someone who wasn't family. You make me determined to continue striving for the best in our business, but you also make me realize that there's more to life than work." He stopped again and looked at her face. He brought a hand up to cup her cheek. "Kate Turner, I love you. I love you with a love I didn't even know I had. The thought of not having you on my side and in my life is not one I want to contemplate."

A tear rolled down her cheek, his thumb quickly swiping

it away. No words were needed, he leaned in and captured her mouth in a slow, soul-searing kiss as if to seal their declarations of love.

An hour later, after cleaning up from another round which may or may not have involved some sticky cherry pie filling, he held her in his arms and they drifted into a sweetly satisfied dreamland.

SATURDAY MORNING DAWNED bright and sunny. Decker savored the feel of her in his arms and the scent of her hair before he even cracked his eyes. He leaned in and kissed her shoulder, moving towards her neck, as his hand roamed over her belly to her hip and landed on her ass. With a quick squeeze, he laughed when she grumbled.

"Morning, Bug." Another kiss to her neck brought a delicious roll of her hips against his quickly lengthening cock.

Another grumble escaped her lips.

"Is my beautiful girl not a morning person?" He chuckled and rubbed his scratchy chin against her cheek.

"I'm not the most upbeat in the morning until I get some coffee, but my issue this morning is compounded by the fact that my insatiable boyfriend tried to fuck me into oblivion last night, several times I might add." There was a smile in her voice.

"If I promise to go easier on you this morning and provide piping hot, sweet coffee afterwards, could you be persuaded to go another round?" His sexy, gruff voice against her ear woke the fire inside of her. Knowing she'd be sore, but already feeling her body preparing for him, she rolled slightly to look at him.

"Well, with an offer like that, who could refuse?" She rolled a little further to accommodate his body on top of hers. "While I like the idea of going easier, let's remember that short and sweet can be very fulfilling."

When he smiled and furrowed his brows in confusion she laughed and smacked at his arm playfully. "I *need* coffee, Decker. It's an addiction, what can I say?"

Smirking at her, he sunk into her without warning, catching her gasp with his mouth and teasing with his tongue. "Well, I *need* you and it's quickly becoming an addiction as well."

Slowly, with strong, measured thrusts, he reveled in her body. On his elbows, he grasped her head and looked deep in her eyes. Their souls met, touched, connected, became one in much the same way as their bodies were one. Katie quickly learned the difference between fucking and making love; Decker knew this was a first-time experience for them both.

Looking into his dark eyes, Katie spoke breathlessly, "I love you, Decker."

"This is forever, Kate. You and me. I won't give you up." He punctuated each word with a thrust. "I love you."

AFTER THEY BOTH CAME UNDONE, a quick shower was in order. It would have been quicker if Katie hadn't decided to play. "I want coffee, but there's something else I want to taste on my tongue first."

Decker's head fell back against the tiles as she dropped to her knees and took him in her hands. How he was still able to be hard was beyond him, but he knew he wanted her mouth on him more than anything. He hissed as she took him in. He started to grasp her head, but she stopped and looked up at him. "Nope, not this time. You're not in control right now; I am and I want your hands above your head, no touching." Knowing how hard it was for him to relinquish his grip on things, she smiled and felt a warm rush through her body when he complied.

Taking him back into her mouth, she used her tongue, lips, and hand to bring him close to his release. Expecting one thing, she was shocked when he jerked her upright, picked her up, and pressed her back against the wall. Impaling her, he swallowed her groan of frustration and satisfaction. "Sorry, Bug, I tried giving up total control, but I couldn't help it. I needed to be in you again." He spoke gruffly as he continued to thrust into her warm body. The water ran cold but neither of them noticed; they saw stars as they came together.

"Mmmm, *now* we can get you some coffee." He kissed her as they both laughed.

WALKING into the kitchen holding her hand seemed like the most natural thing in the world to Decker; he'd never been one for public affection, but he couldn't imagine walking next to her and *not* holding her.

"Well, well, well, if it isn't the love birds. The very *loud* love birds I might add." Kendrick laughed and winked at Katie's blush. "No worries. I'm just a bit concerned. You know, Decker, we do have some young, impressionable cousins who have been given permission to sleep over on occasion, and I worry that your extracurricular bedroom activities may not be the best example to be setting for them, especially as the newest member of Torey Hope's business community." Kendrick kept a straight face throughout his whole speech, and Katie felt her heart drop to her feet.

"Oh my God, Decker! Was Asher here last night? Kendrick's right; you can't be having a girl sleep over. It looks bad on all fronts." She felt so bad, how could she have allowed him to put himself in such a bad position.

"Hear that, BDSM? I'm right." Kendrick winked at Sawyer and Decker both as the other twin entered the kitchen in search of coffee.

"Knock it off, Kendrick." Decker slapped him in the head and poured Katie a cup of coffee, automatically adding her desired amount of cream and sugar.

"Bug, don't listen to him. He's throwing my words back in

my face. I *may* have made a little speech similar to that one upon our return to Torey Hope." Decker rolled his eyes at his brother and cousin's snorts. "Okay, fine, I made that exact speech when we moved back home."

"But, Decker, he's right in a lot of ways. What if Asher had been here? What will people think of their newest, youngest business guru bringing home random girls?" Katie worried her lip as she spoke.

"Stop, Bug. First, if Asher had been here, we wouldn't have done what we were doing or we would have been quieter. Second, we are grownups; you are not some *random* girl I'm bringing home; we are both consenting adults; I'd like to see someone just *try* to cause a problem about us being together." He kissed the top of her head and flipped off Kendrick as he did. "Thanks a lot, fucker."

Smirking, Kendrick apologized. "Kate, I'm sorry. I didn't mean to worry you; I was just giving Deck some shit."

Calming and smiling slightly at Kendrick, Kate tried to let her worry subside.

In hopes of changing the subject, Decker sat next to Katie at the table. Zach entered wearing only boxers and scratching at his bedhead. Glancing around, Decker and Katie both took in, for the first time, the state of undress the other men were in. All three were wearing only boxers; Decker himself had at least donned a pair of shorts.

"Damn guys, I'm pretty comfortable with Kate's feelings for me, but do you think you could dress yourselves a bit more modestly when my girl's over?" He frowned at them. All three glanced at each other and then back at the two sitting at the table. Sheepishly, they sat their coffee down and retreated to their rooms for more clothing.

"Decker, it's not like I'm interested in them, they didn't have to leave." Katie was touched by his protective gesture, but felt bad the other guys had left. "I hadn't even noticed what they were wearing, I've only got eyes for you." She leaned in and kissed him.

"Well, they are grown men, they should have more respect for themselves and you." He knew she wasn't looking at any of them, but it gave him a chance to erase the worry from her face after Kendrick's comments. Taking the moment they had to themselves, he spoke again.

"Hey, I meant to ask you. Do you have plans in a couple weekends? Beckett is getting married, and I wondered if you'd like to go with me as my date?" Decker rubbed her knuckles as he spoke.

"Your date to what?" Sawyer asked as the three reentered the kitchen in sweats or basketball shorts.

"To Beckett's wedding. It's in a couple weeks; you guys are all going, right? Do you have dates?" Decker knew that none of them would miss Beckett's special day; he was their older cousin or brother and had been the epitome of a wise, older, mentor as they were growing up.

"I'm going, but I'm not bringing anyone. I'm not ready to bring a date to something that big and public. Not just yet."

Sawyer had made strides, but he still had a ways to go before he felt confident enough to invite a guy on an in-public date.

"Nah, I'll probably just hang with Zoey." Katie noticed that Zach tried to come off as nonchalant about it, but she saw the slight flush on his cheeks at the mention of Zoey.

"Hell, no, I'm not bringing a date. Weddings are the perfect harvesting ground for desperate pussy." Kendrick spoke and waggled his eyebrows. "Emotional females, sweet cake, champagne flowing..." He threw his head back and closed his eyes as if to savor the image in his mind. "Yep, the pussy will be ripe for the picking, and I plan on picking the juiciest one and bringing her back here. Or at least to the restroom at the reception hall." He guffawed at the look of shock and utter disgust from the other three men; the contemplative look that Katie gave him, though, shot straight to his soul. It was like the girl could see beyond his mask; he didn't like feeling exposed. Standing from the table. "Speaking of pussy, I'll be gone tonight, so you guys can be as loud as you'd like. Have fun." And with that, Kendrick was gone.

"I'm going to hang out with Zoey and Asher, I'll probably just sleep over there." Zach rinsed his coffee cup and headed to his room.

"I have some things to do at The Center+ and then I've got a date. I've asked him if I can crash at his place. As long as the date goes well, I'll stay there. I'll text if I'm coming back to sleep here." Sawyer leaned down and kissed Katie's head.

"It's good to have you here, Katie-girl, you brighten this place up."

Smiling at each other, Decker and Katie imagined the possibilities of having the whole house to themselves for the day.

19

*I*n the middle of their movie marathon, which happened to include several make-out breaks, Decker's phone chirped. "Damn, I hope that's not Sawyer already. Do you think his date backed out on him?"

Katie smiled at his obvious protective streak for Sawyer.

Her smile fell away as she watched him read the text.

"You've got to be fucking kidding me!" He roared and angrily tossed his phone aside.

"What is it?" Grabbing his phone from the floor, Katie read yet another text from the unknown number.

While you're playing house with your little girlfriend, your business venture is falling apart. I thought you were more responsible than that.

Two thoughts struck Kate at once. One, the person who

was sending the texts seemed to know Decker personally. Two, the person seemed unhappy about her and Decker's relationship. What she didn't understand was *why*. Who had Decker pissed off enough to go to the trouble of messing with things at The Center+? And who was mad he was dating her?

"Let's head down there and see what's wrong this time." Decker grabbed her hand and pulled her into a kiss. "Once we get this taken care of, we'll grab dinner and come back here to finish where we left off this morning." His tongue swept into her mouth as his hands caressed down her bottom and pulled her firmly against his hard body.

She bit back a moan and pulled away from him. "Come on. I know it's killing you as much as it is me to find out what's happened now. Before we go, call the police so they can send an officer to take a report if need-ed." She smiled at him and laughed when he smacked her backside; Decker had loosened up a lot in their time together, but she saw darkness swirling in his expression. She knew he wasn't taking kindly to someone messing with his business.

A COUPLE HOURS later Decker held Kate's hand as they walked up the steps to his house. They had spent too much time having to speak to the police officer and combing through the mess that had been left at The Center+. Nothing drastic had taken place, but Decker was pissed that someone was so blatantly messing things up at work.

This time it had been piddly stuff that didn't cause too much trouble, but was just causing a major pain in the ass to clean up. Cut power cords on the tools, sawdust dumped all over the new wing, drywall busted up, and whole containers of nails and such spilled from one end of the wing to the other. No one was hurt and they wouldn't lose more than a couple hours of work getting the mess cleaned up, but it was the principle of the thing that was really getting to Decker.

"I just don't get it, Bug. I'm not the type to have enemies; I'm a fair person in business and my personal life. Someone seems hell bent on messing up The Center+ and causing problems between you and me." Popping the top off a beer bottle, Decker sat heavily on the couch and stretched his arms wide indicating where he wanted her to sit.

"I don't know, Deck. I don't have any sordid past that would be coming back to haunt me; I can't imagine who would be upset that we were dating. I know it's frustrating, but for now I think we have to let the police just monitor and see if they can catch the person in a slip up." She got quiet for a second before continuing, "I'm starting to get concerned that this person isn't going to stop until they are forced to stop. I just don't want anyone getting hurt. So far, it's been annoying, but nothing dangerous; what if this person starts escalating his efforts to mess things up?" She furrowed her brow at the thought and looked at Decker expectantly.

"That thought has been on my mind a lot today, too, Bug. I can't take a risk of going against the law and trying to catch this guy myself, but I also don't want to risk this asshole messing with things so much that someone gets hurt." He sighed as he took a long pull on the beer bottle. "I just don't know, Kate."

20

"Hey, man, I've got a favor to ask, but you've got to swear you won't tell anyone and you won't laugh at me." Decker spoke to his brother hesitantly, heart beating wildly in his chest. Asking for help wasn't something with which he was all that comfortable.

Smirking as if he was already enjoying himself immensely, Sawyer motioned his brother into the room. "In our entire life, I think I can remember maybe five times you've come to me asking for help. What in the world could be forcing the great Decker Morgan to lower himself to asking for help; what knowledge do I, a mere mortal, have that would be of assistance to you, Oh Great One?" Sawyer crossed his arms across his chest and just smiled.

"Damn it, wipe that shit-eatin' grin off your face; you're acting more and more like Kendrick every day, and it's not flattering. You're never going to get in any guy's pants if you act like an ass." His cheeks blushed as he acknowledged his brother was right; he wasn't the one usually coming to ask for help. But, this was important, and this was real. Reluctantly, he let Sawyer gloat for a bit longer before punching him in the arm. "Are you ready to be serious now? I need your help with something, but I don't want anyone else knowing about it."

Sobering slightly, Sawyer punched him back. "Yeah, man, I'll do anything to help you. You know that." Flopping down in one of the over-sized bean bags that decorated the floor of their game room, Sawyer looked up at his brother expectantly. "So, you got me, what do you need help with?"

Taking a deep breath, Decker blew it all out in one quick whoosh. "I need you to teach me how to dance." Looking at his brother, he waited.

And waited.

"Damn it, Sawyer, say something. Stop just staring at me." Decker shifted uncomfortably; he didn't like putting himself out there and then having Sawyer just stare at him was making him more than a little nervous.

"Oh, my God! You totally love her!" Sawyer threw his head back and laughed. "You love her and you need me to teach you how to dance with your girl. This is so classic, so priceless. Please, please let me tell the guys." He rolled off the bean bag, still laughing, to escape Decker's advancing attack.

"Shut up, man. No, you can't tell them. This isn't about

them. This is about Kate; she's asked me to dance before, and I've told her I don't dance and will never dance, but I want to surprise her and dance with her at Beckett's wedding. You're a good dancer, I want you to teach me." Decker had never been one to shy away from fear of doing something, and he wasn't going to stop now. He was surprised at the strength of his emotions about learning to dance for Kate.

"Man, I'm just giving you a rough time, you know I'll help you. Just give me some time to revel in this moment; it's not often you need me AND I get to give you some grief, I just need to savor it for a while." Sawyer smiled and Decker's heart warmed; he knew he could count on his brother.

"Okay, so let's get this started. You won't be able to learn all of my awesome dance skills before the wedding, but we can get a couple moves under your belt. I'm thinking you want something simple and classic for those slower songs and probably something quick and easy for those faster numbers, right?" Sawyer was tapping a finger on his chin, contemplating songs and dance steps. "You're in luck! I just remembered that Katie and I spent one whole summer learning dances for a local competition we were going to enter. Her dad left around that time and we never entered the contest, but I know she knows these moves." Sawyer was almost lost in thought as he mentally planned Decker's dance-related transformation. "So, let's get the slow stuff mastered first; that's the important stuff for weddings. Nothing better than holding that special someone close and swaying to the music while romance floats on the breeze." He closed his eyes and savored the image of holding someone close.

Decker raised an eyebrow at his brother. "No need to convince me, Sawyer, I already want to do this." He chuckled at how immersed his brother had already gotten in this project.

By the end of a couple hours, Decker could hold his own with any slow song. Sawyer had explained that it was basically just hugging the other person and swaying to the music. Decker wanted to practice a few songs with more classic hand positioning; he felt a little silly with his hand in Sawyer's and his other hand grasping his brother's waist, but he was determined to be able to dance for Kate.

Over the next few days, Decker and Sawyer spent several stolen hours a day practicing. Decker liked the dances where the song called out what you were to do or there were set movements. Freestyle was the one that made him nervous; he never knew what to do with his body.

"Okay, so fast songs can be tough if you're not real comfortable. What I want you to do is use Kate and build your dance around her. She likes to dance, you just need to hold her and let the music move you. Dancing is a lot like foreplay. Come here, I'll show you." Sawyer motioned for his brother to join him in the middle of the floor. Decker vehemently shook his head.

Sawyer rolled his eyes and shook his head at his brother's refusal. "Do you want to leave your girl standing on the dance floor to be swept up by Kendrick or someone else just because you won't shimmy your ass with your brother?" Sawyer scrolled through his phone and pulled up "Shut Up and Dance" by Walk the Moon; grabbing Decker's hand, he maneuvered them to the middle. "Now, dear brother, shut up and dance. I'll be Katie, just go with the flow. It's going to feel sexual and that's good. Let your bodies move and touch and feel."

Taking a deep breath and laughing nervously at his brother, Decker shook his head and let the music take over. It was a fun song with an easy beat. Sawyer played up his part as Kate and really got into the song; by the end, Decker was sad the song was over and even more excited to show Kate what he'd learned.

They finished with another fun song, "Dance With Me Tonight" by Olly Murs. The beat and style was different, but just as fun. Imagining himself holding Kate, watching her smile when she realized he was dancing for her, and having fun with his family and her, Decker decided that Beckett's wedding was the most anticipated event he had on his social calendar for the near future.

"Well, you may not win any technical competitions, but you've got rhythm and heart, you're going to have a blast dancing with Katie all night at the wedding. I'll be there for moral support; I'll try not to show you up on the floor, but there's no controlling these moves. Don't worry about the songs, what I taught you will work for any song, but I'll give the DJ a list of some songs to play." Sawyer slapped him on the back. "Decker?" He spoke quietly and waited for his brother to look him in the eyes.

"Yeah?" Decker's eyes were sparkling from the energy of the last dance.

"Thanks, man." Sawyer's sincerity was evident.

"For what?" Decker cocked his head to the side, wondering what his brother could possibly thank him for; he was the one who owed Sawyer his unending gratitude for helping him learn to dance.

"Just for, you know, for coming to me. It feels good to be needed by you. And, after I told you I'm gay, I worried that things would change between us. These dance lessons have meant more to me than you may ever know. So, yeah, thanks for coming to me." Sawyer nodded his head and reached a hand out to touch his brother's shoulder.

Sobering at the thought that his brother worried their relationship would change, Decker stood directly in front of Sawyer and held his face in his hands. "Sawyer, listen to me and listen carefully. I don't like that you've already faced and you're going to face hatred and bigotry because of who you are; if I thought you could change your feelings and avoid that kind of hurt, I would beg you to. But, I know your feelings aren't a switch you can flip on and off; you didn't just decide to be gay, I get that. So, I will stand by your side to fight, to protect, to support through every single situation, every battle, every loss, every victory. You are a part of me, we are as close as two people can be. You hurt, I hurt; you win, I win. Don't think, for even a minute, that I would ever *not* come to you because of what you told me." Decker's heart crushed as his brother's tears fell down his face. "You got me? I'm with you 100% on this. I love you, and that will never change. Any reservations I may have are just because I don't want to see you hurt. I. Love. You." Pulling Sawyer into a strong embrace, he let the love and connection they'd always had surround them.

With a quick sniff of his nose, Sawyer wiped his eyes. "Alright, I think that's enough of that. Thank you, brother. I think I was needing to hear that from you, and I know I needed to spend this time with you. I'm really excited about the wedding; I can't wait to see you bust a move."

THE NEXT FEW days were quiet. A lot of work was finishing up at The Center+; almost everything that still needed done was on the inside. Decker and Katie were very happy with the way plans were playing out. Every class, both the old ones and the new courses, were completely filled with students. The Center+ had always been a central part of Torey Hope, but with the Jordan and Morgan boys' vision, plans, and effort, it was becoming an even more integral part of the town by drawing in all ages of students to take part in the new programs being offered.

Decker found himself with a rare down moment at the end of a productive day. He stood stoically at his large office window and watched momentarily while the workers finished up for the day. Turning, he let his eyes travel to the large blueprint he had drawn up so many years ago, with the help of the guys, and framed as their inspiration. Taking a deep breath, he savored the moment, feeling accomplished and proud. But, all too soon, he realized that these feelings didn't complete him, he wanted someone else to share in the moment with him.

Walking into her office through the back door, he stood and watched as she worked furiously on a last minute report he knew she was determined to get sent off that day. Not wanting to interrupt her, he quietly stood still and just observed. His pants felt tight as he took in the curves of her legs as they traveled from her backside down to her killer high heels. She had piled her hair up on her head, a habit she had when she was busy with a project, and tendrils escaped and framed her face. She hit one final key with a victory cry and stood to add paper to the printer. The sight of her ass, hugged perfectly in the black pencil skirt, was more than he could handle.

He waited until she printed the papers and sent the report, then he walked up behind her and whispered in her ear. "I have the sexiest assistant manager in the history of assistant managers. I think you deserve a reward; why don't you come into my office and let me give it to you." He pressed himself against her backside with his final words and smiled hungrily when she rasped out a sexy chuckle.

Turning in his arms to face him, she wrapped her arms around his neck and pressed herself against the exact reward she knew he wanted to give her. "Mmmm, a reward, huh? That sounds promising. Let me lock up my office, and I'll meet you in yours." As she pulled doors shut and secured her area, Decker walked with a purpose to his office and began quickly and efficiently pulling blinds, closing doors, and flipping locks. They met at his desk mere moments later.

"Hi." She smiled up at him. Her big eyes sparkled with mischief, anticipation, and emotion.

"Hi, Bug." He leaned in and kissed her nose. "I know we work together every day, but I feel like I haven't seen you all week. How are you?" He let his hands caress her face and down her arms. Nibbling her neck, he gave her time to speak if she wanted to.

"I'm good. I'm better now that I'm in your arms. I *can* get along fine without you, but I've found that I don't like it very much. Now, no more talk about work, shut up and kiss me." She wet her lips and smiled at the sexy grumble in his chest.

"Oh, I plan on kissing you and much more. So much more. You deserve a reward, remember?" He took her mouth with force then, his tongue plunging in to meet her waiting one. Swallowing her whimper, he shimmied her skirt up her legs so he could sit her on his desk and stand between her legs.

"Did you bring gym clothes?" He asked as he rubbed his thumbs across her nipples and watched in satisfaction as their peaks showed under her silky shirt.

Momentarily confused, she nodded her head, "Yeah, I have gym clothes, are we going to work out?" He grinned at her obvious disappointment.

"Yeah, we're going to work out, but not in the gym." He fingered the pearly buttons on her blouse. "Was this shirt expensive?"

"Huh? Oh, no. I grabbed it at a thrift shop a while back. Why?" Before she could say more he ripped the silk material and watched the buttons scatter over his office floor.

"I'll get you a new one..." He began to speak, but she put a finger to his lips.

"Decker, I've got a great job, with a really hot boss, I can buy my own shirt." Grabbing his head, she pulled his mouth towards hers, "I want my reward now, please."

Her bra quickly joined the button-less blouse on the floor. Laying her back, he feasted on her breasts. Sliding his hands down her hips, he made quick work of the rest of her clothing. Divesting her of her skirt and thong, he stopped short at the high heels. Kissing from her knees down to her ankles and back up, he whispered, "The shoes stay on."

"Decker, I'm naked on your desk and you're fully clothed, I don't think this is fair." Sitting up, she scooted to the edge of the desk and reached for his tie. "I love you in anything, but you are so damn sexy in these colorful ties." Untying the material she began to pop open each button on his shirt. He watched in breathless anticipation as her fingers worked each tiny button. At first he thought she was having difficulty, but then he realized she was purposely going slowly to torture him.

"Time's up, Bug." He took his shirt off and stepped between her legs. "This is your reward for being such a good manager, so I'm in control here." His thumb found her center with no warning and she threw her head back with a moan. "This one will be hard and fast; at home, I want hard and slow." He pushed her back with one hand as his other hand worked at his waistband. Lowering the material, he smirked at her as she propped herself up on her elbows to watch. "Like what you see?" When she could only lick her lips and nod, he knew this was going to be the true definition of a "quickie."

Before he could make a move, she sat up and pushed at his chest. "Hold on, if we're breaking all sorts of office rules by christening your desk, I think we better do it right. Office sex is always with the girl bent over the desk, right?" Katie raised her eyebrows and smiled seductively.

"I've never had sex with a girl in any office or on any desk, but I think movies usually portray it that way, yeah." Decker had to take a moment to breathe deep and clear his head at the image before him. His beautiful, perfect, intelligent girl was bending over his desk; if he thought about it much longer, he was going to be done before he even got started.

Several quick, sweaty, intense moments later, Decker found himself pressed against her back trying to catch his breath. "That was..., damn, what are you doing to me? I went from refusing to date co-workers to taking my assistant manager on my office desk."

He laughed when she spoke from beneath him, "Oh, how the mighty have fallen. Now, get off me you big oaf!"

Once they were dressed in some semblance of propriety, he gathered her in his arms and kissed her deeply. "Seriously, Kate, thank you for being so very good at what you do here at work. And thank you for just being you and for loving me. I never knew I needed to make changes, until you came into my life and showed me what was missing in my life. All of that control I thought I needed so badly? Turns out I don't need it as much as I thought, as long as you're by my side." He gathered up their things and held out his hand to her. "Come on, we're skipping the gym tonight. Let's go get a drink with the guys and then go home. I've got reservations for you in my bed." He waggled his eyebrows at her and pulled her close as she giggled at his antics.

21

*D*ecker's cousins, Aly and Zoey, had offered to come over and help Katie get ready for the wedding. She didn't really need help getting ready, but she figured it would be fun to have some girl time. She was sort of stuck when it came to the girls in Decker's family; Abby and Megan were older than her and weren't around much, Aly and Zoey were about five years younger than her. Katie liked the younger girls, and they seemed to like her. Having idle chit-chat about random girl stuff was a nice break for her as they primped and prepped for Beckett's big day.

"I can't believe I don't have a date for this wedding, and I can't believe you're just going to hang out with my brother, Zoey!" Aly complained from the shower as she shaved her legs. The girls were practically the same age, but Aly acted much more like an 18 year-old than Zoey did. Katie got an old-soul vibe from Zoey, which made Aly and Zoey being best friends sort of ironic.

"You could have asked any number of boys to come to the wedding, but you complained about each and every one of them, Aly. So, now you're stuck dancing with cousins and uncles. As for me, Zach is my best friend aside from you; I want to spend my evening with him; I'll have him ask you to dance a couple times." Zoey looked at Katie, shrugged her shoulders, and rolled her eyes at the squealing emanating from beyond the shower curtain.

"So, you and Decker, huh?" Zoey smiled at Katie's blush. "You're good for him. I've known him my whole life; being best friends with Zach means I've spent a lot of time with Decker. I really never thought he'd find someone who would break him out of his black and white existence."

"Thanks, Zoey. He's good for me too." Katie chewed the inside of her cheek, contemplating what she wanted to say. "So how did you end up being best friends with Zach when he's so much older than you?" Katie immediately noticed the blush on Zoey's cheeks and the dreamy look she got on her face when she spoke.

"Everyone says he's loved me since I was born. Aly was born just a little bit before me and he loved his sister, but when I was born they say he could always be found glued to my side. We grew up together, like all of the cousins, and we've just always clicked; we get each other. I'm lucky to have such a great group of cousins."

Katie didn't miss the sad emphasis the girl put on the word cousin. Deciding now wasn't the time to delve deeper, she let it go. "Yeah, all of you are really lucky to have such great family."

After the three girls were showered, shaved, and slathered, they worked on their hair and makeup. Katie had to admit that, even though she could do the prep all by herself, it was a lot of fun to have friends to do it with. With about 15 minutes to spare, they pulled on their dresses and shoes.

"Damn, we look fine!" Aly spun around and laughed in front of the mirror.

"Okay, we are going to take off so you and Decker can have your own little greeting time when he comes to pick you up. Zach is driving us from his and Aly's house. Thanks for letting us spend time with you, Katie; it was fun." As the younger girls headed out the door, Zoey spun around, "Oh! I don't know if you know this or not, but Decker does NOT dance. Like, at all. So don't be hurt if you ask and he refuses."

Katie smiled, "Yeah, he has already turned me down once and informed me that he doesn't dance and never will. It's okay, everyone has their faults, I love him anyway." She waved at the girls as they left.

Turning around, she almost ran into her grandma.

"Oh! Grandma, you scared me! I didn't know you were there!" Katie hugged the older woman and laughed.

"So, what's this I hear about you loving that boy?" Grandma squinted her eyes in Katie's direction.

"That boy's name is Decker, you know that Grandma. And, yes, I do love him, very much. He's a very good man; good to me, good to his family, and good in business. I couldn't do much better when it comes to finding someone who fits me perfectly and loves me for me." Katie looked pointedly at her grandmother, waiting for the woman to speak.

"What happens when he leaves? Your father was *good* too, but he chose his work over his family. Where will that leave you when *this boy* leaves?" Grandma seemed to be challenging Katie.

"Mother, don't do this. Katie's father left *me*, not her. It was a mutual agreement that he should leave; he wanted things in life that I didn't have interest in. We were not well matched. Katie and Decker are much better suited; they want the same things. Now, stop meddling; go get ready for the wedding." Katie's mother gently maneuvered the older woman toward the bedroom.

Before she left the room, her grandmother turned around, "Katie, I want you to be happy. But I know how boys are, they just want one thing and then they go looking for it elsewhere. Well, not my Stanley, he was as good as they come. But I didn't give him what he wanted until we were good and married; that's the problem these days, young girls giving it away. 'Why buy the cow when you can get the milk for free?'" Grandma muttered as she left the room.

Katie and her mother just looked at each other and

laughed. "When did she become such a cynic!? I never knew she took it so hard when Daddy and you split up." Katie still felt the sting of disappointment over her parents' divorce, but she knew what her mother stated was the truth; they just weren't well suited. She had a good relationship with her mother, she had a good relationship with her father; they just didn't have a good relationship with each other.

"Her age is really beginning to show lately. She seems to have gotten it in her head that Grandpa Stanley was the only *good guy* and all other guys are scum. She's convinced that Decker just wants in your pants and then he'll leave." Her mother winked at her.

"Mom! I can't believe you just said that!" Katie blushed and thought about the last time she'd let Decker get in her pants.

"Katie, you're a grown woman, if you want to be in a relationship with Decker, you have every right to make that decision. You two really do seem to be good for each other; you balance each other out very well." Leaning in to kiss her daughter's cheek, her mom got up to leave, "I'm assuming you'll be sleeping elsewhere this weekend?" She nodded knowingly when her daughter smiled and bobbed her head up and down slightly.

The doorbell rang and Katie practically ran to open the door. Decker was one of the most gorgeous men she'd ever laid eyes on, but Decker dressed for his cousin's wedding was enough to bring her to her knees.

"Katherine Turner, you are the most beautiful woman I've ever seen on a normal day; today, though, you truly take my breath away." He cupped his hand behind her head and pressed his forehead to hers as if to take a moment to catch his breath. When he pulled back slightly, his eyes glistened with tears.

"Decker? What's wrong?" Katie ran a hand along his cheek.

Nuzzling his cheek into her hand, he shook his head. "Nothing's wrong, Bug. Everything is right. Just right. Seeing you like this just really drove home to me how lucky I am to call you mine. Before you, it's like I was living in a black and white world, then I met you and you brought color into my life." Resting his head on hers again, he breathed her in deeply, "I love you so very much."

"Yeah, yeah, love-schlove. Do lines like that usually get you into the girls' panties sooner?" Grandma's voice echoed from behind Katie and Decker's eyes met hers; both of them trying desperately to control their laughter, they turned to face the diminutive naysayer.

"Good afternoon, Grandma; you look lovely today." Decker leaned in to kiss the old lady's cheek.

Blushing and doing her best not to cave under Decker's charm, Grandma tsk-tsked. "Shame on you, declaring love to my granddaughter and then flirting with me. See, Katie, this *boy* isn't good for you. Once he gets what he wants, he'll move on to the next pair of panties he can find." She turned to

Decker and pointed two fingers at her eyes and then at him, "I'm watching you, *boy*."

Rolling her eyes, Katie leaned in to hug her grandma. "I love him and he loves me, Grandma. He's a very good man. Stop giving him such a rough time."

As they walked out of the house, Katie groaned and Decker threw his head back in laughter when the old woman spoke loud enough for them to hear, "Yeah, well, anyone whose ass looks that good in a pair of trousers is trouble. Trust me."

Once they reached the car, Decker pulled Kate into his arms. "I think your grandmother just accosted my ass with her eyes." She swatted at him, but he just laughed, "Don't worry, I'm not really into cougars. Plus, I've got the most awesome girl in the world on my arm, no need to look elsewhere."

Decker held her door open for her. As he walked around to his side, his phone buzzed. Pulling it out, he stopped in his tracks to read the text.

Have fun at the wedding. I sure hope The Center+ is safe while you're off playing.

Shoving the phone back in his pants, Decker decided he'd ignore the text threat and just enjoy his evening.

"What's wrong?" Katie, always intuitive and perceptive to everything, knew something had upset him when he looked at his phone. The set of his jaw told her that he was pissed.

"Just the stupid unknown number taunting me. This is

our night. Well, actually, it's Beckett's night, but he'll be so busy with his wife and friends that he won't have much time for us, so we'll make it our own little party. No worries. Right?" Katie smiled knowingly as he tried to pretend he wasn't bothered, but she knew he was furious that his business was being threatened again.

"Why don't we swing by The Center+ and take a look around, tell the patrol officer about the threat, ask them to keep an extra close eye out?" Her suggestion was for his benefit as well as her own; she knew she wouldn't be able to relax and have a good time if she thought something was going on at the place she'd come to love as much as Decker did.

"That's a really good idea, Bug. See, not only do I keep you around for the mind-blowing sex, but you're pretty handy in situations like this." He laughed at her mock outrage, and they drove off to check things out before heading over to Beckett's special day.

"DON'T LOOK NOW, but your Grandmother is watching us." Decker nodded his head over Kate's shoulder and waved at the older woman. "I hope we won't be sitting in front of her during the wedding, she may bore a hole in my head with those steely eyes."

Katie smiled and held his hand as they walked to their

seats for the ceremony. "Hush, she's harmless. She'll get to know you and find out how great you are and then she'll move on to being cynical about something else."

The wedding was short, sweet, and extremely emotional. Katie's eyes welled with tears when Audrey did a reading about bringing her son's wife into their family as her own daughter. Those tears spilled over when both Beckett and his bride, Kenja, shed tears and choked up on their vows. When Decker grasped her hand and handed her a tissue, she almost lost it. She didn't know if she was ready for marriage just yet, but the ceremony convinced her that she wanted it one day, and she knew exactly who she wanted her happily-ever-after to be with.

As they left the ceremony and headed to the reception, Decker cocked his head and turned to Kate. "Not that I mind her being here, but how did your grandma get invited to the wedding? Who does she know in my family?" Katie loved how they could have deep, emotional conversation just as easily as they could have random, meaningless chats as well.

"Oh, she's friends with Jack and Judy Jordan. They play bingo together at the senior citizen center at least once a week." Climbing in his car, Katie continued. "Did you know the senior citizen center is going to have to cut a lot of their programming? They are losing some funding. Grandma says that the bingo and other game nights will be the first to go."

She looked out the window, sad to think of her grandma losing one of the weekly activities she looked forward to the most. It wasn't so much about the bingo, it was about the socializing with friends and getting out of the house.

"Decker! What if we started running a few programs just for the senior citizens in town? I mean, I know we already have classes and courses that cater to the older generation, but what if we ran a bingo night and a card game night? Grandma and her friends love Uchre; I know it would be a hit." She gave him an expectant look, waiting for his answer with a sneaking suspicion that he already loved her idea.

"I think it's a great idea, Bug. I know my grandparents would be happy to go to game nights at The Center+; the senior citizen center is on the outskirts of town, it's not always convenient for the older folks to get to. Let's put it on the agenda for our next staff meeting, and we'll see what we need to do in order to get it rolling." He pulled her hand to his lips. "Now, I don't mean to change the subject if you still want to talk about work..." He spoke with a question, and Katie shook her head to indicate she was done talking about work.

"Good. Not to sound as crass as Kendrick, but I can't wait to get that dress off of you later. You are absolutely stunning. If I *was* as crass as Kendrick, I'd be looking for the nearest restroom and locking you inside with me." Katie's body shivered in delight as Decker's words whispered over her as he helped her out of the car. "Mmm, I saw that shiver. Do you want me to lock you in a restroom and have my way with you?" He smiled the coy glance she gave him. "There you go again, my little trouble maker. I told you that song was perfect for you."

"I'm not sure I'd go through with bathroom sex, especially at your cousin's wedding, but I'm already looking forward to our own little after party when the reception winds down." Katie wrapped her arms around his neck and whispered in his ear. "Just to give you something to anticipate throughout the evening, I'm not wearing anything under my dress." She licked her lips and laughed at his exaggerated groan as she walked away with an extra sway in her hips.

KATIE COULDN'T SHAKE the feeling that something was going on. Sawyer and Decker had been trading whispered comments for the thirty minutes they'd been at the reception. Grandma kept walking by and tsking Katie while ogling Decker's ass. And there was just an undercurrent in the air, like someone was watching her.

Decker had gone to do a couple shots with his brother and cousins, and Katie had taken the moment to stop by the ladies' room. Leaving the facility, she started toward Decker and the guys, but she practically ran into a woman she'd never seen before who stepped right into her path.

"Hi, you're Kate, right?" The woman stuck her hand out as if to shake, but Kate was instantly wary; she knew most people in town and this woman was not a local. Trying to remind herself that Beckett and Kenja had friends from school, Katie extended her hand to shake.

"Yes, I'm Kate, and you are?" The cold hand in hers was not comforting, and she couldn't fight the feeling that this woman in front of her wasn't here for good reasons.

"Oh, how rude of me. I'm Angela, Decker Morgan's girl-friend." Angela sneered her words.

Katie took a deep breath, understanding in that moment that she was dealing with a jealous ex-lover. She had heard the guys speak of Angela a couple of times. The woman in front of her was beautiful in a very severe way; she couldn't picture Decker, who was currently smiling and laughing with the guys over drinks, with this angry person in front of her. Knowing that Angela was hoping for a reaction, Kate just smiled.

"Nice to meet you, Angela. Decker has spoken very little of his *ex*-girlfriend, but I recognize your name from the jokes his cousins and brother have told me." Katie couldn't help but get a couple little jabs in with her reply.

Choosing to ignore the barbs, Angela sniffed and spoke condescendingly. "Decker and I parted ways amicably with every intention of rekindling our romance when we were settled with our business ventures."

"Oh? And where exactly is your business venture? Have you gotten yourself all settled? I'm sure Decker will be just *thrilled* to see you've shown up in town for the rekindling." Katie had never had a bitchy or catty bone in her body, but it was obvious they had just been in hiding all of these years.

"You silly little dear. I'm not here for Decker just yet; I'm building a name for myself at a very prestigious company and climbing the ladders quite successfully. I'm simply here to enjoy the wedding. Decker and I will be together when it's right." Angela's voice dripped venom as she spoke down her nose at Katie.

"So, you're here with...who exactly?" Katie racked her brain trying to determine how in the world Angela had landed an invitation to a very small event in a town Katie would guess she'd never even stepped foot in.

"An old friend of mine was a classmate of the groom's; he needed a date, so I did him a favor and accompanied him to this *lovely* little town." Katie didn't miss the nasty emphasis Angela placed on her words.

"Well, if I've got a limited amount of time with Decker, I think I'll go enjoy our evening. So *great* to meet you, Angela." Katie started to back away when she sensed him behind her. She didn't want to look like a simpering female, but her heart kicked up a couple notches when she realized he was there to step in and protect her.

"Angela, what the hell are you doing here?" Decker's jaw ticked rapidly as he waited on an answer. His arms moved Kate from in front of him to behind him.

"Decker, so good to see you; you look great as usual baby. I was just telling your friend here that an old friend of mine was classmates with the groom and he invited me to the wedding. Such a quaint little affair. We should definitely grab a coffee this weekend and catch up." Angela's voice had taken on a sickening sweet tone and Katie fought the urge to gesture with her finger down her throat. She turned her head and caught the guys watching the whole scene go down; when Kendrick *did* put his finger down his throat and pretend to gag, she laughed out loud and knew she'd love that guy and his crass ass forever.

"We won't be getting together for coffee or catching up, Angela. I'd like to say it's been good to see you, but since you seemed to be harassing my girlfriend, I'm going to just have to say goodbye. Come on, Kate, let's go dance." Decker started to grab her hand, but Angela's cackle stopped him short.

"Oh, that's rich, Decker! If you want me to think you're over me, you need to do better than pretending you're going to dance with the poor girl. Don't forget, I dated you for a long time; I know you don't dance. Ever." Angela spoke as if she'd just revealed the biggest secret every kept.

"Well, you obviously don't know a damn thing about me now, because I learned to dance just for Kate, and I intend on spending the rest of the night with her in my arms." Decker did grab Kate's hand then and stalked away, leaving Angela standing gaping like a fish out of water.

"Decker? Decker, slow down. There was no reason to lie, you could have just told her to get lost." Katie found herself almost running to keep up with him. "Decker!"

"Sorry, Bug. I just got angry when I saw her corner you and start giving you a rough time." Decker slowed down and cupped her cheek, running a thumb along her bottom lip. "Are you okay? I'm sorry about that. I had no idea she was coming here this weekend."

She started to speak, but the guys walked up and everyone started talking at once.

"Damn, Katie-girl, where did that little hissy spunk come from? Mee-ow!" Sawyer hugged her. "That was great. I told Deck you didn't need him, you were holding your own just fine."

"Dude, there's something fishy going on here. I call bullshit on her having a date here tonight. I'll keep an eye on her; I think she's up to something. It doesn't make sense that she would travel all this way just to attend a wedding with an old friend." Kendrick narrowed his eyes as he contemplated Angela.

"She said she was basically just counting the days until the time was right for her and Decker to 'rekindle' their romance. Maybe she came with the date just as an excuse to see Decker?" Katie had never really been jealous and she wasn't feeling the emotion as she spoke, but she did feel like something was off.

"Come on, we'll sort of pull together and keep everyone close for the rest of the reception. That way she can't get close to Decker or Katie and we can keep an eye on her." Zach led the group back to the reception tent. Grabbing

Zoey's hand, he explained the situation and had her find Aly and Asher.

"Come on, Bug, let's dance." Decker held his hand out for her.

Laughing, Katie rolled her eyes, "Yeah, right. It's okay, I don't think she's looking, you can stop pretending." She sat down on one of the soft cushioned chairs.

Crouching down to rest his elbows on his knees, Decker spoke softly. "Kate, this isn't the way I wanted to surprise you, and damn Angela for making me blurt it out like that, but I *did* learn to dance for you, and I want to spend the rest of my evening with you in my arms. Now, if I know Sawyer, he's asking the DJ to play a special song just for us right now. So, Kate, will you do me the honor and dance with me?" He held out his hand again and smiled when she reached for him.

Ed Sheeran's "Thinking Out Loud" came through the speakers. "This isn't the song I want to call *ours*, but it will do for now." Decker rested his right arm around her waist and pulled her close to him; grasping her hand in his. "For my debut performance, I plan on doing this right." He smiled and glided her around their small space on the dance floor.

Katie couldn't take her eyes off of his face; he learned to dance. For her. Just for her. Her heart caught in her throat as he leaned in and kissed her softly.

Decker glanced around at the other wedding attendees; he saw his parents dancing and caught the tears sparkling in his mother's eyes when she saw he was dancing with Katie.

His mom had tried for years to get Decker to dance, with no success; she smiled at him through her tears, and he knew she understood why it took Kate to get him to dance when his mom couldn't get through to him all those years.

When the song ended, Sawyer swooped in to steal Katie away for just one dance. It was a fast song; Decker wasn't feeling confident enough for a fast routine just yet, so he let Sawyer take his girl and headed to the restroom.

"Decker, can we talk?" Angela tried grabbing his hand as he exited the restroom.

"No, Angela, we can't talk. We broke up, I have no clue why you're here, I'm in love with Kate; we have nothing to talk about." Decker knew he sounded harsh, but he was not happy with Angela being here or her treatment of Kate earlier.

"You can't love her; she's not good for you. I took a little time from my job so you and I can reconnect; I just want us to give our relationship another chance." Her voice shook and he took a good look at her for the first time. She was shaky and sweaty, her face was pale and she had lost weight. It was not a good look for her.

"Angela, I'm sorry if I wasn't clear when we left school. We are over. I came here to build my life; you went your separate way to start your own life. We weren't meant to be together. I don't want to be hurtful, but I never felt for you what I feel for Kate; she's my perfect match; we just click. Now, I need you to leave us alone, leave town, and go on with your life." Decker walked away, trying to ignore the nagging feeling that jabbed at his brain.

Swinging past the DJ station, Decker asked the man if he could play a certain song. Once the song was found, Decker requested the microphone.

"Good evening. I wanted to start by saying congrats to Beckett and Kenja. You two are truly perfect together, and I wish you much happiness. Now, without stealing the spotlight for too long, I want to dedicate a song to someone special. This song is old, I'm pretty sure my grandparents were fans of it years ago. My brother, a music aficionado, suggested it was the perfect song to describe what this girl has done for me and what she means for me; he was completely right. This song is perfect. Kate, this song is for you; this is our song. Before you, my world was black and white; when I met you, you brought color into my life. I never knew what I was missing until you showed me how to live. So, thank you; I love you." He handed the mic back as the song floated from the speakers.

Wrapping Kate in his arms, he held her close and nuzzled her neck. "Listen closely to the lyrics. It's called 'You Decorated My Life' by Kenny Rogers. That's what you did, Bug, you came along and added your spark and flare to my life; you balance me perfectly. This is our song, forever. I love you, Kate."

Katie's heart was full-to-bursting wrapped in Decker's arms listening to beautiful lyrics. She didn't think she could get any happier...until Sawyer dragged her out on the dance floor with Decker, Zach, Kendrick, Zoey, and Aly and made them dance to a couple fast numbers. Watching Decker let loose, laugh and have fun with his family and friends touched her heart in a deep way; knowing that he was having fun because he learned to dance just for her was overwhelming.

Decker really played it up during both songs. "Shut Up and Dance" by Walk the Moon was a lot of fun; Katie got to pull some attitude on him and get a little sassy. "Dance With Me Tonight" by Olly Murs was just sweet, silly, fun; they all got into the moment by acting out the video. By the end of both songs, everyone was sweaty and laughing and having the time of their lives.

Heading over to grab drinks for Kate and himself, Decker was waylaid by Grandma. "Is it true that you'd never danced before tonight?" Her rheumy old eyes squinted at him as if trying to gauge his answer for truth.

"Yes, ma'am, it's true. I've never been a dancer; never felt the need. But, Kate wanted me to dance with her one night, and I felt bad saying no. So I had my brother teach me so I could dance with her tonight." Decker drank from a bottle of water while he waited on their drinks to be prepared.

"So, let me get this straight. You learned to dance just so you could come here tonight and make an absolute fool of yourself shaking your ass all over the dance floor, and you did it all for my granddaughter?" She spoke unbelievingly.

"Well, I didn't plan on making a fool of myself, but if I

did, so be it. Yes, I did it all for Kate." He smiled as he realized what he'd said was true, he *didn't* care if he'd looked like a complete idiot out there. The smile on her face had been worth it.

"Well then, *boy*, I think I may have misjudged you. My Stanley learned to dance just for me, and he was the best man I've ever met. So, I'm willing to give you a chance with my Katie. But, so help me God, if you hurt her, you'll answer to me. It will be awfully hard to dance or run a business with your cock-n-balls missing." Water spewed from Decker's mouth and nose. She had turned and walked away before he could dry himself off and stop coughing. Turning around, she walked back to him. "If you want to shake that sweet ass of yours later, come find me when they play The Cha-Cha Slide." She winked as she smacked his ass and shuffled away.

Laughing as he carried the drinks back to his beautiful girl, he couldn't help but shake his head at the old woman. When Katie saw him laughing and looking a bit shocked, she raised an eyebrow in question.

"You don't want to know." Decker grabbed her and kissed her as he chuckled.

Exasperated, she persisted. "What? Did Kendrick say something ridiculous?"

"Are you sure you want to hear this?" Decker questioned. At the look of impatience on her face, he held up his hands and gave in, "Okay, okay, but don't say I didn't warn you."

Pulling her closer, he look down into her waiting eyes.

"Your grandmother is giving me a chance; she likes the fact that I learned to dance just for you. I guess your grandfather did the same thing for her." As Kate's face softened and her eyes teared up, Decker delivered the blow. "And, she said she would cut off my 'cock-n-balls' if I hurt you." At the wide-eyed look of mortification on her beautiful face, he threw his head back and laughed. "I kid you not, Bug, she used that exact phrase and told me it would be hard to dance or run a business with my package missing. That woman is scary, but I think I love her."

He leaned in and captured her embarrassment with a long, lingering kiss. When she had gotten over some of her humiliation, he felt the kiss change direction. No longer was her mouth lazily accepting his; she increased the pressure of her lips on his and easily opened when his tongue sought entry. Wrapping her arms around his neck, she moaned a bit when he rubbed himself against her middle.

"You ready to head out of here?" Decker spoke huskily into her ear and reached down to covertly adjust himself; saying their goodbyes to family while he was sporting a tent in his pants would be more than a little awkward.

With desire flaming in her eyes, Katie nodded. Taking her hand he led her to say farewell to Beckett and Kenja along with the rest of his family. The guys all just smirked when he said they were calling it a night and heading home.

"Is that what we're calling it these days? 'Calling it a night?' I thought the popular phrase was still 'fucking like rabbits' but what do I know?" Kendrick winked at them as he sauntered off in search of his next warm body.

Rolling their eyes at Kendrick, but their breathing ramping up in anticipation of getting home and in bed, Katie and Decker all but sprinted to the car.

22

"The ceremony was beautiful, huh?" Katie shifted in her seat, attempting to calm the desire and anticipation she felt.

"Yeah, it was really nice. It was so great to see Beckett so happy; he's been a friend and mentor to the four of us for as long as I can remember. He's always been a little different, a lot like Uncle Nicky, so it's nice to see him get his someone special." Katie's heart warmed as she listened to Decker talk about the older cousin he loved so much.

Decker reached over and took her hand; bringing it to his mouth, he placed a warm kiss. "When I get married, I want something small like they had. I don't need hundreds of guests; I just need my family, my friends, and the woman I love." Katie blushed as he spoke, but her heart fluttered at the thought of marrying him one day.

"I don't want anything big either. Heck, I'd be happy with the courthouse or Vegas; maybe a celebration with family and friends after the marriage." She couldn't say that she'd put a ton of thought into her future wedding; she'd actually not thought a lot about it until she met Decker. "I think the most important thing is that two people who love each other get to say their vows to each other in front of God; anything other than that is just icing on the cake."

"Bug, it's good to hear we're on the same page. Although, I won't be marrying you in the courthouse. Maybe we could do a wedding on the beach or in the mountains; definitely not Vegas, it just seems trashy to me." He winked at her as he spoke, and her breathing hitched; he was openly talking about marrying her. She loved him, but were they ready for marriage?

Hoping to change the subject, Katie laughed at his Vegas comment. "Kendrick says he's getting married in Vegas if any girl ever manages to tie him down."

Decker gave her an I-told-you-so look and chuckled, "Exactly. Anywhere Kendrick plans on getting married is not the place I'll be marrying you."

As they neared his place, Decker's hand began to roam up her thigh. "Okay, enough talk about marriage for now. I'm pretty sure I remember you saying something about not having anything on under that dress, am I right?"

When she laughed and let her legs part slightly, he caressed higher and moaned, "You wicked, wicked woman."

Pulling into his covered parking spot, Decker let his hand continue its journey until he found exactly the spot he was looking for. When she whimpered against his touch, he cupped her neck and pulled her face close to his. "So hot, so ready. Should I put you out of your misery or tease you a bit like you've teased me all night?" Letting his mouth hover just over hers, he nuzzled her nose and brushed the barest of kisses along her lips.

"You can tease all you want, Decker, but I have another secret that may spur you into action." She nipped at his lips, and he knew that no matter what the secret was, he wasn't going to be able to hold off possessing her body sooner rather than later. Whispering softly against his ear as she palmed the steely heat under his pants, "I brought some of my toys." With a final kiss to his lips, she giggled as he threw his head back against the seat and groaned. When she exited the car, she was sure she heard him mutter, "Gonna fucking kill me, Bug."

Sauntering with a purpose to the front of the car, she made sure he was watching as she walked towards the door of the house. The sway of her hips and the sexy smile she threw over her shoulder were completely ad-libbed, but damn if he didn't feel himself grow harder.

She had him in the palm of her hand the second she opened the door earlier that day; the no-panties and toys were just an added bonus to the time he planned on spending with her. Adjusting himself, he all but catapulted out of the car;

with a wicked gleam in his desire laden eyes, he began to take slow and purposeful steps towards her. When she noticed he was gaining on her, she squealed and began to run; he caught up with her right as she reached the front door.

Pinning her between his hard body and the door, he breathed in deeply as his face nuzzled into her neck. Searching for the key in his pocket, he growled, "I've got you now, what do you think I should do with you?"

Never one to back down from a challenge or temper her thoughts and feelings, Katie grabbed his chin and leveled his gaze to look straight into her eyes. "I think you should get the door open, strip my clothes, and take me up against the door before anyone else gets home. After that, we can play things by ear." She finished off her request with a scorching kiss, letting her hands roam down his back until she was gripping his hard ass and pulling him toward her center.

"I like the way you think. Now, where in the hell is that damn key?" She maneuvered them around so that he was facing the door and she was against his back. He switched to searching the other pocket, but gasped when he felt her slender hand slide seductively into his front pocket. If she kept rubbing him with her hot little hand, she was going to find more than just a key in his pants. "Bug, you keep that up and we'll have to postpone the against-the-door sex until I've had time to regroup." He immediately missed the heat of her hand, but had to smile when she let out a victory cry and produced the key to the door.

Handing it to him, she smiled and pulled her bottom lip into her mouth. "Hurry, Decker. I've got hot fantasies about sex against a door, but they don't include being walked in on by your brother or cousins."

Swinging the door wide, he ushered her inside and immediately locked the door behind them. He pulled her into a tight embrace and placed hot kisses from her jaw to her neck to the creamy swell of flesh just above the neckline of her dress. "Turn around." His command was gruff and sent shivers through her body.

Turning around she glanced over her shoulder and watched as he reached for her zipper. She couldn't help but breathe faster in anticipation as he lowered the tab and reached his big, warm hands under the material at her shoulders to slide it from her body. She hadn't been lying when she'd said she didn't have on panties; she also wasn't able to wear a bra with the dress she had chosen, so he got the full effect when the fabric hit the floor.

She started to step out of the shoes as she turned around, but he grunted a negative, "Keep the shoes on." He grasped her hip and turned her the rest of the way around to face him; hands on her waist, he dropped his head back against the door and breathed heavily.

"You are every man's fucking wet dream, and I've got you standing right here in front of me ready to wrap those gorgeous as sin legs around me. I don't know how I got so lucky, but I thank my stars for you every day." Spinning her around so that her back was flush against the cool wood of the door, he dropped to his knees and ran his nose from her belly button to where she was clearly wanting him to be. Gripping her ass and lifting, he nudged forward until her legs fell over his shoulders. Running his tongue slowly over her, he gruffly chuckled when she arched her back in an attempt to get his mouth closer to where she wanted it.

"Easy there, babe, I'll get you to where you want to be; you just have to be patient." His tongue made two more complete trips around her core, before hovering just over the spot she was practically begging him to pay attention to.

"Damn it, Decker, lick me!" She grabbed his head and positioned him exactly where she wanted him. Already hard enough to pound nails, he felt himself harden even more when she spoke with such fever and wanting.

Allowing his tongue to flick and taste, while his lips and teeth nipped and sucked, he took pride in the orgasm that ripped through her, knowing that he was the only man to have ever given her that.

Head thrown back against the door, chest heaving, she slowly lowered her legs from his shoulders and let him steady her into a standing position. "That was amazing; we can try the sex part some other time." When he cocked an ever-sexy dark brow at her in a questioning way, she shook her head with a small smile, "Surely you don't think I can go again so quickly? And the guys could be home any time." Watching as he made quick work of his belt and the button of his pants, she yelped when he gripped her hips and lifted her body quickly against the door. Moaning when she felt the steel heat of him pressing against her, she acquiesced and wrapped her legs around his waist.

"That's it, babe. We still have several rounds to go, but we're getting our first door-sex tonight. Right now." He filled her as he said his last words and then no words were needed. Locking her legs behind him, she held tightly to his neck and felt her body stretch with each slow thrust.

In all of her fantasies, sex against a door had been hot and heavy and hard; in the stories she'd heard in college, door-sex was clumsy and not nearly as sexy as the movies. Decker somehow took her wildest fantasies and threw them out the window as he loved her against the door; his long, slow movements reached deeper inside of her than she'd ever felt him. When his thumb moved between their sweat-slicked bodies and found her center, she whimpered his name and let her body's release rush over her; with one final thrust, he stilled and cried out her name as he found his own release.

Using his weight to hold her against the door, never wanting to leave her warm body, Decker leaned his forehead against hers and breathed heavily as her breath mingled with his. The scent from their bodies hung heavy in the air, and he knew there would never be another woman who could love him the way she did. "Kate, you are my life, my world, my love. I meant every word of that song tonight; you truly have brought color to my otherwise black and white existence. I love you. Now, not to ruin a special moment or freak you out, but I just saw headlights. I'll be damned if any of those fuckers are seeing you like this, so I need you to gather your stuff and make a run for my room." Wincing as he pulled out of her and dropping her gently to her feet, he laughed as she grabbed her dress and the bag she'd brought in with her and sprinted toward the stairs.

Realizing he'd not even got his pants completely off, he quickly pulled them up and swept his shirt off the ground. One quick look around, he felt sure they'd left no evidence of their activities. He was darting up the stairs when he heard the key in the door. He didn't take time to investigate what all the laughter was about before he quickly shut the door to his room.

Taking in the sight of Katie on his bed, sound asleep, curled under his comforter, was enough to tug at his heart. He wanted to see her in his bed every damn day, not just for sex, but for life; he wanted her hugs and smiles and laughter. The thought almost brought him to his knees. Reverently he reached out and stroked her cheek; when she murmured and rolled over, he pulled the blanket back and crawled in behind her, pulling her close to his chest and savoring the warmth of her body against his. "Forever, Kate, I love you. Always." His whisper ghosted across her ear, and she snuggled closer to him. "Always, Decker," she said on a sigh before succumbing to a deeper sleep.

KATIE GRUMBLED against the pillow as the intruding noise attempted to invade her peaceful slumber. She was awake enough to know that deliciously warm arms and legs were wrapped around her body, but she hadn't come fully to her senses enough to comprehend what the buzzing sound was. "Make it stop, Decker, I just want a few more minutes of sleep." She mumbled and attempted to roll over, grateful that the buzzing had stopped.

Instead of being allowed to move, she found herself quickly on her back and a warm hand was caressing down her stomach to a point on her body that had definitely already awakened. Continuing to come awake slowly, she savored the warmth of his touch; her ears perked and her brain attempted to place the low buzzing sound which was once again filling the room.

Whimpering at the loss of his warm fingers, Kate was instantly awake when the head of her purple vibrator was placed against her folds. Grasping the sheets in her fists, her eyes popped open and found his dark eyes, hooded with desire, watching her with a ferocious intensity.

"Good morning," he all but growled, "I found your toys." He smirked sexily and flicked the vibrator slightly, causing her to moan deeply. "I don't know if this one is your favorite, but it's the first one I found when I opened your 'Bag of Fun'." Continuing to watch her, he slid the purple head inside and pulled himself level with her; bracing on one elbow, while the other arm worked the vibrator in slow pulses, he kissed her deeply. "Come for me, Kate. Come for me now, and then while your body is still shaking, I'm going to fill you and make you come again."

Swallowing her cries of pleasure, he removed the vibrator and replaced it with himself. Entering her while her body was still rippling with aftershocks, he took up a forcefully slow pace. Not able to tell where her first orgasm ended and the second began, he increased his speed. Pulling back enough that he could see their joining, he groaned in satisfaction; the sight of his body possessing hers was enough to send him over the edge. Burying his head in the crook of her neck to muffle his groans, he thrust one last time and moaned her name in one deep, long breath.

"Mmmm, I think I like your toys. Maybe we can schedule a play date again soon so you can share all of them with me." He stood behind her in the bathroom as she attempted to brush her teeth and fix her hair. The bathroom was steamy from the shower they had shared; her body was well-sated from the loving they had shared.

"I'm really surprised you picked the purple one to use for the first time, did you not like the pink one? I figured you'd get a kick out of that one." She winked at him as she finished brushing her teeth.

"I told you, I picked the first one I found when I opened your secret little stash. By the way, where in the hell did you get all of your toys? You could open a sex shop, you little sexual deviant." He kissed her shoulder and watched her face in the mirror.

She blushed as she spoke, "My college roommate one year was a sex toy consultant; she'd have all these parties and get free stuff. Since I wasn't dating, she'd give some of them to me 'so your vagina doesn't close up shop,' her words, not mine." She walked to her bag to find the huge dildo she'd brought as a joke.

"Funny, Decker, where's the pink one?" She continued digging through all of her sexual paraphernalia, most of which she'd never even attempted to use, hoping against hope that she'd find what she was looking for. Her roommate had dated a guy for a while who was supposedly 'very well-endowed,' she had given the gigantic pink vibrator to Katie as a joke, "So you'll know what I'm screaming about if you ever hear us through the wall," her roommate had almost pissed herself laughing at the look on Katie's face when she saw the toy. It was easily as long as her forearm and as wide as a pop can; she'd never even fathomed using it. She had also never understood the looped string on it, did people hang their dildos from strings? Shaking her head, she continued looking for the big pink one. She had kept all of the toys her roommate had donated to her in the bag for several years. Figuring Decker would be curious, she'd left the pink one in there to see his reaction when he saw it. Where the hell was it? Nothing that big could hide for long.

"Babe, I didn't see anything pink, I don't know what you're talking about. I grabbed the purple one because it was on top and seemed the least intimidating. But, watching your reaction to it, I'm pretty sure I'd be willing to play with more of your toys any time you'd like." He grabbed her hand and led her down the stairs; Katie had a hard time letting go of the missing vibrator. She didn't think Decker would take it and not tell her, but she knew it should have been in that bag; so where was it?

Walking into the kitchen, Katie felt her face flame red-hot in a matter of seconds. Kendrick stood in a pair of basketball shorts, hard, hot body leaning against the kitchen counter. In his hand, swinging from a string on his right index finger, was the huge pink dildo. Covering her face with her hands, Katie groaned, but Decker just busted out laughing.

"Um, Bug, I think we found your missing toy." Looking at his cousin, Decker gave him a look that warned against embarrassing his girl too much.

"Damn, Decker, if you're living up to this monster, you must have grown quite a bit since we were sharing baths at Grandma and Grandpa's house. This thing is enough to scare *me*, yet you're obviously satisfying your girl here, so bravo, man, bravo." Kendrick laughed and waved the pink monstrosity in front of Katie's face. "Missing something, Katie?"

She knew he meant no malice with his teasing, but that didn't stop her mortification from growing. Knowing it would be pointless to try and explain she'd never used this particular toy, she just shook her head. Holding her head high, she poured herself some coffee. "May I ask where you got that?" She was proud that her voice didn't break in embarrassment even once.

Zach and Sawyer came walking into the kitchen at that moment and just chuckled at the obvious merriment being had at Decker and Katie's expense.

"Well, after we had the extreme displeasure of watching Deck's ass streak up the stairs when we got home last night, we happened to find this beauty rolled halfway under the couch. We probably wouldn't have found it, but the flashing neon lights gave it away." Sawyer took the offending apparatus and gazed at it longingly. "I think I'm in love with this big beauty."

"It flashes neon lights? I never knew that." Katie realized too late that she sounded much too interested in this undiscovered function, and hid her crimson face in her hands once again.

Hitting the vibrator with the palm of his hand, Kendrick demonstrated how it flashed with neon lights. "I'm guessing in your haste to get your naked asses upstairs and away from our innocent eyes, this big guy fell out of your bag, Katie, and the force of the fall turned on the lights as it rolled under the couch. Imagine poor Zach's surprise when he pulled this from under the couch." Swinging the flashing pink dildo from his finger, Kendrick continued to torment Katie.

"Okay, Kendrick, I think you've embarrassed my girl enough." Decker spoke with a smile, but it was clear he didn't want Katie to have to put up with anymore teasing.

"No, it's okay, Deck. Thanks for finding my toy, boys. Decker more than made up for its loss though, so I don't plan on needing it back anytime soon. Sawyer, would you like to have it? The way you're gazing at it so lovingly, it may be just the thing you're looking for. Kendrick? I hear you're not against some experimentation; maybe this can be your intro-duction? Zach? Got any special girl you'd like to show a wild time to? No? Hmmmm, I thought differently." Katie narrowed her eyes wickedly at the guys, proving once again that she could give just as well as they could dish it out. The smiles of love and respect which shone from the eyes of the three men confirmed that her place in Decker's life was abso-lutely perfect. The adoration and hunger which shone from Decker's eyes proved that she'd be spending much of the day captive in his bed. Right where she belonged.

23

"Hey, Deck, can you come here for a second?" Katie called through their shared office door. The wedding had been a week ago and she was chomping at the bit to share a surprise she'd cooked up for him.

When he walked in, her heartbeat doubled immediately. Decker wore a suit better than any man she'd ever seen. His eyes looked hard as he read the report in his hands, but when he lifted his eyes to her, they softened and she saw love and desire there.

"I need to tell you something. It's sort of important." Katie tried to look serious, but she was giddy with excitement; she also felt anxious that he might balk at her idea, and all of her planning would be pointless.

"What's wrong, Kate?" He immediately looked concerned, and she felt a little bad trying to deceive him, even if just for a few moments. Laying the report on her desk, he pulled her from her chair and held her face, looking deep in her eyes. "It's okay, we can fix it, whatever it is."

"Well, you see..." Katie widened her eyes and bit her lip, really playing up the whole innocent, damsel in distress act. "I feel like we've been working really hard lately; the construction is almost done and once it is, we'll be even busier. So, I took the liberty..." She paused and watched as he looked askance upon her; she could tell he was curious, but also a little nervous.

"I planned a trip for us. I cleared everything with your dad, he said he and Jeremiah can easily take care of things while we're gone. It's a three-day trip, we can be back at work on Monday. But, we leave tonight." She stopped talking and looked expectantly at him. Would he refuse? She knew asking him to give up a Friday at work was a huge deal, but Nate had told her that it wasn't a problem at all.

"Katie, Decker is a good guy, but sometimes he doesn't give those of us around him enough credit. We were running this place long before he took over; I'm sure we can handle it again for three days. Don't ask him about it, just make the plans, and don't let him turn you down." Nate had smiled softly at her as he spoke of his son. She had blushed when he continued, "I think some sand and sun with his girl is exactly what Decker needs; help him take his mind off of work for a while. It will all be here when you guys get back." He'd hugged her and ruffled her hair like she was 5-years-old. Katie had smiled at his

retreating back, thinking that the older man would possibly be her father-in-law someday. She knew she couldn't do much better.

All of that ran through her head as she watched Decker process her announcement.

"So, let me get this straight. You planned a vacation for us, without me knowing, and spoke to my dad about running things while we're gone? And you expect me to just drop everything and leave to go running off into the sunset with you? Is that about right?" His voice had an edge to it, and Katie immediately felt a bit defensive.

Holding her chin high, she spoke firmly, "Yes, that's exactly right. You, me, sun, sand, and sex. You dad thought it was a good idea. Your brother thought it was a good idea. Your cousins thought it was a good idea. It IS a good idea. You and I need this. YOU need this. So yeah, Decker, you've got it all pretty much straight." Instead of getting weepy that he possibly didn't want to go on vacation with her, she was pissed. She ended her little speech with a finger poking into his rock-hard chest.

He resisted the urge to smile at the fire in her eyes; his girl was so strong and exactly who he needed by his side. He continued to play as if he wasn't onboard with her plans. "So, let me clear up this one last thing..." He looked at her, trying to appear harsh.

"What's that, Decker?" She all but spit the words out.

"Am I understanding it correctly that you can play all

innocent and 'something's wrong' and act all nervous trying to make me worry, but when I try to act like I don't like your idea, you get all pissy?" He finally gave into the smile that was threatening his lips and realization dawned in her eyes.

"You were playing me that whole time?!" She smiled, but she shoved his chest.

"What? You played me just as much as I played you." He pulled her close and kissed the corners of her mouth. "I think your idea is a great one and I'll gladly run away with you for three days. Bug, I'd run away with you forever if it meant keeping you by my side." They gazed into each other's eyes and smiled big, cheesy smiles.

"Yo, yo, yo! What's up, bitches!? Why are you still here? I thought you were leaving. I was planning on using your office for some hot sweaty sex. She'll be here in ten minutes so I need you guys to make like trees and leave." Kendrick laughed at Decker's soured expression.

"I'm kidding, I'm kidding." But then he waggled his eyebrows and chuckled, "Or, am I? Hmmm, guess you'll never know. Don't worry, I'll make sure all fluids are cleaned up." Slapping his cousin on the back and pulling Katie into a tight hug, he whispered in her ear, "Be careful on the sand, it's a bitch to get out of all your crooks and crannies. If you get some in the wrong spots, Decker here will have a sand-blasted pecker come Monday." Kissing her cheek he laughed at Decker's growl of possessiveness. "You know, we used to laugh at how his name rhymes with pecker. 'Decker, Decker, where's your pecker?' we used to sing on the playground."

"Get your lips off my girl, prick; and no one ever sang that song. Get out of here; no one is using this office for sex except us." At Katie's surprised gasp and pink cheeks, Kendrick looked back and forth between the two of them and cracked up.

"Well, well, you naughty, naughty children." Walking toward Decker's desk, Kendrick ran his hand over the edge of the wood. "Mmmm, is this where the magic took place? I guess I can leave this spot alone; your couch will do just fine."

He ducked quickly when Decker picked up a notebook and threw it at his head. "Get out, fucker."

Kendrick left laughing and whistled as he walked down the hall. "Have fun, love birds! Everything here will be fine." He called out as he disappeared around the corner.

Turning to her, Decker shook his head and rolled his eyes. Taking a deep breath, trying to clear his head from Kendrick's visit, he quickly organized all of his stuff and headed toward the door. When he reached for her hand, she cocked her head in question.

"Don't you want to finish that report you were working on?" She hadn't expected him to drop everything right then.

"Nope. I can do it on Monday. Don't we have a plane to catch? Come on, Bug. I'm ready to get you naked and keep you naked in the warm sunshine for three whole days. Let's go." His eyes twinkled as she took his hand and they headed home to pack.

KATIE HAD WORKED FEVERISHLY to plan their trip to Cayo Espanto, a private island in Belize. Their plane trip was long, but afforded them the chance to sleep so that when they arrived at their island paradise they were rested enough to explore; the fact that the island was two hours behind them helped as well.

After a delicious meal of fresh seafood and island vegetables, Katie and Decker allowed a very excited tour guide to show them around the island. Making plans to snorkel the next day, they bid their guide goodnight and settled into their private bungalow.

"Oh my God, Decker, this place is breathtaking. I don't want to sound like I'm bragging, but *damn,* I did a good job." She smiled at him and flopped herself onto the king size bed.

"You did do a good job, but I don't think this island is the only thing that's breathtaking." He dimmed the lights and walked toward the bed, his eyes never leaving hers.

Smiling seductively at him, she shimmied up the bed and escaped from his reach. Wagging a finger at him she tsked, "Nuh-uh-uh, you're not the one in charge here, I am; this was my plan. Now get naked and lie down while I set the mood." She began opening the bungalow so the warm ocean breezes could flow throw, bringing the briny scent of the sea with them.

"What's my girl up to?" He asked with a smirk as he removed clothing from his travel-weary body. He knew whatever she had planned for tonight would be slow and luxurious because they were both fatigued.

"Don't you worry about it, just get naked and look glorious like you always do; I'll take care of everything else." She lit candles throughout their private hut.

Completely naked, he stretched his body out on the cool, silky sheets of the bed. Positioning bent arms behind his head, he propped himself up enough so that he could watch her every move. His curiosity peaked to full when she brought a handful of sexual paraphernalia to the bedside table.

"I have a blindfold and ties; I'll use them if you want or if I have to, but I'd like to think you can follow directions like a good boy." She winked at him and thumbed through her phone for the playlist she'd programmed in before leaving home.

Soft, sensual music filled the night and he felt himself grow harder as she stepped to the foot of the bed. "Tomorrow we can take in what the island has to offer, but for tonight, I'm your entertainment." She began a slow discarding of her clothes, each piece revealing more of the body he'd come to love and crave.

When she was naked, she walked to the bedside table and flipped the lid on a bottle of lotion. "Roll over onto your stomach." She rubbed the lotion in her hands to warm it; the scent of the sea, the candles, and the lotion assaulted his senses.

Straddling his back, she began a gentle massage of his back with her lotion-covered hands. She felt his tight muscles ripple and relax under her ministrations. Working her way down, she worked his lower back and spent extra time filling her hands with his perfect ass. When she had reached his feet she softly whispered, "Turn over."

Knowing this part of the massage would be much quicker because she was anxious to get to her reward, she began to rub her hands up his tight, muscular legs. Hands reached for her, but she sat back, "Nuh-uh, put those hands back up behind your head unless you want me to tie them up." His throaty growl spurred her on and she continued her way up his magnificent body.

She forced herself to bypass the one part of him that was straining for her attention, and worked her way up his abdomen and chest. Allowing her body to settle on top of his, she forcefully repositioned his wayward arms back behind his head.

Placing her hands on his chest, she leaned in and sucked his bottom lip into her mouth. "Are you feeling relaxed yet?"

He growled out a strangled chuckle, "If by relaxed you mean I could paddle a boat with my dick right now, then sure, I'm relaxed."

"Awww, does my poor boy have a *hard* problem? Does it

need taken care of?" Katie loved the feeling of control and power she had as she rubbed her body over his.

"Damn, Kate, I want you to have your fun, but I'm about two seconds from flipping you over and taking you. *Hard.*" She watched sweat break out on his forehead as he spoke.

"No, you'll control yourself because that's what you're good at, and you'll let me play my game. Don't worry, I won't make you wait any longer." She moved so that he was right where they both wanted him to be, and lowered herself ever so slowly; her body stretching to gloriously full.

Rocking herself on him, they found a rhythm. "Damn it, Kate, let me touch you." He gritted his strained request out almost painfully.

"Hold me," she panted.

Sitting up, he engulfed her in his arms as she continued her rocking motion. Kissing her deeply, he thrust up to meet her movements. Holding the back of her head with one hand and wrapping his other arm around her back, he cocooned her body; his lips drank from hers, swallowing her cries of pleasure.

When they were both spent, they sank into their silky sheets. Surrounded by the perfume of the island, and the lingering fragrance of the lotion and candles, they gave in to a deep sleep wrapped in each other's arms.

THEIR NEXT COUPLE days were full of fresh ocean breezes, warm sun and sand, delectable island cuisine, snorkeling and parasailing, and hours spent with bodies wrapped around each other in bed. All too soon it was time to head back to Torey Hope; Kate knew Cayo Espanto would be a destination they'd visit time and time again.

24

"*D*id you have fun?" She laid her head on his shoulder as they buckled in for take-off late Sunday night. Her skin felt warm from the sun she'd gotten over their little vacation, and, thanks to their private cottage on the beach, she definitely didn't have any tan lines. The scent of coconut and sand and sex seemed to still linger in her brain; her body was deliciously sore from the activities of the past couple days.

"Did I have fun? Well, I just spent three magical days with the woman I love being naked in my arms, under the most gorgeous sun, on the most exquisite sand, next to the bluest water I've ever seen. Did I have fun? No, Bug, I had the time of my life. I'm not sure how we'll top it, not even with our honeymoon. Thank you for dragging me away." He kissed her nose and settled her into the crook of his arm so they both could sleep a bit during the late flight. Being at work Monday morning was going to be a bitch, but he knew he couldn't keep himself away another day.

THEY WALKED, arm-in-arm, to the car and climbed in. "Do you want to stay at my place or go to yours?" Decker asked as he plugged his phone in. He'd forgotten his charger so he'd lost battery power yesterday. Surprisingly, he'd found it was sort of nice to not have to worry about every ding and beep sounding from his phone while they were away.

"Better take me to mine, I need to grab some clean clothes; plus, you know we won't sleep if I'm at your place tonight. And, as much as I've loved our time together, I *really* need some sleep if I'm going to function at work tomorrow." She kissed him, but he could see she was about to conk out again.

Turning toward her home, he drove silently as his hand absently rubbed her thigh. As they drove the last block to her house, he noticed his phone had finally pulled enough charge to start beeping about texts and messages. As he pulled into her house, he grabbed his phone and his heart stopped when he read the first message.

Sawyer: *Hey, man, don't freak out. Everything is fine. There was a little accident at work. Uncle Nicky got a pretty* *good bump on his head, but he's going to be fine. Call me when you get this. And stop freaking out; everyone is fine.*

"What the hell?!" Decker immediately put the car in reverse and peeled out of the driveway. "Sorry, Bug, I'll explain on the way; I can't drop you off right now."

Katie felt the worry pouring off of him in waves; Decker's Uncle Nicky had been born with some challenges and he'd struggled with many things throughout his life. Nicky Morgan was probably the nicest, most direct, unassuming person Katie had ever met; she knew it was killing Decker to think that his sweet, innocent uncle had gotten hurt.

She listened as Decker called Sawyer. From what she could gather, Nicky had been treated for a contusion on his head at the hospital and was now back home. The whole family was over at John and Cindy Morgan's home and that's where Decker steered his car.

It was late, but Katie knew Decker wouldn't rest until he saw Nicky and heard the story of what happened at The Center+. She wanted to believe it had been a random accident, but her heart felt sick that the "accident" hadn't really been an accident at all; with all that had been going on with the mysterious texts and questionable issues at work, she feared this wasn't just random. One look at the hard set of Decker's jaw and she knew he was thinking the same thing.

WALKING INTO DECKER'S GRANDPARENTS' kitchen, Katie was overwhelmed by the outpouring of love and concern. She saw Decker walk straight to his uncle and pull him into a tight hug.

"Uncle Nicky, are you okay?" Decker was younger, but Katie noticed that people who spoke to Nicky often took on the appearance and demeanor of being older than him due to his somewhat limited understanding of things sometimes.

"Yeah, Boss Man, I'm fine. My head hurts, but the doctor said it shouldn't hurt for too long. I have a 'goose egg' on my head; don't worry, that doesn't mean that I actually have an egg on my head, it just means that I have a big bump. They took some pictures of my head and gave me some medicine." Nicky patted Decker on the back as he assured his nephew he was fine.

"What happened?" Decker turned to the rest of the family when he asked his question. The air was heavy; tension floated thickly, and Katie could tell that her fear was about to be confirmed. This hadn't been an accident. But why Nicky?

"Let's all grab some coffee or tea and sit down." Nate nodded to Libby who started pouring steaming mugs. Decker gratefully took the brief distraction from his parents and sat down with his coffee while everyone else found a seat with their warm mugs.

"So, the best we can figure, Nicky interrupted someone who was trying to find something in either Katie or Decker's offices." Nate spoke quietly, obviously trying to ease the sting of this blow.

"Start at the beginning, please." Decker sipped his coffee, but Katie noticed the hard glint in his eyes already showing that his head was leading him to conclusions that weren't ones he wanted to accept.

"This morning, I was going to go over some of the financial reports, but I was missing that one that you told me you were taking a last look at on Thursday. I was going to head down to The Center+ to grab it from your office, but Nicky stopped by the house before I left and said he was going down there anyway to finish up some things for a talk therapy session they were planning for tonight. He offered to grab the report; I knew it was in the red folder and it would be front and center on your desk, so I told him where to find it." Nate took a sip of his hot tea as Libby ran her hand along his thigh; the anger Decker was feeling was reflected in his father's eyes, but Nate's eyes also showed guilt, guilt that he'd let his twin brother walk into getting hurt the way he did.

"When I got to The Center+, I finished up what needed done in the room we were going to use for tonight's talk therapy, then I headed to your office, Decker. I was surprised at how messy your desk was, you never leave anything messy. I was looking for the red folder when I heard something in Katie's office; it scared me because I knew no one should have been in those offices. I walked to the doorway between the offices and looked around, but I didn't see anything or anyone.

When I turned back around to take one last look for the red folder, I felt someone come up behind me. I'm not sure what they hit me with, but they hit my head and then ran out of the room. I fell down, but I was able to get back up and call Nate. He and Jeremiah came to help me. The police came and asked me a lot of questions." Nicky finished his story, but Katie had a feeling there was something he wasn't saying.

Decker must have gotten the same feeling because he looked around at the stoic faces surrounding the kitchen table. "What are you not telling me? What else happened? Damn it, something like this happens, someone I love gets hurt when it should have been me, I deserve to know what you're not saying." Decker slammed his fist on the kitchen table.

"Decker, I'm glad you and Katie weren't there. I didn't get hurt that bad, and I'm glad it was me and not either of you." Nicky looked Decker in the eyes before letting his head fall; his voice was quiet and shook as he spoke again, "I think the person who hit me would have hurt Katie worse than me."

Decker's eyes snapped toward his father after hearing what his uncle had said. "What's he not telling me, Dad?" He reached over as if to hold Katie's hand, but pulled back at the last moment. That single movement stung worse than salt in a paper cut; she felt like miles were between them; she had no hard proof, but her gut told her that this incident was going to cause issues between them. Issues she wasn't going to like.

"Go ahead, Nick, tell him what the person who hit you

said." Nate nodded at his twin; Nicky's eyes shone with tears and his wife, Carly, reached over and took his hand.

He sniffed his nose and then spoke softly, "I don't know if it was a man or a woman, I don't really remember the voice, I just remember the words. 'You're lucky you aren't that bitch Katie. I'm going to kill her. And soon.' That's when they hit me, and I just remember getting up later to call Nate." Nicky wiped his eyes and looked between Katie and Decker. "So, you see, I'm so glad you weren't there. A sore head is better than Katie ending up dead."

A short while later, the group dispersed. Katie found herself being driven home by Sawyer while Decker stayed to talk some things over with Nate. She felt a bit spooked as Sawyer walked her to her door, but he got her settled in bed and promised to lock the door behind him as he left. "Sawyer? Why do I feel like I just got the proverbial brush off from your brother?" Tears threatened her eyes as she spoke; Decker had kissed her cheek absentmindedly and basically pushed her into Sawyer's arms. No promises to call her, no words spoken in love, no assurances that everything would be fine. Her heart hurt, and her mind was running in circles trying to get inside Decker's head to figure out what he was thinking.

"Katie-girl, if I know my brother, this is going to play out in one of two ways. The first option is he's going to get pissed, pull you closer, and solve this shit. The second option is he's going to get pissed, push you away in order to protect you and get control of the situation back, and solve this shit." He leaned in to kiss her head and tucked the blankets around her tightly. "If I'm being honest with you, I think Option 2 is the most likely right now. He's going to blame himself for not being there, for Uncle Nicky getting hurt, for putting you in danger. He was off having fun in the sand and sun when this happened. Someone is purposely fucking with him and The Center+, and you're in danger; he's going to tick each of those things off on his well-manicured fingers and add them up to one thing: 'I need to get this under control,' and the way he'll do that is to push you away to protect you." Sawyer rubbed her hand through the blanket as tears poured from her eyes.

"Yeah, that's what I was afraid of. I think I've felt this coming since he first got your text tonight. Do I have a chance of fighting him on this? Or do I just have to sit by and watch as he closes in on himself again and pushes me away all in the name of controlling a situation and fixing whatever is going on?" She sniffed and wiped angrily at her tears.

"Well, I guess you could sit by and watch, but that doesn't seem like my Katie-girl. And I know sure as shit that Kendrick, Zach, and I aren't going to let him go running back to the uptight douche he used to be. I love my brother dearly, but he's been a lot more fun since you came into his life; I'm not going to let him throw that away." He laughed as she giggled. "Now, all of that being said, I think it will get worse before it gets better. And, I'm in 100% agreement with him that YOU need to be protected. I don't get why someone seems so dead set against you and him being together, but that threat against you tonight isn't something any of us are going to take lightly." She shivered as Sawyer spoke of the menacing threat Nicky had shared with them earlier.

"Sawyer? In any other situation, this would be a totally fucked up request...." She looked up at him from her pillow and he just laughed, already knowing what she was going to ask.

"No worries, Katie-girl. Let me text Decker to let him know where I am. I'm going to check the locks on all the doors and windows, grab a pillow from the couch, and lose the jeans. I'll be right back." She smiled as he walked out of her room. Her heart hurt because she was so far from Decker, but she trusted Sawyer to take care of her until she could be back in his brother's arms.

Sawyer checked the locks, called the police department to be sure an extra patrol was watching Katie's house and texted his brother.

Sawyer: I know what you're doing. Pushing her away isn't what she needs. She needs you, and you need her. I'm staying with her tonight. Think about that. By 'protecting' her and getting your damn precious control back, you're leaving her alone; she's sobbing in bed, and I'll be the one wrapping her in my arms and comforting her. Great plan, brother. I love you, but if you do what I think you're going to do, I'm not supporting you.

He headed back up the stairs and crawled into bed with her. Wrapping his arms around her, he whispered, "We will get through this, Katie-girl, and I'll be here by your side until we do. I love you."

She sniffed her nose and whispered, "Thank you, Sawyer. I love you, too."

KATIE'S HEAD was aching so badly the next morning, she had Sawyer let Decker know that she would be in later. Sawyer had briefly filled her mother in on what was going on, telling her to keep an eye out for anything suspicious and to call the police with any concern.

He had hugged her tight before leaving, "Don't lie down and take this. Maybe I'm wrong and he'll choose Option 1; I hope to hell he does. But, if he goes with Option 2, you have to fight. It won't be easy, but he's got to see that he needs you by his side and pushing you away isn't the way to fix this. I'm going to talk to him first thing to see where his head is at, but I want you to get a hot shower and some breakfast and get your ass to work. And talk to him." A quick kiss to her cheek and Sawyer was gone.

WALKING into The Center+ a few hours later, Katie smiled at Decker's parents and held her head high in regards to their crushed expressions. Did they already know what he was planning on doing? Holding her steaming coffee in her hand, Katie checked in at her mailbox.

"Katie? Could I talk to you, sweetie?" Libby Morgan was probably the sweetest person in the world, and Katie could tell that what she wanted to talk to her about was not making her happy.

"Sure, Libby, what's up?" Katie tried to play nonchalant, but she knew talking to Decker's mom was going to be hard.

They walked side-by-side to the conference room. On the way, they passed the gym and Katie's heart stopped when she saw Sawyer and Decker speaking. Kendrick and Zach stood off to the side. None of the four men looked happy; there was definite tension in the air, and it broke her heart knowing that Decker was indeed choosing Option 2. Her heart, wounded as it was, warmed to know that the other three men were standing up for her.

"Katie, my son is very special to me; both of my boys are absolute gifts and I treasure them. That being said, I don't agree with the way Decker plans on handling this situation. Both his father and I tried to speak some sense into him last night. Even Jeremiah and Kyle tried to talk to him; his Aunt Audrey all but castrated him with her words, but he's not backing down right now. I know I don't really have the right to ask you to do this, but I'm going to anyway because I feel it in my soul that you two are meant to be together. Please don't give up on him; every person in his family will stand by your side and fight him on this. He's mad and scared and hurt right now; he thinks he's let us all down. The only way he knows to fix things is to pull the reigns tight and shut himself down to everything but protecting his business and you. He doesn't see that shutting you out isn't protecting you, it's hurting you; he thinks that he's doing what's best. Give him some time, Katie, but don't give up on him." Libby's eyes shimmered with tears. Patting the girl's hand, she stood to leave. "Don't let him forget how beautiful you made his life, because you did that, Katie. You made his life so much more than what he allowed it to be before."

Katie dried her tears and walked with determination to her office. Setting her coffee cup down, she checked her mascara in her small compact mirror and then headed to Decker's door. He had barely had time to dry his hair after his workout with the guys and the scent of soap emanated from him, teasing her senses and choking her with emotion.

"Good morning, Decker. Could we talk?" She spoke professionally, not knowing exactly how he was going to play this off. Would he pretend like their relationship hadn't happened and just treat her as his assistant manager? Or would he address the huge white elephant in the room; the beast was so large, Katie felt like it was seated on her chest. Did he feel it too?

"Good morning, Kate. Yeah, I think we should talk. Pull up a chair." Decker avoided meeting her eyes, not a good sign. This lit a spark of anger inside of her. *I won't let him do this. Not now, not this way.* Making up her mind, Katie pulled a chair in front of his desk and sat down. Pulling herself up to her full height, she sat on the edge of the chair.

"Decker, before you speak, I have something to say, and I want you to just listen until I'm finished." Leaving him no chance to argue, she started speaking.

"When I first met you, years ago, you were this serious, controlled, unapproachable young man. I adored your brother, but I fantasized about you." The tick in his jaw was the only indication that he was hearing her words. She plowed on. "Years later, I found the absolute perfect job for me in my perfect little hometown, working alongside the perfect boss. Fighting the immediate attraction we had for each other became pointless, and you soon became my perfect match, my missing puzzle piece. You are it for me, Decker; I gave you myself, I gave you my love, my heart, my soul." Taking a deep breath, she steadied herself and went on.

"I hate what is happening to The Center+; I don't understand it any more than you do. I am woman enough to admit that I'm scared to death of that threat Nicky shared with us," her breath hitched when his jaw tightened yet again and his nostrils flared in anger over the threat to her. As long as that emotion continued to show on his face, she knew she hadn't lost him forever.

"I spent last night in the arms of your brother. Stop growling, you know there's nothing there, even if I wanted there to be. I tell you this so you'll stop being so pigheaded; your brother held me and comforted me last night. Your mom offered me her support this morning. I love your family, Decker, but I want *your* arms and *your* comfort and *your* support." Taking another deep breath, she readied herself to deliver her ultimatum.

"Decker, I watched my father put his business and his professional goals in front of his marriage for far too long. You are not my father, I know that. I know that in your heart-of-hearts, in your misguided head, you are doing this to protect me. But, I won't stand by while you shut me out. One week, Decker. You have one week to figure your shit out. I will stand by your side and we will fight this and work it out, together, as a team, or, I'm gone. I will walk away from the most wonderful job, family, and man I've ever known; I won't be second to your business, Decker. I can't, and I won't. One week." She willed away the tears which threatened to fill her eyes and waited for his response.

He looked at her with hard eyes. Not hard, hateful eyes; hard, broken, determined eyes. "Kate, you are the best thing that ever happened to me, both personally and professionally. The threat against The Center+ and you is just too much. I can't risk you, and I can't risk my business. Whoever is behind this seems to be pissed that you and I are together; if they see that we've cooled it on a personal front, maybe they'll give up and leave us alone, or, they'll mess up and we'll catch them. I'd never choose the business over you, but all of this started happening when I brought you on board, and we started a relationship. The Center+ keeps taking hits, you're in danger, and my Uncle Nicky was hurt because I've lost my focus." He pinched the bridge of his nose before he spoke again. "I can't promise you anything will be solved in a week; I want to ask you to give this thing more time, but that would be unfair of me. So, take your week, but I can't guarantee anything, so be sure you're ready to follow through on your ultimatum. I won't put you in more danger; if that means I lose you in order to protect the business and you, so be it." He looked at her with sad but unwavering eyes.

"So be it, huh? So you'd throw away all that we have instead of fight for us? You'd go back to that cold, bleak existence you called life, all in the name of protecting me and your precious business? Why, Decker?! It would be so easy to let me stand by your side and fight with you. Everyone else sees it, why can't you?" She started to crack, her voice was beginning to quiver with emotion. "You know what? Forget it; there's obviously no talking to you right now. I'll give you some time. Until the end of the week, you know where to find me. I hope you also know that I won't be sitting idly by, waiting for you to come up with a fix for this. I love you Decker Morgan. Even though you aren't willing to fight for us right now, I am; I'll fight for both of us." She stood from the chair.

"Damn it, Kate, I *am* fighting for us! Why can't you see that? I lost my control, I lost my focus, and that led us to where we are now. My family, my business, and the love of my life are in danger. I can't split my focus, so for now, I will do what I have to do to protect everyone and everything that I love. You're the one handing out ultimatums, Kate. Not me. I'm not pushing you away, I'm protecting you." He leaned towards her, palms flat on his desk.

Her body, heart, and mind wanted nothing more than to lean over that desk and kiss him until he stopped this asinine plan of his. But she wouldn't do that; their love was more than a physical attraction. He needed to come to her because of his love for her, not because he wanted her back in his bed.

She turned and walked out of his office. Knowing that she was shot for today, she gathered up her bag and headed to the gym; a good punishing run on the treadmill would maybe help clear her mind and comfort her broken heart.

25

a few shots into his evening drinking with his brother and cousins, Decker was more pissed off than when he'd arrived at the bar. The three fuckers who were supposed to be his best friends, supposed to support him and stand by him, were clearly not on his side; they were on Kate's side. Everyone was on Kate's side. Damn it, why couldn't they see that he couldn't pull her any further into this mess? If it wouldn't be the worst move ever for the business and it wouldn't crush her spirit more than he already had, he would fire her from her position in hopes of keeping her away from danger. But, he already feared for his 'cock-n-balls' when her grandmother found out that he had essentially ended things with her. It wasn't a permanent separation; it was just temporary until he could get things at the center under control and get Kate out of danger.

"Okay, I feel like we need to run down the list of possible suspects again. Who in the hell would be so out to get me and ruin The Center+, putting Kate in danger at the same time?" Decker racked his brain, trying to come up with names.

"What about Ted Nelson? That guy was a total douche in high school, always trying to compete with us on everything. I heard he was trying to coach the high school basketball team, maybe he's trying to cause problems at The Center+ to thwart Kendrick's teams." The motive sounded flimsy at best, even as he spoke it.

"Know anyone at the senior citizen center? Zoey said that it was going to have to cut some programs to save on the budget. Would anyone there be trying to mess with The Center+ in hopes of keeping more business coming through their doors?" Zach offered a slightly more plausible idea, but Sawyer shook his head almost immediately.

"No, no way. First, all of those people are either close personal friends with our families, use The Center+ just as much as anyone else in town, or don't even know Katie; they'd have no motive. Even if The Center+ went down completely, the senior citizen center would still be losing some of their funding. It wouldn't make sense for them to shut down the only other viable option for most of the seniors in town." Sawyer wanted to come up with a suspect in this whole mess just as much as the other guys, but pinning it on the wrong person or group wasn't going to help anyone.

"I think we need to focus more on who hates Kate so

much that they'd go to the trouble of messing with The Center+ and threaten her life. I brought a couple yearbooks; Sawyer, you were the closest with her, you can help us go through the pictures and see if anyone sets off any alarms in your mind." Kendrick pulled out some books and passed them around. The four men stopped drinking, opting for water at that point, and poured themselves over the books, looking for any face that would clue them in to someone wanting to hurt Katie and/or Decker.

Two hours later, eyes crossing from looking at so many thumbnail photos and small print, the men were no closer to coming up with a name than when they'd walked into the bar. Packing up the books and paying their tab, they headed home.

Decker drove by Kate's house. He told himself it was just to be sure everything looked safe; he knew the lie he told himself was weak. God, he missed her. His heart hurt; his heart literally burned inside of his chest. Rubbing his hand over the pain, he closed his eyes and tried to block out the fact that he knew he had hurt her. His only hope was that his strong-willed, determined girl wouldn't give up on them before he had a chance to fix everything; he prayed he'd be able to fix everything. With a last glance at her house, his heart stopped. There in the front window, he saw her. With a sad smile, she lifted her hand in a slight wave; he raised a hand in return and drove off. What would she think knowing he'd driven by to check on her? He hoped she'd realize that it meant he wasn't giving up, he was fighting, but he was fighting in the way he felt was best. Keeping her as far away from him as possible was the best for now.

KATIE WASN'T sure what to make of Decker's car being in front of her house. She watched for several minutes as he rubbed his chest, closing his eyes he laid his head heavily against the head rest. He was hurting, she could feel it. When he noticed her watching, the helpless wave he gave her was enough to bring her to her knees; the pain in her heart was overwhelming.

"When will you stop being so stubborn you stupid, stupid man?" She muttered angrily through her tears. Turning around she almost ran over her grandmother.

"Come sit, dear. I made tea; we need to talk." Grandmother's eyes were hard, but a fierce love and protection shone through them.

Sipping her tea, loving the way Grandma always made it perfectly strong and perfectly sweet, Katie waited for the older woman to speak.

"Well, before I begin dismembering your young man, I feel like I need to hear the whole story." Grandma motioned for her granddaughter to speak.

"It's a long story, Grandma." Katie hesitated. How much should she tell her?

"Well, I'm not ready to die just yet, I've got the time. Go on, girl. Speak." Grandma set her chin, and Katie knew there was no escaping.

"Someone is messing with things at The Center+. It seems like the problems started when Decker hired me. When we started dating, the issues at The Center+ continued and got worse. This past weekend when we went on vacation, his Uncle Nicky was hurt by someone snooping in my office. The person made a threat against my life. We don't know who is behind all of this. We don't know who would hate me so much. The police are trying to help, but they really can't do much with the little evidence we have to go on." She paused to catch her breath, knowing Grandma already wasn't happy with what she had told her; the older woman was going to pitch a shit fit when she heard that Decker was pushing her away.

"So, Decker feels like it's in the best interest of The Center+, his family, and me if we stop seeing each other. He seems to think he can't divide his focus between the professional and the personal, and he feels I'll be safer if he sticks to just the professional. He loves me, or so he says, but he's pushing me away in order to protect me. At least that's what he thinks he's doing. I gave him one week; I told him he needed to get his shit figured out in one week or I was gone." Katie held her chin high and waited on Grandma's response.

Shaking her head, Grandma sipped her tea quietly as if contemplating all that she'd just heard. Setting her cup gingerly down on the tea tray, Grandma leaned back in her chair and just stared at her granddaughter.

"He's being an ass, right Grandma?" Katie had wanted Grandma to love Decker as much as she did, but at that moment, she needed the older woman on her side.

"Well, girl, if I agreed with you, we'd both be wrong." The old woman delivered her blow as softly and lovingly as she could, but Katie felt it as sharply as if she'd been slapped.

"You're taking his side? How could you? I thought you wanted to cut off his male parts and feed them to rabid dogs; now all of a sudden you think he's making the right decision?" Katie sputtered her words, shock at what she was hearing settling over her.

"Calm down, Katie-girl. I'm not 100% on his side, but I'm not totally against him either. Same for you; I see where you're coming from, but I don't think you're dealing with the issue at hand very well." Grandma closed her eyes and leaned her head back against the chair momentarily as if to gather her thoughts.

Katie poured herself more tea, wishing she had something a bit stronger to sip; she had a feeling that she needed to steel herself against Grandma's words.

"Katie, I'm sorry you're hurting, but I think Decker is doing what's for the best right now. The best way for him to protect you is to make the person who is pissed off think you're not dating. He can't exactly fire you to keep you out of danger, so he's doing the next best thing. That boy loves you, any fool can see that." When Katie raised her eyebrows in disbelief at her grandmother's words, the old woman sighed, "Girl, he learned to dance for you and made an absolute fool of himself at that wedding just for you; his eyes light up when he sees you, he puts up with a crotchety old woman just to be near you. It's true, the boy has it bad." Leaning over to pat Katie's knee, she smiled softly. "I think he's doing the only thing he can do for right now. I hate that he has to hurt you in the process, but I'm proud of him for being man enough to do it, even though it hurts, if it means protecting my girl."

Grandma let that sink in for a bit. When Katie sniffed her nose, the woman continued. "Now, as for you....I think you're making a big mistake issuing ultimatums. You're giving this boy a week to sort things out that the police haven't even been able to sort out in months; you're not being fair to him. I know you're strong and determined and proud, maybe a little too proud sometimes, but it doesn't show weakness to be patient and wait for the one you love. At least give him longer than a week. If he says he wants out completely, then let him go. And *then* I'll do the dismembering. But, until he says he's out or he figures this out, give him time and don't give up on him."

Katie felt like a petulant little girl who had just been reprimanded by her grandmother. She sat, brooding, sipping her tea for several moments. Not sure where to go in the conversation, she was about to excuse herself when Grandma spoke again.

"Okay, let's get our Angela Lansbury hats on and solve

this mystery." Grandma's eyes lit up and she wiggled in her seat like a giddy little schoolgirl.

"Who is Angela Lansbury?" Katie was a little concerned that Grandma seemed so excited about a threat being made against her life.

"Oh my goodness. Where did I go wrong? I've failed you, child. Angela Lansbury? *Murder She Wrote?* Only one of the best mystery shows on television for several years beginning in the mid-80s. I can't believe I never introduced you to super sleuth Jessica Fletcher." Shaking her head in dismay, Grandma drained her tea cup and poured another, this time adding an extra lump of sugar. "Anyway, let's hash it out and see if we can figure out who might hate you enough to hurt you and Decker."

Katie nodded her agreement, although she wasn't sure how her elderly grandma was going to be able to help her solve something that even the police hadn't been able to put a stop to.

"Let's start with townsfolk who hated you in high school. Anyone come to mind?" Katie shook her head in the negative.

"College. Jilted lovers? Jealous roommates? Professors whose love for you was unrequited?" Katie rolled her eyes at her grandma's imagination.

"Grandma, you know I barely dated in college. My professors were all women or over 70. My one roommate sold sex toys and I lived by myself the other years before I returned home. I think you've had too much sugar or caffeine or both." Katie had to giggle at her grandmother's antics.

"Okay, that leads us to the here and now. Who hates you? Who is mad at you and/or Decker? Townsfolk jealous of his or your success? Local guy wanting to date you and feeling let down when you picked Decker? Ex-lover of Decker's?" Grandma continued to rattle off possibilities, but Katie sat bolt upright on the chair.

"Oh my God! How did none of us see this? Grandma, that's it! Decker's ex-girlfriend of three years. He broke up with her right before he moved back home. He thought it was a mutual, amiable breakup, but she showed up at the wedding and started talking about how she and Decker were destined to get back together. Oh my God, we didn't even put it together." Katie drained her tea, rushed to the bathroom, and called the guys' house. After telling them she was coming over, she kissed her Grandmother on the head. "Thanks for the talk, Grandma. You're the best. I love you."

"Love you too, Katie-girl. Love you too. Now, go get your man. But, remember, good things come to those who wait. It may not happen right away. It may be like a good bowel movement, you may need to give it time to work itself out." She cackled at her granddaughter's grossed-out expression and closed her eyes for a short little catnap.

BOUNDING up the steps into Decker's house, Katie felt exuberant with the thought they could solve this problem tonight, but she worried how things would be between her and Decker after this tense time apart.

Sawyer met her at the door and drew her into a warm hug. "Katie-girl, it's good to see you. I hope you haven't come to poke the sleeping bear. That's a metaphor obviously; my brother isn't sleeping, but he *is* being a total bear." Walking with him into the living room and watching him close the front door, she was bombarded with memories of that door just a short time ago. Her heart constricted and she cast sad eyes Sawyer's way before linking arms with him.

"It will get better, Katie-girl, I promise. If it's any comfort, he's just as sad and miserable as you are." He kissed her head and turned her toward the kitchen. "You ready for this?" He was talking about walking into the kitchen and facing Decker. She nodded and took a deep breath.

"With any luck, this will be over soon." She smiled hopefully at Sawyer.

"There's our girl. Hey there Katie. Come here and give me some love, girl." Kendrick stood and walked toward her. She knew he was laying it on thick in hopes of pissing Decker off. From the red-hot daggers his cousin was shooting his way, it appeared that Kendrick had been successful. She let herself be pulled into Kendrick's arms; they weren't the arms she wanted wrapped around her, but she would take the love and comfort for now.

"Good to see you, Katie." Zach kissed her on the cheek and pulled a chair out for her. He really was such a sweet, good guy; total boy next door vibe coming in waves off of that fit, tight, hot body. "You want some coffee? I was just making some when you called." Katie nodded and dared a looked at Decker.

He was staring at her intently, but she couldn't read his expression. Was he glad she was here? Mad? Did it hurt him to be so close to her and not be able to take her in his arms? She felt the pain shoot clear through her heart.

"What's up, Bug?" He caught himself right as the nickname tumbled out of his mouth. She almost had to laugh as she watched him attempt to stop it, to pull it back in. *Sorry*, he mouthed with a wince. She smiled slightly. Funny how that silly nickname could warm her heart.

"Well, my grandma and I were talking." She laughed out loud at the expression on his face when she mentioned her grandmother. "Rest easy, Decker. I know you'll find this as surprising as I did, but it appears that Grandma is mostly on your side, so your manhood is safe. For now." She smirked at him shifting in his seat.

"Anyway, Grandma and I were running through possible suspects and motives; she mentioned thinking of someone who would hate me or be jealous, perhaps an ex-lover of yours." She stopped talking long enough to let her words sink in. Within seconds, three of the guys had wide eyes and understanding had dawned.

"Fuckin' bitch!" Kendrick slammed his fist against the table. "I knew that bitch was up to something."

Zach rubbed his temples and shook his head while Sawyer pushed back from the table to start pacing the kitchen.

Decker looked around, confused. "Someone want to clue me in here?" Four pairs of eyes turned to look at him in disbelief.

"Are you kidding me, man? For someone as smart as you are, you really are dumb as shit sometimes." Kendrick leaned back in his chair and looked skyward as if asking God for patience with his cousin. "Angela? Angela Ford? Ring any bells? Damn man, how did we not put two and two together before this? She was beyond pissed when you dumped her sorry ass. She showed up at Beckett's wedding, with a shady-as-fuck story as to why she was there, cornering both you and Katie, declaring her never ending love for you and promising you'd be together again." Standing with disgust, Kendrick almost toppled the kitchen chair.

Understanding dawned on Decker's face. He grabbed his phone and scrolled through quickly. "She found out my number somehow and texted me her office number. I'll call and see if she's there; it's after hours, but at least we may get an answering service if she's not there working late. If she's there, she's got an alibi; there's no way she could be hours away at her office and be here in Torey Hope causing trouble." He looked around at the others to see if they were in agreement with him making the call.

"Do it, man." Zach nodded and Sawyer added his agreement.

Decker hit the number, and waited for it to ring through. The group watched intently, holding their collective breath. When the line connected on the other end, Decker placed the phone on the table and turned the speaker feature on. "Thank you for calling Angela Ford; this is her personal assistant, Lori, how may I assist you today?" The voice on the other end floated through the air professional and crisp.

"Yes, hello. My name is Decker Morgan. I'm an old friend of Ms. Ford's, and I was hoping to speak to her if possible." Decker glanced around at the group, as if looking for approval on what he was saying. Katie fought the urge to giggle hysterically; she felt like they were in elementary school making prank phone calls.

"I'm sorry, Mr. Morgan, Ms. Ford isn't available at the moment." Lori spoke with sorrow along with finality.

"Well, Lori, I wonder if you could help me out with a little information. I'd like to surprise Ms. Ford with a little visit; is there any way you could help me coordinate my schedule with hers so I can figure out a time to surprise her? Does she travel a lot?"

"No, not really. Ms. Ford is in the office 90% of the time. She's just recently traveled out of town for a wedding, but that's the only traveling she's done in a few months. She returned the Monday after the wedding and has no plans of being out of town for several more months. She normally has meetings in the morning, but her afternoons are easier to clear. Give me a date and I'll see what I can do on her schedule." Lori was busy clicking away on the computer keys.

"Um, actually, I don't think I've thought this surprise through as well as I should have. Can I take a look at my own schedule for the next couple weeks and get back to you about an acceptable weekday afternoon?" Decker quickly created the story, impressing everyone around the table with his fast thinking.

"Yes, of course, Mr. Morgan, that would be just fine. I'll look forward to taking your call." Lori said a polite goodbye, and the call was ended.

The five of them sat around the table, looking defeated and dejected. Angela had an alibi, she couldn't have been in Torey Hope when the problems took place or when the threat was issued. Katie hung her head in disappointment; she had truly thought Angela was the person messing with their lives. She was so ready for the mess to be over.

After a bit of depressed chit-chat, Katie excused herself and started toward the door to leave. She stopped at the kitchen doorway and glanced at Decker; she longed for him to cross the room and walk her to the door. Instead, he turned his back on her; Kendrick grunted in disgust and walked towards her.

"Let me walk you out, Katie. I'd hate to be a total douche

and not walk my girl to her car." Kendrick threw daggers at this cousin before placing a hand on the small of her back and leading her out the door, down the steps, and to her car.

"Okay, Katie, I'm only saying this once, and I'll deny it if you mention it in front of the rest of them; although, I'm pretty sure Sawyer and Zach would be on my side with this. I think Angela is the guilty party, 100%. Just because someone answered the phone and offered an alibi, that doesn't mean she wasn't here in Torey Hope. She could have anyone answering her phone and giving the answers she needs given. I say you and I play detective and nail this bitch; however, I need you to promise me you won't act on anything without me by your side. Decker the Pecker is already going to be beyond pissed that I'm going behind his back to do this; he'll have my balls if something bad happens to you because of this little undertaking of ours." Kendrick spoke stealthily, as if he was afraid someone would overhear their conversation.

Katie's eyes shone with excitement and hope. "Thank you, Kendrick! I think you're exactly right; Angela has the perfect motive and the perfect opportunity. I think you and I should do a little research on Ms. Ford and her place of employment." Kendrick chucked her on the chin and laughed.

"I like the way you think, Katie. Swing by my office tomorrow at work, and we'll make plans to dig in this shit up to our elbows."

26

"Okay, Decker just left to go to the police station; he wants to run over the timeline and happenings with them to make sure they aren't missing anything. He's sent Zach to speak to the security technician; he wants the cameras and alarms updated. We've got at least an hour or so before he's back." Kendrick spoke quickly and quietly as he led Katie by the elbow inside his office to sit.

She had been in Kendrick's office a couple times, but it was always to drop something off or to ask a quick question. She'd never really sat down and looked around. He had decorated in a sports theme which fit his position very well. Before taking a seat, she took a quick look at pictures hanging around his office and scattered along tops of bookshelves. She saw him with the other guys in many sports team photos; Kendrick with his parents and siblings filled some of the frames. As she walked from behind his desk to take her seat, she noticed a small wooden frame placed, almost hidden, in front of his paper trays. She saw a much younger Kendrick, early to mid-high school age, with a beautiful girl held in his arms. Katie instantly recognized the girl as one that Kendrick had dated; if she recalled the story correctly, the girl had moved away from town; Kendrick had seemed lost for quite a while after that. She blushed when he caught her gaze on the photo; he quickly laid the frame face down and sat behind his desk.

"I've been doing my research. You told me that Angela was leaving school at about the same time as all of you and was heading to New York to take a position with Starsky Enterprises. I checked out the company and it seems legit, so I think we should start with a call to Starsky's main offices and see what we can find from there." Katie laid out paperwork containing the information she had been able to gather.

"Sounds like a plan. Let's play it off like we're a potential employer; that way, if we find out it's all legit, we can at least cause a little awkwardness for Angela if her current employer thinks she's applying for other jobs." Kendrick waggled his eyebrows with a menacing smile.

Picking up the office phone, Kendrick hesitated. "Do we take a chance calling from this number? Or should we call from a cell and block our number?" Thinking it over for a bit, he hung the desk phone up and pulled out his cell. "Let me use mine. That way, if she somehow learns of this and figures

out the number that called, she'll find me rather than you."
He dialed the information desk at Starsky Enterprises.

"Good afternoon, thank you for calling Starsky Enterprises, this is Suzanne. How may I direct your call?" Suzanne
was pleasant, but seemed to want nothing more than to
transfer the call and answer the next one.

"Hello, Suzanne. I'm Rick Roberts with Colglazier Incorporated here in Santa Fe, New Mexico." He had a comical
expression on his face and shrugged his shoulders as if to say,
What? We didn't plan this part out; I'm improvising. "I'm
calling about a potential employee, a Ms. Angela Ford. I need
to speak to someone in a supervisory position who is familiar
with her work history."

"Yes, Mr. Roberts, let me look Ms. Angela Ford up in our
system." A few clickety-clacks of the keys and Suzanne was
humming while she seemed to be looking through a list of
search results. "Ah, yes, here is an Angela Ford. She worked
under Mr. Tim Rose; shall I forward your call to Mr. Rose's
office?" At Kendrick's go-ahead, Suzanne sent his call
through.

"Good afternoon, this is Mr. Rose's office, how may I help
you?" A perky little voice answered the call.

"Hello, this is Rick Roberts of Colglazier Incorporated,
I'm calling to inquire about a Ms. Angela Ford." Kendrick
stopped there, feeling that less was more in this situation.

"I'm sorry, Angela Ford is no longer employed by Mr.
Rose *or* Starsky Enterprises. Is there anything else I can do

for you, Mr. Roberts?" The perky voice took on a bit of snooti-
ness when it spoke Angela's name, and Kendrick and Katie
were both intrigued to find out more behind that.

"Well, miss, I'm researching Ms. Ford's professional background in hopes of hiring her at my company. However, I
only hire those who come with high recommendations.
Would you be in a position to speak of her work history at
Starsky Enterprises?" Kendrick knew he was pushing his luck
asking this question; any secretary or assistant worth her salt
would *never* disclose information regarding a former
employee. But Kendrick sensed the voice on the phone was as
ditzy and shallow as they came, so he cast out the line and
began reeling it in.

"Well, Mr. Roberts, I really shouldn't say, but what I *can*
tell you is that Angela Ford was nothing but a trouble maker,
and she didn't last here more than 3 weeks." The voice picked
up in cattiness and seemed eager to spill more dirt; Kendrick
played along.

"Oh dear, that doesn't sound like a raving review; may I
be so bold as to ask what type of trouble she caused?" He gave
Katie a hopeful look as he waited for Ms. Voice; from the
shuffle and the soft click, it appeared she was closing the door
to gain privacy for the rest of the conversation.

"Well, I will deny I *ever* had this conversation; you don't
even know my name, so don't think you can pin this on me."
Her voice was a whisper now. "When Angela was hired, she
immediately slept her way through at least 3 of the entry level

management positions; that was in a span of 9 days, tops. When she threatened all three men with allegations of rape and contacting their wives, upper management quickly shut her up by promoting her three positions higher. I guess they thought that getting her into a higher level would remove her from the chance to cause problems; no such luck. She started hitting on my boss, Mr. Rose, almost immediately. When the dear man turned her down flat, she tried the rape allegation and threatened to contact his precious wife; lucky for Mr. Rose, he's a bit paranoid and has his offices on 24-hour surveillance and bugged. That's why I'm having to sit in the only corner where the cameras don't reach and whisper to you right now. Mr. Rose immediately told his wife about the psycho who had come to work for him and pulled all of the tapes as proof of his devotion to her." The girl chuckled before continuing, "The only thing they were able to see or hear on those tapes was Angela Ford fucking one of the night custodians and trying to bribe him into disconnecting the security cameras."

Kendrick and Katie's eyes were bugged out and she mouthed the word, *Whoa*, to him as they waited for Ms. Voice to continue.

"Mr. Rose called the authorities and had Angela escorted out of the building and off the premises. He took out a restraining order on her. The last known address she left, so that I could send her sorry ass her last paycheck, was...hold on, let me look it up." From the sound of heels clicking, she was apparently walking across the office floor and opening the door. Upon settling back at her desk, they heard her clicking around on the computer keys. "Aha, here it is. The day she left, she listed a local address, but a few days later, she had a private courier deliver her new address. 1341 State Street, Torey Hope, IL 71006." She covered the speaker with a hand and could be heard speaking in a muffled voice.

"Excuse me, Mr. Roberts, I'm needed in a meeting, I really must go. Again, you didn't hear any of this from me, but I would highly advise that you *not* hire Angela Ford." A quick goodbye and silence echoed from the phone.

Katie grabbed a piece of paper and scribbled down the address they'd just been given.

"Oh my God, Kendrick, she's been here almost the entire time you guys have been back. This is all the proof we need." Her eyes were wide with shock, and Kendrick felt his heartbeat increase at the thought of Angela being in their town, watching, waiting, planning.

"Hold on, girl, let's think this through." Kendrick rubbed the top of his head, trying to organize his thoughts. On one hand, he felt they should go straight to Decker and the rest of the family and let them know what they'd just learned; call the police. On the other hand, he thought of Nicky Morgan getting hurt, the threat to Katie, all the fuck-ups at The Center+, and he just wanted one round with Angela Ford to let her know that she was in way over her head if she thought she was going to fuck with the Decker/Morgan/Jordan boys.

"Tell me what you're thinking, Kendrick." Katie felt a nervous excitement mingling with a sick knot of fear in her stomach.

"Well, part of me wants to go over there, rip her a new one, and send her packing. The other part, the smarter part, knows we need to share this with the family and police." His eyes sought hers; he knew immediately that she was completely on board with the first suggestion.

"Slow down, Katie, we've got enough proof here to at least have the police bring her in for questioning. Decker would have my balls on a platter if he knew I took you anywhere near that bitch now that we know she's been behind all of this." Kendrick was shaking his head, trying his best to convince Katie that they shouldn't go check out Angela's last known address.

"What if we just go drive by and get a look at it? Then we can tell Decker and the rest of the family; we can give all the info we have to the police. Let's just take a gander; what do you say?" She raised her eyebrows and smiled hopefully. She couldn't explain the deep-seeded pull inside her to see where Angela had been living this whole time; she just knew she needed to see for herself.

"Fine. We will drive by, but then we are calling Decker and having the whole family meet up so we can discuss this situation." He stood and motioned her toward the door. He didn't completely understand it, but he felt the same need

Katie was feeling; he was pulled to see Angela's home in Torey Hope for himself.

Knocking quickly on Sawyer's office door, Katie and Kendrick were both a little surprised to see a very disheveled Sawyer answer the door. With a quick excuse about a killer headache, he told them he'd meet up with them later and all but slammed the door in their faces.

"What the hell was that about?" Kendrick frowned at the door and then at Katie.

"If I wasn't so hyped to go check out Angela, I'd totally be looking further into whatever just happened here." Katie's eyes narrowed and she cast a speculative gaze upon the door which had just closed on her.

Climbing into Kendrick's gray Ford Mustang, Katie glanced around furtively; she knew Decker would be pissed beyond belief if he knew what they were doing. But, he pushed her away in order to protect her; she felt justified in looking into Angela's whereabouts and activities if it meant saving herself and The Center+ anymore trouble.

"I think if you go down a couple more blocks you'll turn right and we should run into her address. If I'm not mistaken, it's a small cluster of about 6 townhomes." Katie gave directions as Kendrick drove.

"There, that's hers. 1341; well, isn't that just the cutest little homey abode you've ever seen? Looks like she's been playing Suzy Home Maker; nice little decorative touches. I bet she even introduced herself to her neighbors with a plate of cookies." Katie's voice sneered as they took in the humble townhome that Angela was calling home.

"Oh my God, Kendrick, isn't that her?" Katie all but threw herself out of the car. Without waiting to hear what Kendrick was yelling, she barreled across the street and practically tackled Angela on the sidewalk.

"Fuckin' shit, girl. So much for just driving by; damn it, my ass is grass when Decker finds out about this." Kendrick threw his door open and rushed to join Katie; as he walked, he quickly formed a plan in his mind in hopes of keeping Angela calm.

"Baby, I thought we were going to tell her together?" Kendrick grabbed Katie by her waist and swing her around, burying his face in her neck. His voice was low, but very serious, "Play along with me, Katie. No questions, just do it." Letting her body press up against his as he lowered her to the ground, Katie fought to contain the shocked look from taking over her face.

"Hey there Angela. Didn't get to talk to you much at the wedding; hope all is well. I know you've met my girl, Katie. Are you still in town? I thought you were just visiting your old friend for the wedding weekend?" Kendrick talked to Angela as if they were close personal acquaintances; Katie stared up at his face entranced that he could talk so smoothly to the woman they both knew was fucking with their lives.

"Kendrick." Angela gave a small, friendly smile; Katie noticed when the woman wasn't being a psychotic bitch, her smile was quite pleasant. "*Katie.*" The smile disappeared and a hateful sneer took its place. "To what do I owe this pleasure?" She looked over her shoulder as if she were hoping to avoid anyone seeing her. "You'll have to excuse me. I'm staying with that friend from school and he's expecting me back inside soon. Why are you here, Kendrick?"

"Well, we were taking a drive and we saw you; Katie wanted to thank you personally for what you did for her at the wedding. I told her that she shouldn't come running up and interrupt your day, but she was insistent that you hear her appreciation straight from her." Kendrick put his arm around Katie and pulled her close to his side.

Still not quite catching on to what game he was playing, Katie just smiled up at him and snuggled into his warm embrace. She wasn't sure why he was hugging her, but he seemed to want her to play along, so she really hammed it up. "Oh, Kendrick, you're so right; I couldn't wait to tell you thank you when I saw you were still here in town!" Turning her head to speak to Angela, she poured every ounce of acting skill she possessed into her speech.

"Really. What exactly do you need to thank me for?" Angela's skepticism was clear and the hatred written all over her face was scary.

Racking her brain trying to figure out exactly what Kendrick wanted her to thank Angela for, Katie buried her head in his chest; voice muffled, she spoke tearfully, "Kendrick, I'm just too overcome with emotion right now, can you tell her, Kendrick?" A couple sniffles for good measure were thrown in and Katie was reminded just how much she enjoyed theater in high school.

"Shhhh, baby, it's okay. Of course I'll tell her." Kendrick kissed her head and rubbed her back. "Angela, when you confronted Katie and Decker at the wedding it really opened Katie's eyes to the real Decker. After leaving the wedding, Decker couldn't talk about anything but you, and Katie realized that the sham of a relationship they had was completely over. They broke up that weekend; she just couldn't continue listening to Decker pine away for you." He cast a pitying look upon the top of Katie's head as she continued to sniffle into his chest. "Honestly, I have to thank you as well. My heart broke for Katie when she had to admit that Decker wasn't the one for her, but that gave me the opening I needed to let her know how I really felt about her. It will take a while and we aren't rushing anything, but you coming to that wedding was quite possibly the very best thing that ever happened to me if it means I get to hold this girl in my arms for the rest of my life."

Angela's shrew eyes narrowed even tighter. "You and Decker broke up? Because of me? And now you're dating Kendrick, the biggest male whore I ever met?" She questioned Katie as if she clearly wasn't buying it. "I thought you two went on a vacation recently?" Angela didn't seem to realize she'd just given away the fact she was stalking Katie and Decker.

"Yes, I broke up with Decker; we let people think we went on vacation together. I actually went out of town to heal from the break up. Decker took a road trip to clear his head." *Sniff, sniff.* "I just couldn't stay with someone who was obviously still so hung up on his ex-girlfriend. He'd told me you were beautiful, but I knew I didn't stand a chance once I saw you at the wedding. After we left, he spoke of you for hours; it was immediately evident that he wasn't over you. I guess he'd been fooling himself along with me when he said it was over; one look at you and he was right back under your spell." Taking a deep breath, Katie shuddered and dried a few tears. "We ended amicably, but it was for the best. And, like Kendrick said, maybe it was all meant to be if it led me to find him." Leaning up to place a kiss on Kendrick's cheek, she batted her lashes at him. "I know all about his past, but that's where it's going to stay; it's his present and future I'm the most interested in." She let out the most ridiculous giggle and rubbed her nose against his.

"Wow, I really didn't see that one coming. Oh, not about Decker, I knew he'd have to admit he was still attracted to me; what we had was just too special to give up on. I just didn't see you and Kendrick finding each other, but it almost seems like it was meant to be, so I'm happy for you. Now, you'll have to excuse me, I need to get back inside." With a curt nod, Angela took off up the stairs.

Gritting his teeth and talking in a growly whisper, Kendrick grasped her hand in his and began walking her slowly back to his car, "Keep playing it up, Katie-girl. She's going to be watching. Now, get your pretty little ass in the car; that little stunt just about cost me my balls. Smile sweetie, and pretend like you're a little in love with me; I'm going to kiss you now." Still walking, he leaned down and captured her lips with his. His mouth was warm and pleasant, but Katie felt no spark between them at all; this kiss was the very definition of what it would feel like to kiss a brother.

"If I'm going to get my balls busted for letting you get in this situation, I might as live it up while I can; won't Decker just about shit a brick when I tell him I had to kiss his girl all in the name of acting out a scene in front of his psycho bitch of an ex; here's an extra little improv to really add insult to injury." He let his hand move from her shoulder to cup her ass right as they reached the Mustang.

Laughing for real, no longer acting for Angela, Katie faced him and cupped his face in her hands. "Kendrick Jordan, I love you, you wicked man; you just pulled off the perfect little lie. I love Decker with everything I am, but you will always hold a very special place in my heart; even when you lose your balls once Decker finds out about this. Thank you for jumping in and saving me when I acted without thinking." Kissing him quickly, she opened the car door and climbed in.

Kendrick's heart fluttered and warmed unexpectedly in his chest.

Driving off to meet up with the whole family, Katie

wondered what Angela's next move would be now that she thought Katie and Decker were finished. She shivered with dread at the thought of Angela watching close enough to know about their vacation; she could only hope Angela bought the story about why they were both out of town that weekend. With any luck, they were one step closer to their problems being over.

27

"**Y**ou fucking did what?!" Decker roared at Katie and Kendrick, standing up and slamming his hands on the kitchen table in his grandparents' home.

"Son, you need to calm down. Let's listen to the whole story and figure out what the next step should be here." Nate laid his hand on Decker's shoulder and forced him to sit down.

"Libby, dear sister, I think some of your calming tea is definitely needed in this situation." Audrey cocked her head at her baby boy and wondered just what Kendrick and Katie had been up to. She walked with her sister to the counter and began preparing mugs of steaming hot tea.

"Let's take this to the living room, shall we? I think we'll all be a bit more comfortable." Judy Jordan suggested and the clan trouped toward the couches.

Once they were settled, Decker all but barked, "Let's hear it."

"Decker..." Katie knew he was mad, or upset, but she needed him to look at her. She needed to feel that connection and see the love in his eyes; right now he was acting as if she wasn't even in the room.

"Kate, not now." Decker held his hand up and cut her off.

Hurt and fuming mad, Katie took a deep breath; this would not be something that was worked out or solved within a quick five minutes, she knew she was going to have to be patient. Knowing she'd hurt Decker bothered her, but the childish part of her wanted to stick her tongue out at him and say, "See how it feels to not have any say in someone's actions? You hurt me, I hurt you, we're even." She knew this wouldn't solve anything and in the end it wouldn't even make her feel any better, but she had to work hard to control her response.

Decker's hard, angry eyes drilled into Kendrick's; the two of them were cousins, as close as brothers, Decker would do anything at all for him, but at this point in time, all he wanted to do was take him out back and beat the ever loving shit out of Kendrick.

"Deck, I know you're mad, and you have every right to be." Kendrick spoke sincerely to his cousin. Looking around at the rest of the family, he gave a sheepish half-grin, "You all know I'm the type to act first and think about it later. I'm sorry for doing that yet again."

"No, Kendrick, you're not taking all of the blame on this one." Katie interrupted him and openly made eye contact with each family member, including Decker. "Kendrick and I gathered some information and made a plan; I took a huge detour from that plan, and Kendrick stepped in to save me from what could have been a really bad situation." Katie finished and looked at Decker; the heat in his eyes was hard to read. Anger? Desire? Fear? All of the above?

"Kate, can I talk to you for just a second?" Decker was on his feet in 2 seconds flat and stalked towards the kitchen.

Katie looked around helplessly, meeting curious expressions, smirks, and wide eyes. Standing slowly and rubbing her hands down the front of her thighs, she gave a small nervous smile and quipped, "Well, I guess I'll be back in just a second." She walked to the kitchen with the awkward laughter of Decker's family echoing behind her.

"If you're not back in 10 minutes, we'll send a search party." Sawyer winked at her as she walked by him.

Feeling defensive the moment she stepped into the kitchen, Katie crossed her arms over her chest and stood with her feet planted wide, as if ready to fight. "What is it Decker?" Her heart was hurting so badly, but she'd be damned if she'd let him try to control her and reprimand her like a wayward child.

Taking a deep breath, pinching the bridge of his nose in

his signature *get it under control* move, Decker took a step toward her. His face twisted in pain, he rubbed his hands over his face and then held his hands out to the side as if to surrender.

"Kate, I don't want to fight. This is all so very hard. I'm scared for you, for us, for The Center+; I'm also angry as hell that you and Kendrick dragged yourselves into a dangerous situation." He stopped for a moment and looked at her with a strange sad expression. "Please don't take this the wrong way, but I can't listen to you tell this story right now. When this is completely over, you and I can sit and talk things through and figure out where we go from here, but for now I need you to let Kendrick tell the story."

Katie's foggy brain cleared slightly as his words sunk in. "What are you talking about, Decker? Talk things through and figure out where we go from here? What the hell? What is there to talk about, where else would we go?" She pinned him with a questioning glare. And then, it began to make sense. "Oh my God, you're not sure about us? You've curled back into that cocoon of tight control and all you can focus on is keeping it. Fine, let's go listen to Kendrick tell the story, but understand this: I told you I wouldn't sit idly by and let go of what we had. While you were so busy pushing me away and reigning in your damn control, Kendrick was there to listen and help me. I guess I was wrong thinking you'd welcome me back with open arms." She shook her head sadly, disappointment with him evident on her beautiful face.

Turning on her heel, she returned to the living room and took a seat next to Sawyer. Noticing her defeated expression, he put an arm around her and pulled her in close. "Give it time, Katie-girl. Remember I told you it would probably get worse before it got better?" He placed a kiss on the side of her head and turned to listen to Kendrick.

"Long story short, those who want a longer version can ask me for it later, I believed Angela was involved the moment Katie brought up her name. I didn't feel the phone call we made was enough to proof to end the suspicion on her. So, I told Katie where Angela was planning to work after college. She and I called Starsky Enterprises, pretending to be interested employers, and got all sorts of dirt on Angela. I'll spare you the details, but let's just say the psycho we thought we knew has developed into a *stark raving mad* psycho in the last several months. The main information we got to help in this whole scenario is that she's not been working there for a long time, almost the whole time we've been back in Torey Hope. And, here's the nail in her coffin, the last known address she gave to Starsky was 1341 State St., *Torey Hope*. Yep, Angela Ford has been living here in Torey Hope almost as long as we've all been back home. Which means she's been watching Decker and Katie; she's had perfect motive and opportunity to wreak havoc at The Center+." Kendrick stopped for a moment; that was the easiest part of the story. He knew the hard part was going to be telling Decker about their run-in with Angela.

"Now, here's the part you're probably really going to get pissed about. Katie and I decided we'd just drive past Angela's place and then we'd meet up with the family and take the information we'd found to the police. Angela's place is that little group of townhomes along the edge of town. She's got it all spiffy and looking quaint and lovely, total façade obviously; that is one crazy ass bitch. Anyway, we were sitting in the car across the street from her place when we spotted her on the sidewalk. Well, my girl here let her emotion get the best of her, and she bounded from the car and approached Angela." Kendrick gave Katie a sympathetic smile, knowing she regretted not thinking her actions through.

"I hauled ass out of the car and followed her; I didn't really have time to plan anything through, I just came up with the most plausible sounding story I could within the 20 seconds it took me to catch up with Katie." Kendrick gave Decker a look that communicated sorrow, regret, but also a little bit of payback, as if he was rubbing it in his cousin's face that it was wrong of Decker to push Katie away.

"After a few minutes of conversation, we had convinced Angela that Decker and Katie broke up. Then we headed over here to tell all of you and hopefully head to the police." Kendrick ended the story so abruptly that everyone in the room cast suspicious eyes upon him.

"I don't know Angela, but how did you convince her that Katie and Decker broke up? She saw them together at the wedding and she's seen them together in town since she's living here. Surely she didn't just take your word for it?" Nicky spoke slowly, trying to piece together the story without all of the pieces needed.

Zach leaned forward on his knees, "Feels like something's missing, cousin." Zach's eyes gleamed in anticipation, as if he could read Kendrick's face and knew what was coming. The guys never passed up a chance to give each other a hard time, and Zach was sure the rest of the story was ramping up to be perfect fodder.

Wincing and glancing at Katie, Kendrick hung his head. When he lifted it back up, he spoke regretfully, "Just know, this was a spur-of-the-moment plan, and it sounded much better in my head than it's going to when I speak it out loud." Stalling for time, Kendrick stole a look at Decker and steeled himself against the molten anger simmering there.

"Spit it out, fucker." Decker spoke menacingly, clearly already having a slight idea of where this story was headed.

"So, we told Angela that Decker's feelings for her were brought to the surface after seeing her at the wedding, and that Katie had refused to be second place and had broken up with Decker." At Decker's raised eyebrow seeming to say, *And that's all?* Kendrick rushed on, "And we thanked her for coming back into Decker's life because it brought Katie and me together. Angela thinks that Katie and I are taking it slowly, but that we have a real chance at a relationship because Decker still has feelings for Angela." Deciding to throw it all out there, Kendrick went all in, "And I may have laid it on pretty thick with some kisses and ass rubbing." He winced and ducked as Decker came across the coffee table at him.

"Decker, that's enough. Outside, now." Nate spoke to his son gruffly. He stood and ushered the younger man towards the door. Jeremiah Jordan and Kyle Martin following with the nod of Nate's head.

NATE SHOOK his head as he watched Decker pace in the backyard. "Decker, get your ass over here." Decker walked towards the three men he'd looked up to all of his life. Crossing his arms over his chest, he was closed-off and defensive.

"Son, I realize you're angry with Katie and Kendrick for going after Angela on their own. They made some mistakes, and they've owned up to those mistakes. I'm guessing your pride is stinging a bit at the thought that your own actions of pushing Katie away may have actually led her to working with Kendrick." Nate watched his son's jaw tighten and knew, even without a confession, that Decker was feeling responsible for a lot of things at that moment.

"I'm sure knowing your cousin was kissing your girl isn't the easiest thing to swallow; but, Decker, there's absolutely no spark between those two. That girl is crazy about you. Sure, she loves your brother and cousins, but she's *in love* with you.

I think this is one of those situations where you need to admit you were wrong, let some things go, and move on." Nate put his hand on Decker's shoulder.

"Decker, you know that Kendrick loves you with every ounce of his being; I know he doesn't have the best track record with his dating history, but there's no way he'd every purposely take your girl from you." Jeremiah spoke with a sureness of his son.

"Don't let something like this ruin what seemed to be the start of something really good, Decker. In the grand scheme of life, this is just a bump in the road. Drive over it and don't look back." Kyle spoke with understanding; knowing his history, Decker had no choice but to listen to his words.

"I'm not sure what's going to happen with Katie and me. But, I know we need to get this information to the police station." Nate rolled his eyes and shook his head at the stubbornness of his son.

"Nathaniel, I seem to remember a certain young man who wouldn't give up on fighting for what he thought was right so many years ago. There's no question in my mind where Decker got his stubbornness from." Cindy Morgan had joined them in the yard and touched her son's arm as she watched her grandson stalk toward the house.

IN THE KITCHEN, Decker caught Katie alone for a moment.

"Kate, we're going to the police station. I'd like you there, please."

"And what happens after that, Decker?" Katie turned sad eyes upon him.

"I don't know, Kate. Right now I can't think about that, I need to know that you and The Center+ and my family are safe. We can figure us out when this is all over." Decker looked at her as if he wanted to reach out and pull her close, but he sighed and turned away.

KENDRICK, Katie, Decker, and Nate went to the police station. The officer, Smitson, who had been assigned to the case from the beginning took notes and nodded appreciatively. "Now, this isn't the way we'd usually advise citizens to gather information; we don't like thinking that any of our residents are putting themselves in danger, but I have to say this is really good information. Knowing about the break up, her words at the wedding, her behavior at work, and that's she's been living here this whole time, all of that is at least enough to bring her in for questioning."

Taking a sip of his coffee, the Officer Smitson continued, "I don't want you to get your hopes up too high. There's a very good chance that the questioning won't garner enough for us to hold her, and she'll be released. At this point, we have reason to believe she's the perpetrator, but not enough evidence for an arrest. We'll probably question her and then keep close eyes on her, waiting for her to mess up."

Katie's heart fell; she had thought that the information they'd gathered would be enough to end this whole mess with Angela.

"Ms. Turner, I have to advise that you take extra precautions. I'd assume, based on her actions and threats, that Ms. Ford is going to be especially angry with you when we release her from questioning. Do you have somewhere you could go, out of town, for a while? At least a few days? It would make me more comfortable knowing we were just watching the suspect instead of watching her and trying to protect you." Smitson spoke sympathetically, as if he understood he was asking a lot of Katie.

"She can go to her dad's, it's pretty far out of town, I'll call and let him know what's going on." Decker spoke to the officer as if Katie wasn't sitting in the room.

"Damn it, Decker, I'm right here. Stop acting like I'm invisible!" Turning to the officer, she spoke. "Do you really feel this is necessary? Leaving town? Leaving my place of employment? All because a jealous ex-girlfriend doesn't like me?" Katie was exasperated, but deep down, where the threat against her life kept playing loudly in her psyche, she knew that leaving would be the best. She just didn't want to appear like she was running away.

"Ms. Turner, I really do think it would be safer for you to go to your dad's, or someplace, for at least a few days until we see how Ms. Ford is going to react to the questioning." The officer gave her an *I'm sorry* look and finished with the paper work on his desk.

As the group left the station, Decker walked away from them and headed toward his car. The look of dismay on Katie's face was more than Kendrick could handle. He looked at his Uncle Nate and shook his head in disgust and disbelief. Nate nodded toward Decker as if indicating to his nephew to go stop his son. Grabbing Katie's elbow, Nate stopped her on the sidewalk.

"Katie, I get what he's doing, but I'm sorry for how he's doing it. He's going to come to his senses at some point and be embarrassed about the way he's handling this whole thing." Nate held her hand and patted it in a fatherly way.

"Nate, I'm glad you *get it* because I don't. Not at all. Protect me? Fine. Focus on fixing this problem? Okay. But shutting me out completely, and throwing a little pissy fit because of what Kendrick and I did? That's not okay." She wanted to stomp her foot as she spoke, but she refrained.

They looked over to where Kendrick and Decker were having heated words in the parking lot. "Come on, I'd rather not see those boys in a knock-down-drag-out in front of God and everybody, let's go see if we can calm them down." Nate put his arm around her and held her close, feeling very much like a dad comforting a daughter upset about a boy.

"Boys, I think coming to blows in the police station parking lot would possibly be a bad idea. Could we talk about this calmly?" Nate took a step to place himself between his nephew and son.

"Dad, I'm worried that Angela is watching us; she's clearly been watching us for a while, I'm afraid if she sees Kate and I talking, she won't believe we've broken up. Douche-bag here is mad because I'm giving Kate the cold shoulder, but I don't want to risk that Angela may see something to contradict that ridiculous story these two told earlier." Decker glanced around nervously as if looking for any sign of someone watching. The hair on his neck stood up, and he had a bad feeling in the pit of his stomach.

"The least you can do is talk to her and say goodbye before she has to pack up and leave. Don't just walk away from her; don't leave her with no explanation of your thoughts or actions." Kendrick was almost growling at his cousin. When Decker shifted uncomfortably, Kendrick let out an exasperated sigh. "Oh my God, what are you? Ten? I get that this is sort of awkward, but your dad and I standing here will help camouflage anything that may appear like you're still together; talk to her, try to pretend we aren't here."

"Kendrick, thank you for standing up for me," Katie reached out and placed her hand gently on his arm. "But, I'm a grown woman, I don't need you fighting my battles." Turning to Decker she spoke softly in case someone was listening, but her voice was laced with hurt and anger. "Decker, I'm so torn over this. One side of me gets that you're doing this to fix things at The Center+ and to protect me from Angela; that side of me is appreciative, and I'm so hopeful this will be over soon. The other side of me is so angry at the way you're going about this, I could just spit. You took what we supposedly had and you've wrecked it; you've wrecked me, my heart is in shambles. How are you able to be so cold toward me? How are you able to ignore me so easily? How are you so eager to get me out of town? I get that we need to keep up the appearance of a break up, but some phone calls or texts or secret meetings where you tell me it's all going to be okay would be nice. Do I get that from you? No, I get nothing, zilch, nada. You're mad at the situation, you're mad because you think we were meddling where we didn't belong, you're mad that your ex-girlfriend is a psychotic bitch and your business and love life have been fucked up because of her...FINE! But don't give up on what we had, don't give up on us." She let the tears fall from her eyes unchecked.

Decker rolled his neck to ward off the tension headache that was looming; he felt it, someone was watching. Cursing himself for what he was about to do, he spoke to the whole group, but kept his eyes on Kendrick. "I feel like someone is watching us, this needs to look like you and Katie are together; put your arm around her and lead her away." Between gritted teeth he lowered his voice, *"So help me, God, if you touch her in any way other than friendly, I'll hand you over to her grandmother."* Ignoring Katie, not even a glance in her direction, he pretended to throw his hands up in exasperated anger, pointed his finger at both Katie and Kendrick, and shouted, "I'm done with both of you, done." and then turned and walked away.

Angry devastation rolled off of Katie as she felt herself pulled into Kendrick's embrace. "He's trying to keep you safe, Katie. I know it sucks how he started this by pushing you away, and I know it sucks that we're all having to keep up this lie, but he's doing the best he can. We don't have to like it, but we need to play it out." He walked her toward his Mustang.

Decker drove off with a rev of his engine and squeal of his tires. Nate watched his son drive away and remembered his mother's words; she was right, his son was just as stubborn as he himself was when he was younger.

When Kendrick pulled up to Katie's house, he looked over at her; she was curled up, eyes staring unseeing out the window. "You want to talk about it?" He was pissed that Decker had hurt her like this, and he was even more pissed that Angela had brought her own brand of crazy to Torey Hope; he didn't like his family being hurt.

"I think the thing that hurts the worst, the thing I'm the most worried about, is that he has shut me out so completely. Earlier, in the kitchen, he acted like we'd have to see where things stood between us when this was all over. If he was just pretending to push me away, if he was staying in contact with me to let me know it was hard on him and he hates it as much as me, if he was making an effort to comfort me...then I could play it off for the ploy it is and pray that we get rid of Angela sooner rather than later. But, he's gone from pushing me away to being pissed at what I did, and now he's talking about reassessing our relationship when this is all over. I feel like I'm losing him to that damn obsession he has for control. What happens if this all gets worked out and he decides he can't risk letting go again? Where does that leave us? I won't be able to work side-by-side with him after what we've been through; I'll leave The Center+, I'll lose him, the whole family. I just don't know if I see this ending well when it all does come to an end." Katie leaned over and kissed Kendrick on the cheek. "Thanks for bringing me home. I'm going to pack and head to my dad's. It's a couple hour drive, so I better get going."

Thinking about Katie taking off by herself made Kendrick uneasy. "Wait, if Angela is watching you, it's going to look weird if you just up and leave town. I'll drive you to your dad's so it looks like we're leaving town together; maybe I'll stay a day or two, then sneak back into town. Go ahead and go pack, I'll be back in an hour." He waited until she walked in the front door before driving away. He didn't like to admit it, but he got the same feeling as Decker; they were being watched.

28

*D*ecker pulled his car over and sat with his head against the steering wheel. After several moments of getting himself and his emotions in check, he glanced around and realized he'd stopped near a local park. Needing a minute to clear his head, he exited the car and began to stroll the walking paths through the park.

Coming upon an ancient oak tree, he was reminded of the night he kissed Kate against an old tree. The feelings came in wave after painful wave and bombarded his heart and mind. Leaning against the tree, he laid his head back and tried to sort through this whole mess. Playing it over in his mind, he knew he reacted wrong when they first realized Angela was behind this. He should have listened to his family, but instead he pushed Kate away thinking it would keep her safe. Now he had to play through those choices, at least until the Angela problem was solved.

The part of the whole situation which was bothering him the most was Kate and Kendrick running off and confronting Angela. His mind couldn't figure out what he was the most upset about; he didn't like that Kate was reckless. She was usually calm, cool, and collected. He hated that Kendrick was getting to spend time with Kate; deep down he knew that he had basically pushed them together with his own actions, but it didn't mean he had to like it. He wasn't worried about his cousin making a move on Kate. He trusted Kendrick with his life, and Kate definitely wasn't Kendrick's type. But the thought of them off somewhere, without him, Kendrick consoling Kate, it wasn't setting well with him.

His life was in turmoil. He wanted The Center+ finished and running smoothly. He wanted his family and friends safe. He wanted Kate back in his arms, but...when he closed his eyes and weighed out his options, he was torn. Kate brought color to his life, but she also threw his life into a hectic, out-of-control chaos. Thinking of the business and his family, maybe things would be better in the long run if he went back to being the black and white, cut and dry Decker. He would miss Kate terribly, but he owed it to himself, the family, the business to run things in a responsible manner.

The thought of living his life without Kate though... he didn't know how he'd get through each day without seeing her smile and knowing she was on his side. Not to mention, he knew his family would not be happy if he cut Kate loose.

He missed the days of being able to make tough decisions without emotions being involved. Taking a deep breath, he made just one decision for that point in time; he would continue to have no contact with Kate. He wasn't sure about a lot of things right now, but he was definitely sure that keeping her away from him and Torey Hope would be the best for her safety.

Pushing himself off the tree, deciding it was time to head to The Center+ to get some work done, Decker was startled, but not really surprised when he almost ran smack into Angela. He had known, deep down, that she was around and watching. Not really feeling in the right frame of mind to play games with her, he steeled himself for what was to come. How was she going to approach the situation?

"Decker, baby, I'm so glad to find you here." She reached out a trim, pale arm and ran her hand from his shoulder to elbow. "I saw you at the police station earlier."

When his eyes snapped up in surprise that she would admit that, she cooed, "No worries, sweetie, nothing illegal going on. I was walking past and saw you in the parking lot. Please tell me all is okay; you looked distressed when you were talking to your cousin and that woman. Are they causing problems for you?"

Decker relaxed slightly to know she didn't realize why he'd been at the police station; since she was claiming to have seen him by chance, he'd play along for now. He wondered to himself how soon the police would bring her in for questioning.

"Oh, no, no problems; just some issues with The Center+ that we needed to take care of." Decker glanced nervously around. He'd spent three years of his life with this woman, but she was genuinely freaking him out now. Her eyes had a scary look, vacant, disconnected, and vengeful. He was seriously beginning to worry about how he was going to get away from her and what her next move was going to be. Scenes from psycho thriller movies were running through his head; would she drug him and drag him to her basement, keeping him prisoner until he admitted his undying love for her? Damn, he needed to get away from her.

"Decker, I can't begin to tell you how thrilled I was when I heard you'd gotten rid of that other woman; she was *not* the right woman for you." Angela sidled up closer to him and pressed her bony body into his side. Had she always been this thin and sick looking, or was this a result of her obviously taking a flying leap off the deep end? "I'm sorry if the breakup has been messy with her and Kendrick hooking up right after you dumped her; but at least you got to see her true colors before it was too late." She was almost purring in his ear at that point and his body felt the deep instinct to run.

"Thanks, Angela. Yeah, it's always good to find out someone's true colors before it's too late. A lot of trouble could be avoided in the long run." He wasn't exactly sure what he was saying. He knew he was speaking, but his mind was playing through excuses as to why he needed to leave. He was a grown man, he should just knock her clinging body off of his and tell her he had to go; the words she had said to Uncle Nicky and the whacked-out look in her eyes prevented him from doing that.

"Decker, baby, I know you're just coming off a breakup, but I also know that what we had never really died for either of us. I'd really like for us to get back together and see how it works out." He swallowed hard, trying to force down his disgust.

"Angela, I'd be happy to see where things could go for us, but I'm going to have to be honest, I'll need some time. This breakup and resulting hookup between Kate and my cousin has really done a number on me." He looked at her, trying his best to come across interested and sincere when all he really wanted to do was smack her. "And, what about your job with Starsky Enterprises? I'm sure they wouldn't be thrilled to let such a highly respected employee go." He was interested to see how she would explain her work situation since she clearly didn't work there anymore.

"Oh, work, yes. Work has given me a unique opportunity; they've offered me 6 months to set up three new divisions of Starsky. One will be close to Torey Hope, the other two will be in neighboring states. What a perfect setup for us to be together and still work for our respective companies." The lie rolled easily off her tongue and Decker fought the urge to shudder.

"Wow, that's great. I'm sure you're really pleased with that opportunity." He made a show of looking at his watch. As he was beginning to speak, hoping to offer a plausible sounding reason why he needed to leave, a voice came from behind him.

"What the hell, Decker? I thought you were meeting me 20 minutes ago so we could go over that paperwork before I have to meet with the new instructor?" Turning to Angela, Sawyer smiled and spoke politely. "Hi, Angela. Good to see you again. Listen, I hate to steal Deck away from you, I'm sure you have a lot to talk about, but he and I really need to get some things ironed out at work or my ass is grass." Sawyer, not giving Angela a chance to speak, walked around her and headed toward Decker's car. Throwing over his shoulder, he spoke to his brother, "Come on man, I had a friend drop me off here when I saw your car, I need a ride."

Decker tried to look sheepish and regretful as he offered Angela a slight smile. "Sorry about that, but I really am late to meet him; I need to get going." He walked around a sputtering Angela, almost laughing at the indignity of being dismissed so quickly written all over her face.

"I'll call you, baby. We can grab a coffee and talk about what's next for us." She attempted to catch up with him, but her ridiculously high heels snagged in the dirt and she was forced to stop and watch as he retreated quickly.

Throwing open the door to his sleek black Camaro, he all but collapsed into the driver's seat. Holding everything in, not even looking at Sawyer, Decker drove. He drove until the road took him around the corner from the park and then both he and Sawyer let out the breaths they'd been holding.

"Brother, I've never been so glad to see you in my entire life. She'd had me trapped there for what seemed like forever and I couldn't figure out how to give her the slip. How did you know I was there? You completely saved my ass; that girl has gone from 'not the right girl for me' to completely insane." Decker continued to drive, but glanced at his brother momentarily.

"I guess it was that whole 'twin connection' thing, I don't know, man. I was at home and just felt the urge to walk; while I was walking, I got the strangest feeling that you were scared or upset. I kept seeing us playing on the swings when we were little and my heart told me to head to those swings. From the second I entered the park, I could feel you; I just kept walking until I saw you by that tree. I know we've felt those connections before, but I'd never felt it as strongly before as I did today." Sawyer just shook his head in disbelief.

"Well, I'll forever be grateful for that gut feeling you had." They pulled into The Center+ and got out of the car. Slamming their doors, they both looked around uneasily. "When do you think the police are going to bring her in for questioning?" Sawyer asked as they walked into the building.

"I don't know, but I'm calling the officer in charge of the

case to let him know about our little run-in at the park. I want the whole confrontation on the record." Decker and Sawyer stopped in to chat with Zach and Zoey as they prepared for their next fitness class. Once they had updated them on the happenings with Angela, Sawyer and Decker went their own ways, promising to meet up later.

"Mr. Morgan, I'm glad I caught you in your office. May I sit down?" Officer Smitson held his cap in his hands.

"Please do; may I get you some coffee or water?" Decker shook the man's hand and began to pour himself a coffee before fixing up a mug for the officer.

"Thank you, Mr. Morgan. I just wanted to stop by and brief you on where things stand with the Angela Ford case." Taking a sip of the hot drink, he gently sat the cup on a coaster in front of him. "We brought Ms. Ford in for questioning a few hours ago. We had eyes on her and saw she had followed you to the park, so we went ahead and brought her to the station upon her return to the townhouse." Another slurp of his coffee; the man was stalling, Decker didn't like it. He nodded his head at the man in an attempt to keep him talking.

"Decker, I have to be honest with you, our psychiatrist on the force, Dr. Sai, listened in on the questioning as she does with many cases; she is very concerned about Angela's mental well-being. Ms. Ford presented extremely aloof and professional, but her answers uncovered a very detached and vengeful nature underneath the put-together exterior. Dr. Sai believes that Angela has absolutely no connection to human emotions; she was very void of normal emotions throughout the questioning. Most people brought in for questioning are nervous or angry at what they perceive as injustice to their innocence; Ms. Ford didn't even bat an eyelash throughout the entire procedure. Many times, our questioning will scrounge up old hurts or angers or wounds; Ms. Ford kept to a very scripted story and never once veered from it, she showed nothing and gave us nothing. But, for Dr. Sai, all of what she wasn't saying was enough for the doctor to worry about her ill-intent towards Kate Turner, you, and your family."

Decker felt sick to his stomach; he had a feeling the real gut-punch was coming next.

"All of that being said, Decker, there's absolutely nothing in her history or the questioning that would allow us to hold her or arrest her. We had no choice but to let her go. Dr. Sai worries that Angela will now be angrier and use that anger to make plans. Plans against you and those you love. I'm really sorry to have to tell you all of this; I know you were hoping to get this thing swept under the rug sooner rather than later." The officer finished his coffee and stood to leave. "We are going to keep additional eyes on her and do daily reports of her activity to Dr. Sai. We'll keep you updated; for now, please let Ms. Turner know to stay away and don't let her whereabouts be known. Call me if you need *anything*." Turning to leave, the man stopped briefly, "If I were you, I wouldn't be caught alone with that woman; this is completely off record and I'll deny ever speaking these words, but she's certifiably insane if you ask me. If she messes up, does something wrong, we'll bring her in; until then, keep your eyes open."

Decker stared at the door the officer had walked through for several moments. Fear, anger, and uncertainty coursed through his body. Picking up his stapler, fighting the urge to hurl it against the wall, Decker pictured Kate; taking deep breaths and pinching the bridge of his nose, he fought to control the deluge of emotions overtaking him. Still wanting to throw something, he forced himself to gently lay the stapler down before stalking down the hall to find Zach.

Entering one of the fitness studios, Decker was momentarily thrown off when he saw Zach holding Zoey in his arms. Forgetting his own turmoil for a second, he watched his two cousins in a very intimate embrace. Like the observer of a terrible accident, unable to look away, Decker watched as Zoey lifted her head to look into Zach's eyes. Determined to forget everything he had just witnessed, Decker cleared his throat gruffly before he saw something he wasn't sure he was ready to see.

Gasping and jumping out of Zach's arms, Zoey quickly grabbed her bag and headed to the changing rooms. "Um, I've got one last class in an hour. I'm going to see if my mom needs help with the art supplies until then." Retreating quickly, an awkwardly flushed Zoey all but ran into the changing room.

At a loss for words, Decker simply stared at his cousin for a few moments. When Zach crossed his arms over his chest and quirked an eyebrow, Decker shook his head to clear it and tried to recall why he'd sought Zach out in the first place.

"Do you have a bit? I need to punch something, and I didn't think my wall would be a good idea. Want to go a few rounds?" Decker inquired hopefully.

"Sure man, I've got time. We can punch, talk, or both." Zach slapped him on the back, almost seeming glad Decker was having issues so as not to have to address his own misstep. That being the huge elephant in the room of Zach being caught with his much younger cousin in what appeared to be a personal and intimate moment.

When both men had changed into their gym shorts, laced up their shoes, and donned their gloves, they walked into the small boxing ring which sat off to the side of the gym facility. With some warm up swings, Zach struck first. Decker, stunned from the sudden punch, gathered his wits and realized that Zach needed this form of therapy right then as much as he did.

Throughout their jabs and crosses, hooks and uppercuts, they bobbed and weaved and they talked heatedly.

"Want to tell me why you had our much younger cousin wrapped in your arms like you wanted to devour her?" A quick jab followed this question from Decker.

"No, I don't want to talk about it. At all." Some quick footwork by Zach and he deflected Decker's next blow. "But, I will remind you that she's not blood related to me. There's nothing else to talk about." And with that, Zach landed a heavy blow to Decker.

"Fair enough, man. For now." Decker ducked and popped up with an uppercut.

"What's got you in such a pissy mood?" They took a quick break for a drink and to wipe the sweat from their bodies.

Heading back to the middle of the ring, they went through the motions of boxing while not landing any real punches so that Decker could tell Zach what Smitson had told him about Angela.

Pausing for a moment, Zach rested his arms above his head. "Shit, man, that doesn't sound good. Not good at all. I mean, we already knew she was crazy with the way she hit my dad and threatened Katie, but this sounds like some serious psycho shit." Beginning with some light jabs again, the men continued to slog it out.

"So, what are you going to do about Katie?" Zach's question came with a right cross to Decker's jaw.

"Nothing I can do right now. If I'm going to keep her safe, I have to keep my distance." He was immediately defensive and followed with a quick jab cross to Zach's midsection.

"Are you kidding me right now, man? Angela is a fucking psycho, but keeping Katie away from you isn't the right thing to do anymore." Zach stopped throwing punches and looked his cousin straight in the eyes. "I'm not kidding here man. Maybe you thought you were doing the right thing in the beginning, but you need to man up and admit that keeping her away isn't going to help anyone right now. We need Kendrick back here, Katie needs to be with us, we are her family and friends; she's good at what she does here at The Center+. I say we bring her back home, circle the wagons, and protect the family and business until Angela screws up and they can arrest her sorry ass." Zach's voice had grown heated as he spoke.

"Fuck, man, don't you think I want to bring her home? But if she comes home, Angela has easy access to her and anyone who is around to protect her. I can't put people at risk like that." Decker had begun to pace the ring.

"I call bullshit, Deck. Want to know what I think? I think you realize you screwed up, but instead of just calling it for what it is, you're trying to control the situation from the backside of it." When Decker started to defend himself, Zach help up a gloved hand to stop him. "I'm not finished. I also think you're scared; you know you screwed up with Kate by pushing her away and then by getting so pissed at her and Kendrick. That whole thing about reassessing your relationship when this is all over, that was a total bonehead move; you let your anger speak to her through that, and it didn't come out well."

When Decker looked puzzled as to how Zach knew about

his misguided words to Kate, his cousin shrugged. "You know the family grapevine is more efficient than those celebrity gossip sites. Anyway, you know you screwed up and now you're taking the easy way out by keeping her away in the name of protecting her; in reality, you just don't know how to fix things, you're not sure you can fix things. So, instead of admitting that your relationship is out of control, you're clinging to that one shred of control you have left and keeping her away. Not to protect her, but to protect yourself."

He had barely spoken the last word when his head jerked violently to the side as the deadly powerful punch was delivered from Decker's glove. Immediately fighting back, Zach ignored the gloves on his fists, and barreled himself into his cousin's midsection. When his right shoulder plowed into Decker's abdomen, he heard the air whoosh out of him before they were both on the ground. They rolled around, kicking and punching for a few moments before a voice was heard above them.

"Knock it off, both of you." Nate Morgan stood, hands on hips, glowering down at his son and nephew. "We have clients, paying customers, here in the building. Could you two stop grappling on the ground and act like you've got some common sense?"

Nicky Morgan stood beside his brother. "I don't like seeing my son and nephew fight; fighting makes me sad. Why are you guys mad at each other?"

Wiping sweat from his eyes and a trickle of blood from his

nose, Decker yanked off his boxing gloves and refused to answer his uncle.

Licking the blood which seeped from his busted lip, Zach laughed in disgust, "He's mad because I called him on his bullshit and the truth hurts." Pulling his own gloves off, he jabbed a finger at Decker's chest. "Fix this shit, man. Angela is crazy no matter what; I'd rather have family all together, ready to fight and protect each other, rather than have us spread out. Bring her home man."

Decker pushed his cousin's finger away from his chest and lunged at him. "Decker, stop." Nate held his son back from continuing the brawl that Decker so badly wanted to see to the end.

"Zach, go hit the showers. You two need to cool off; I know you'll work this out, but no more fighting for now." Nate spoke to his nephew while he kept an eye on Decker.

Zach shook his head and gave Decker one final look, and walked away to take a shower.

Nicky spoke quietly to Decker. "You'll do the right thing, you always do. Ever since you were a little boy, you've had a hard time admitting when you were wrong, but you always come around and do the right thing." Nicky delivered his subtle blow and advice all in a few soft-spoken words before he turned to leave.

Leaning against the ropes, Decker felt his body sag as heavily as his heart. Dropping to the ground, he let his head fall between the knees he had pulled up to his chest. He felt rather than saw his dad lower himself to sit beside him.

"So, does everyone think I've totally screwed this up?" Decker's muffled question sounded from between his knees.

"Decker, everyone loves you and thinks you were doing what you thought was best." Nate spoke surely.

"But?" Decker knew there was more.

"But, we also know that sometimes our first reaction to things isn't always the right one or sometimes our plans need to be changed when the situation changes." Nate delivered his words diplomatically.

"Zach says I'm scared to bring Kate home for fear I've messed things up with her too badly by acting like I wasn't sure where things would stand with us when this was all over." Decker hated repeating those words.

"Are you?" A simple question from his dad.

Decker took a moment to gather his thoughts. "Yeah, I guess I am. I just wanted her to be safe and for all of this to be over. I was scared to death when I found out about the threat against her, I was beyond pissed when she and Kendrick put her in a potentially dangerous situation, and I spoke out of anger instead of speaking to her as the woman I love. And, if I'm being honest, I'm afraid I've messed things up and we may never get back what we had."

"Well, you're never going to know if things are beyond repair until you get her back by your side. Once she's home, talk to her, admit you were wrong, tell her what you just told me. But let her decide where things stand now instead of taking that control from her like you did in the beginning of this whole mess." Nate patted his son's arm and then pushed off the floor, leaving Decker to stew in his own thoughts.

DECKER WALKED into the house he shared with his brother and cousins just as his cell phone rang. "Decker Morgan" he barked into the phone.

It had been a few days since Angela was brought in for questioning, and he'd yet to be able to reach Kate. He knew she was okay; Kendrick had been keeping him updated. His cousin was sleeping at Kate's dad's house and spending the days with her. There had been nothing suspicious going on, and they didn't expect there to be since Mr. Turner probably wouldn't be on Angela's radar. Kendrick reported to Decker a couple times a day. Kate was sad, she was angry, she was bored, she wanted to come back home, she wanted this to all be over. Decker wanted to put his hands through the phone screen and wring Kendrick's neck when his cousin sent a snapshot of Kate pulling on a pair of yoga pants. The caption, "Today's underwear of choice is a beautiful teal and matches perfectly with the bra she has on" had Decker seeing red. He called Kendrick.

"What man, I thought you wanted to know everything about her days. Yesterday was pink. She's got a purple pair she hasn't worn yet." Kendrick just laughed as his cousin cursed him.

"Fucker, stop looking at her underwear and stop taking pictures of my girl's ass." Decker knew Kendrick meant no harm and was simply trying to get a rise out of him; it worked.

"Your girl? Really? *Is* she your girl?" Kendrick taunted.

"Shut up. I've been through this with Zach and my dad already. I messed up man, I get it. I just want to give it a little longer to see what Angela does, then I'll let her come home." Decker noticed the tsk, tsk, tsk from his cousin.

"Man, first you better hope she'll speak to you. She seems to be getting angrier each day we're here. Second, you better rephrase that 'let her come home' bullshit; that's one of the things that got you in deep shit earlier. You don't 'let' a girl like Katie do anything; you talk to her, you stand beside her, you support her. She wants nothing more than to be on your team, working with you, but you've got to stop trying to control everything; she's your equal, treat her like it." Kendrick had hung up then, but teased Decker once more with a cleavage snapshot as he ate dinner across the table from Kate that evening.

Now Decker took the phone call from the police department.

"Mr. Morgan, it's Officer Smitson. There's been a development in the Angela Ford case. Are you able to speak to me for a moment?"

Decker walked straight to his office, laying down on the

couch to hear what the officer had to say. "Of course, Officer Smitson. What developments?"

"Well, it appears that Angela Ford has left town. The eyes we had on her reported that she packed a few boxes and drove off last night. One of our officers discreetly followed her all the way to the bus station. She left her car there and boarded a bus to New York. Upon running the plates of her car, we found it registered to a Robby Thomas who lives in Torey Hope. Mr. Thomas was questioned and says he knew Angela through a mutual friend and had let her borrow his car. The officer checked the records of that bus headed to New York; Angela rode it all the way, never disembarking or switching buses." Decker had sat upright on the couch to listen to the information Officer Smitson was delivering.

"The second officer who we'd assign to watch Angela checked out her townhouse; it's completely empty. Not a stitch of clothing, a pillow, or even a random piece of lint was left." Officer Smitson spoke in a way that lead Decker to believe he was just as shocked by this turn of events as Decker was.

"What do you think this means, Officer?" Decker wanted to be happy that Angela was gone, but it was such a surprising turn of events that he wasn't sure what to make of it.

"Well, I spoke to Dr. Sai. She said it's unclear to her why Angela would up and leave so abruptly when she obviously doesn't have a job to return to in New York. Right now the best she can advise is to keep eyes on her. I've contacted the

PD where she is staying; they've got an officer assigned to watch her. If she makes any moves to come back here, we'll be the first to know. I don't want to give any false hope, especially since Ms. Ford seems very unpredictable and volatile, but for now it looks like you can breathe a little easier." Officer Smitson ended the call and Decker sat in stunned silence.

29

"Katie, can I talk to you for a minute?" She and Kendrick looked up from the TV program neither of them were really watching. She could tell Kendrick was bored out of his mind, as was she, but he refused to leave her alone while she was at her dad's.

"Kendrick, I'm safe here. You are missing out on all kinds of work; you'll have a mountain of paperwork and phone calls to return when you get back. What about signups and tryouts for the teams you're running? Don't you still have some coaches to hire? I love you, and I love you for what you're doing, but you don't have to babysit me." She had spoken to him a couple days before.

"Katie, my cousin loves you like I've never seen him love anyone except his family. I'm not going to leave you here to wallow and convince yourself that you two are over. We'll take

care of this and get things back to normal. Plus, I like sending Decker texts about your underwear just to piss him off. And, another bonus, when this is all over, I'll be able to rub it in his face that I was the one here comforting you and spending time with you; I'll get plenty of mileage out of this little bump in the road." Kendrick had kissed the side of her head and turned back to his cell phone where he was happily enjoying her father's WiFi connection to play games, and probably to torture Decker about the color of her underwear. With any other guy, finding out he was talking about her underwear would have seemed creepy; with Kendrick it just made her shake her head and laugh.

She was surprised when her dad asked to speak to her, but she patted Kendrick on the leg and told him to go do something while she talked to her dad. Kendrick nodded and pulled himself off the couch; keys in hand he returned from the kitchen to kiss her head and strolled out the door after a respectful nod to her father.

"What's up, Dad?" Katie and her dad had a pretty good relationship. It had hurt when her parents divorced, but as she grew up she realized that they were not a good fit for each other. She wasn't sure how they had ever thought they were a good fit in the first place. But, in the end, going their separate ways was truly for the best for everyone involved. She spent time with her dad growing up, when he wasn't on business trips or too busy at work. He was the type of guy who could only focus on one thing at a time; if Katie was at his house for a week in the summer, he took off work (the one week a year he'd take off for non-holiday related activities) and spent every minute with her. But, when he was working, he couldn't split his time or focus between his daughter and business. It made Katie sad, but she had come to accept him for who he was.

Watching her dad's face as he spoke now, she wondered if that was also who Decker was. Would he ever be able to split his time and focus between his professional and personal life? Assuming they got back together, although Katie knew what happened when one made assumptions....if they married and had kids one day, would Decker be the type of dad who couldn't make it to sporting events, was always stuck at the office, never made it home for dinner?

She had lived with that her whole life both when her parents were together and when they split up. She only got her dad's full focus on holidays and one week in the summer. She didn't want that for her own children. Painfully, she thought about the rest of Decker's family. Without a doubt, she knew they would step in and fill the void if Decker couldn't pull himself from work, and she already loved them for that, but it wouldn't be the same.

She was a talented, smart, confident woman; if she let her heart lead, she would walk straight back to Decker when this was all over...but, if she let her head lead, she wondered if it would be wise to end things completely. Recalling his words from several nights ago, about seeing where things stood when this was over, she briefly contemplated that maybe Decker had the same thoughts about letting this end before it got too deep. Marriage and kids would complicate things tremendously; she knew those things weren't on the agenda at the moment, but she didn't want to bring kids into a situation and have it end the way her parents did.

Her dad must have noticed she was deep in thought because he let her sit and think for several moments before he spoke.

"Katie, I love having you here and you're welcome anytime for as long as you'd like to stay." He spoke genuinely, but Katie sensed a 'but'.

"But?" She smiled softly at her dad. She knew he'd seen her occasional tears and heard her conversations with Kendrick about Decker.

"But...I know you're missing your job, your mom and grandma, your boyfriend. His cousin seems like a great guy and I really appreciate him being by your side as the police try to take care of this situation, but I know you miss Decker." He cleared his throat before going on. "Katie, I wish like hell I had realized what a gift I had in my life before I went and threw it all away on my business endeavors. I thought I could have my family and my business; when it became apparent that I couldn't divide my time, I foolishly chose my business over your mother and you. It breaks my heart that I gave up on that love and the years I could have had with you. Hindsight really is 20/20, and I can see now that I made the wrong choice." He sighed heavily.

"Dad, I'm sorry you have these feelings. I wish things could be different too, but they can't be; don't beat yourself up, we have a pretty good relationship, I'm not scarred for life. Let's just make the most of what we've got and not dwell on the past." She paused and thought over his words. "Plus, I think maybe your speech would find a better audience with Decker than with me. It's him who I worry about not being able to divide his time and feeling pressured to choose his business over love. Not pressured by anyone but himself, but pressured all the same. He's got this crazy need to control everything around him and a notion that everything in life is his responsibility; he doesn't like the idea of letting people down." Rubbing hands over her face, she sighed, "I love him, but I'm not sure if it's enough. I don't want to end up like you and Mom; if he can't pick me 100% or truly divide his time between work and love, I may have to admit this needs to end." A tear threatened to fall from her eye. "The problem is, how will I know if he can or will divide his time until it's too late? Whew, I think my no-dating status was a lot easier than this falling in love thing is." She laughed sadly and leaned over to hug her father. "Thanks, Dad. I love you."

Kendrick had pulled back into the driveway while they were talking, but he continued to sit in his car talking on the phone. Katie walked to the door and waved him in. As he bounded up the steps, he wore a huge smile. Pulling her into a hug, he spun her around. "We're going back to Torey Hope, girl! Angela left and the police think it's reasonably safe for you to come home."

A FEW HOURS LATER, after packing up and saying goodbye to her father, Kendrick and Katie drove in relative silence. She was thrilled to be heading home, getting back to work, putting this behind her, but something just wasn't sitting right with her. She couldn't decide exactly what was bothering her, but she waffled between Angela's abrupt departure and the fact that Decker had called Kendrick to tell him they could come back rather than calling her. Both of those things were weighing heavily on her.

"What's going on in that head of yours?" Kendrick smiled at her as he drove.

"Why didn't he call me? This whole time, we've all talked about 'when this is over' everything will be okay. But, now it's 'over,' and he still hasn't spoken to me. I guess I'm just scared that too much has happened, and he's had a moment to pull back on the reigns and get that tight control back, and now he's going to close in on himself. I love that man, but I hate what he does sometimes. I just get a feeling that I'll get the 'let's just be friends/colleagues' thing when we actually do talk." Katie glanced sadly at Kendrick and realized with dread that he was afraid of the same thing.

"You know my cousin very well. Just give it some time."
Kendrick patted her hand and drove on.

THREE DAYS. Three days is how long it took before Decker
spoke to her as anything but an employee. She had hoped
beyond hope that Decker would call her or come over when
she and Kendrick got back, but he kept his distance. Keeping
her calm and realizing that this time to decompress from the
whole Angela thing would probably be good for them, she
promised herself she would give things time, let work get back
to normal, before addressing things with him. She knew that
running back to him the second she arrived home would have
been too emotional, and emotions make it hard to have
rational conversations.

Emotions were what he was going to get though. Three
days! She'd seen the heat in his eyes, the hurt haunted his
expression every time he spoke to her about the budget or
expense reports or new hires. Decker Morgan was a stubborn
asshole and Katie was tired of waiting.

"Mr. Morgan?" She smiled inside when she saw his jaw
tick and his body stiffen at the sound of her saying his name
that way. "I was hoping to have a business dinner meeting
with you tonight. I took the liberty of checking your schedule;
you have no plans. I've set up reservations at that little Italian
place off the courthouse square. I'll see you at 7:00 p.m." She

smiled genuinely, knowing he was pissed that she was ordering him around. *Yeah, well, I'm tired of you being in charge here. It's time for you to relax the reigns a bit, bucko.* And if he refused to relax the reigns? Well, his brother and cousins told her to keep at him, but she wondered if she'd be better off just to hand those reigns back over and let him go.

Damn it. Things had gone from bad to worse, and he didn't know how he'd gotten in the mess he was in. Decker kept telling himself things would be fine once the Angela fiasco was done. But, here he stood, three days since Kate came back home, and he'd not even spoken to her. Well, he'd spoken... but it was more like he'd spoken *at* her, not *to* her. He wanted to go back to the way things were; he wanted his sexy, beautiful, fun girlfriend back as his assistant manager and friend. But, he feared letting go and allowing her back into his life in that capacity. Last time he did that, all hell broke loose. Now, this huge problem was sitting between them, and he didn't know how to address it. He felt like a stupid high school kid, letting emotions and miscommunication or *total lack of communication* cause this riff between them; pride was a vicious bitch, and he didn't know how to overcome this.

His body ached to hold her, laugh with her, kiss her. Hearing *Mr. Morgan* on her lips was enough to have him growing hard; having her tell him what to do both pissed him off and turned him on. And now he had a business meeting with her.

Before she had left his office, he'd blurted out, "Can I pick you up for this business meeting?" The longing in her eyes almost did him in; he wanted to cross the room and gather her in his arms and never let go. But he watched her steel herself and shake her head. "No, I'll meet you there." Seemed he wasn't the only one being stubborn.

He pulled his sleek black car into the parking lot at 6:55 p.m. He watched as Kate pulled in as well. She stood from her car, adjusting her gray dress. His eyes traveled down her legs and his gut clenched at the sight of her shiny red shoes. Exiting his car quickly, he strode toward her attempting to look casual. Stopping in front of her, he looked to the ground sheepishly and rubbed the back of his neck. When he lifted his eyes to hers, he smiled bashfully. "Kate, it's good to see you, you look gorgeous." Leaning in, he meant to just place a kiss on her cheek, but his heart and body had other plans. One hand slid around her waist and he found himself pressed hard against her as he breathed in her scent. "God, Bug, I miss you." He swallowed deeply, took a deep breath as if to fortify himself for what was to come, and kissed her cheek softly.

They turned to enter the restaurant. He reached to hold her hand, but she moved it from him; shaking her head no. He knew she was fighting her feelings, but he also knew she had a motive for this meeting. Upon being seated, Kate excused herself to the restroom and Decker placed an order for wine.

Staring at her reflection in the mirror, Katie attempted to get her breathing under control. Hearing him speak that ridiculous nickname had brought stinging tears to her eyes; feeling his body against hers had shook her to the core. She wanted him and what they had back more than ever, but she needed to make sure he was clear on where she stood.

Returning to the table, Katie gratefully sipped the wine placed before her. After placing their orders, an awkward silence fell over the table.

"Decker, I feel like we slipped off track and instead of righting ourselves we've let that one little slip derail us completely. We went from confident, mature, intelligent people in love, to ridiculously immature, ignorant, stubborn people who don't talk. This dinner isn't to point fingers or place blame; all of that is water under the bridge and there's no reason to rehash it." Sipping her wine, enjoying the sweetness on her tongue, she continued.

"My dad was, is, a lot like you. I watched my mom compete for his attention with his job. He couldn't divide his focus or his time between the two, so they split up. I could never compete for my dad's attention when he as working. I spoke to my dad while I was out of town and he floored me by admitting he was wrong; he wishes he had divided his time or chosen my mom and me over his work. It's too late for him to do that now, but his admission had me thinking about us. I'm not planning marriage and kids right now; heck, I'm not even 100% sure about *us* right now. But, if we work through this issue and decide to make it work, I have to know that you will *always* choose me and our life over your work. I can't ever think of bringing kids into this life if I'm not assured that their father will always put his focus on them and me before anything in his professional life. You'll have me on your side at work, I'll support you and help you run The Center+ like the kickass business it is. But, home and love and family will always come first." Draining her wine and looking at the hard expression etched on his face, she drew in a deep breath. "If you can assure me of that, then I want to ask that we try to work this out. If you can't assure me of that, then I want to ask if you think we can still work together; if not, I'll give my two week notice and begin searching for another job." Grateful that the waiter took that moment to fill her wine glass and deliver their plates, Katie took another gulp of her wine.

She had said what she'd come to say; she felt strong. Daring a look at Decker, she tried to read the look on his face. His expression gave away nothing. Katie wanted him to assure her; with every fiber of her being she wanted him to promise her forever and choose her over all else. But, she knew Decker almost as well as she knew herself, and she knew what she'd just laid out to him could easily go the other way. She was prepared to only be his assistant manager if that's what he wanted; in her heart, she knew it would be best if she tendered her resignation and began searching for another job. But, for the moment, she sat and waited for Decker to respond.

THROUGHOUT AN EXCRUCIATINGLY LONG DINNER, she waited for him to process what she'd told him. After paying the bill, arguing that he'd put it on The Center+ since it was a business dinner, Decker took her hand in his. "Can we walk?" The heat from his hand shot straight to her heart, and she nodded mutely.

"Is this okay?" Decker held their intertwined hands up between them as he asked the question.

"It's the only place I ever want my hand to be, Decker. But, I guess it depends on what you're thinking and what you're going to say." Katie smiled a little regretfully at him as she removed her hand from his.

Breathing deeply, Decker stared at the sidewalk. "I don't know if I can offer assurances, Kate. I love you more than I love breathing, but this is who I am. I take the responsibility of the business and my family very seriously. I want you by my side, as my partner and my friend, as my life, but I can't promise that things at work will never take me away from you or our family. Rationally, I want to say that I would always choose you and any children we may have one day. But, I know how I am; if something were to come up at work, I know I'd drop things to be there. I'd like to think I'd never miss a ballet recital or baseball game, I'd like to think I'd be at every school function, home for dinner every night, and there for bedtime. But, I'm devoted to my family's business; I've been devoted to The Center+ since I was old enough to know I wanted to run it and make it bigger and better. I want to say I could split my devotion and my focus and my responsibilities, but it's not something I can promise." He stopped walking by a bridge. Listening to the gurgling water flow, Katie took in his next words. "I love you, Kate. But, years from now, I don't want you disappointed in me or angry that I've not lived up to what you want or need. If promises and assurances are what you need for a future I can't see, I'll have to step aside; when I give my word, it's as good as gold. You're wanting my word on something, but it's something I can't predict or control; I can't give my word on something like that. This is killing me, Kate. But, I'll understand if you can't do this without those assurances." He cupped her face in his hands and pressed his forehead against hers. "I love you, Kate. I want to beg you to stay, but I understand why you need what you need. I'm so very sorry that I can't give you that. I don't want to make any decisions about your position at work tonight. Let's give it a few days and see how we're feeling; I don't want to lose you at The Center+, but we may find it's just too hard to work together." His breath mingled with hers, and she closed her eyes against the onslaught of feelings.

With a tearful sniff, she spoke quietly. "I knew this outcome was a possibility; I just kept thinking that what we had would be enough, that our love would pull you out of your cocoon of control. I know this is how you are, I think I was just hoping that I'd been enough for you; I wanted you to choose me." Her lips met with his, a mournful mating; love and goodbye mixed together. "Decker, I love you. So very much. Thank you for all that we had. I will cherish it always." A last kiss, one last embrace, and she turned to go. Stopping briefly, she spoke, "I'll work from home for a while. Let's discuss my position in a couple days." Retreating quickly before he could see the tears streaming down her face, she dropped into the driver's seat and drove off.

Decker stood, rooted to the sidewalk, and watched his life fade from view.

30

"Katie, you're an idiot." Grandma glared at her over a steaming mug of tea.

"Excuse me?" A stunned Katie was instantly defensive. She'd been working at home for two days; moping at home for two days was a more accurate description. When she'd finally told her grandmother about her conversation with Decker, this wasn't the reaction she thought she'd get.

"Child, I understand you want to protect yourself from what your mother and you went through with your dad. I get it, I really do. But in attempting to protect yourself, you've basically done the exact same thing to Decker that he originally did to you when he was trying to protect you from Angela. You're pushing him away, but worse than that, you're asking that boy to make promises about something that hasn't even happened yet. You aren't married and you don't have children, but you want him to promise he'll never take a work call or have a meeting that runs into dinnertime. Can you promise him that you'll never miss a day of work with a sick child? Can you promise him that you'll get up with a hungry baby every night, even when you've got an early morning meeting?" When Katie started to protest, Grandma held her hand up to shush her. "Think about what I'm saying Katie. Some promises are easy, but some are hard. Life gets in the way of promises sometimes. You're not being fair to Decker. You know his word is everything to him. Asking him to give his word on something like this, it's unreasonable." Grandma watched Katie's face as she processed the information. Hanging her head, Katie felt defeated.

"I just want him to say that he will always choose me and our family over work. Daddy didn't do that, I don't want my kids to go through being second to a business." Katie's eyes shone with tears.

"What if I asked you to promise me something? Would you try your best to do it?" Grandma spoke softly and rubbed Katie's hand.

"Of course I would. I love you. That's what I want Decker to do; I want him to say he'll try his best to keep that promise." Katie nodded her head emphatically at her grandmother.

"Okay, what if I asked you to promise me you'll be with me when I die. I want you to prove your love to me by being by my side when I die." Grandmother held her chin high and challenged Katie.

Annoyed, Katie tried to avoid the question. "Grandma, I don't like talking about you dying; you're asking for something you know I can't do. I'd have to be glued to your side 24 hours a day in order to keep that promise; we have no clue when you're going to die. That's a totally unfair example to use against me."

"But you're doing the same to Decker, hon. You're asking him to predict soccer schedules and piano recitals and family dinners along with expense reports and staff meetings and water main breaks at work." Grandma nodded sagely at the younger girl. Watching her granddaughter, she knew the information was sinking in, even if she didn't like what she was hearing.

"Fine, Grandma, you've made your point. I'm going to run into work. The Center+ is closed, but I've got some files I need to grab. I may also use the gym to work out some of the millions of thoughts in my head right now. I'll be home by 11:00p.m., but don't worry about waiting up. Just let Mom know where I am, okay?" Katie gathered the tea cups, and leaned down to kiss the old woman on the head. "Thanks Grandma. Once again, you gave me the ability to see things for what they really are instead of allowing me to look at things through fogged-up glasses."

"Well, Katie, when you're as old as I am, you've had a lot of time to see things for what they really are. Get your thoughts together, but don't waste too much time. That boy loves you, don't make him sit around being as miserable as you've been." Grandma smiled and leaned her head back to catch a little shut-eye before her favorite program came on TV.

KATE: *Can we talk? I'm heading into The Center+ to get some files and run on the treadmill. Can I come over around 9:00p.m.?*

Decker read the message and smiled to himself. He was miserable without her. His only consolation was Sawyer and Kendrick reporting to him that Kate was just as miserable. He wasn't happy she was miserable, but he hoped maybe this text meant she'd reassessed her stance on their future. He wanted more than anything to be able to promise her what she wanted to hear, but he just couldn't; he wished she could see that.

Decker: *Sure. Text me on your way.*

The events which unfolded over the next hour would haunt Decker for the rest of his life. Thirty minutes after his text to Katie, he got two texts within seconds of each other. First thinking it was her telling him she was skipping her run and coming over early, the blood in his veins froze as he read the words.

Officer Smitson: *Where is Katie Turner? The NYPD officer who was trailing Angela Ford was just found dead; his throat was slit. He's been dead over 24 hours. No idea where Ford is, but probably heading to Torey Hope.*

Angela: *Hope those kisses she gave you were enough to last a lifetime...she won't be around to put those filthy lips on yours for much longer. Say goodbye to your precious Kate.*

Calling Kendrick, he bolted to his car. "Angela is back in Torey Hope. Call the police, tell them to get to The Center+. Kate's there, Kendrick, she's there. Angela's going to kill her." The fear that gripped him was enough to take his breath, but he pushed it aside and focused on Kate. "Bug, be smart. Fight her, fight like you've never fought before." He had tried her cell, but it just rang through; he knew she wouldn't have it on her while she was running because she didn't like it strapped to her arm.

Pulling up to The Center+, he swallowed down bile when he saw the glass on the front door had been shattered.

He took small comfort in knowing Angela couldn't have been there long; the alarm company would have alerted the police the second the glass was shattered and they would have been there in 5 minutes. Stopping briefly in the equipment room, he grabbed a baseball bat and walked stealthily through the semi-dark halls. He tried to listen for sounds to determine where they were, but the blood roaring in his ears from the beating of his heart was too loud.

He heard the sirens pulling up outside, voices on the radio speaking, and Officer Smitson yelling, "Mr. Morgan, I need you to stop. Let us go in first, sir."

Ignoring the man, Decker progressed down the hall toward the gym. Knowing Kate, she probably grabbed the files first thing and then headed to the gym. Angela was most likely to find her there, so Decker proceeded that way. Finding the gym dark, his heart sank.

A shrill scream, the loud pop of a gunshot, and deathly silence echoed through the building. He tried to control his breathing, tried to control his fear, but everything was out of control. He ran into the darkened gym and straight toward the light coming from under the locker room door.

The sight that greeted him would forever be fodder for his nightmares.

∾

KATIE HAD GRABBED the files and headed into the gym.

Picking her favorite treadmill, she turned it on and started running. Before she'd even broken a sweat, the treadmill shut off and the lights went out.

"Damn it." Knowing the lights were on a timer, she headed toward the only light she could see streaming under the women's locker room door. As she reached for the handle, her brain registered that the men's locker room didn't have light; the entire gym was on the same timer. Why were all the lights off except the women's locker room? And what had caused the treadmill to turn off? Too late, she pulled open the door and screamed when a hand grabbed her hair and pulled her inside.

"You stupid bitch. I knew you'd come running back from Daddy's as soon as I left town. I just had to bide my time and get rid of that cop they had trailing me before heading back to this shitty little town to finish you off. Anything you want me to tell Decker? He'll be so distraught from your death, he'll have no recourse other than to turn to me." Spit flecked against her cheek as Angela's deadly whisper spoke into her ear.

Katie knew there was no reasoning with this woman; she had gone absolutely insane. Fighting back was her only chance. Thinking of the time, she knew Decker would be expecting her soon; her only hope was to fight Angela off until he got worried and came looking for her. When Angela pulled out a gun, Katie's hopes of fighting deflated.

Laying the gun on the counter next to the sink, Angela

produced a knife from her boot. "I think I should do a little decorating before I put a hole through that damn ugly head of yours. I'll make you so hideous, Decker won't be able to stand the thought of your body; he'll long for me instead." The grip on her hair tightened and she gritted against the pain.

She felt the knife trail down her cheek, the sting of her flesh being opened, the warm trickle of blood as it oozed from the wound and ran down her neck. Pain and fear mixed together in her head, but anger took precedence. She'd let Angela run the show for way too long; Angela was the reason she and Decker were in the position they were in. Katie was done being the victim to this woman.

With all the strength she could muster, she jammed her elbow into Angela's midsection. A growl from Angela was the only warning before the knife sliced into her side. The searing pain brought tears to her eyes, but she threw another elbow and kicked backwards, landing both her elbow and foot in hard contact with Angela's body. It was enough to cause Angela to let go. Grabbing the gun off the counter, Katie leveled it at the woman and hoped against hope that she wouldn't have to use it; never in her life had she held a gun, let alone shot one.

With fire in her eyes and hatred on her face, Angela let out a shrill scream and threw herself at Katie. As they fell to the floor in what felt like slow motion, Katie heard the loud pop of the gun, and then her world went black.

31

"*D*ecker, you need to get some sleep." Nate stood over him as he clung to the side of Kate's bed. "Your mom and I are here, Katie's parents are here, we'll let you know the second anything changes." Decker lifted red-rimmed, bleary eyes to look at his father.

"I can't, Dad. I can't leave her." His voice caught, and he brought the hand he was holding to his mouth to brush a kiss across her skin.

"Well then, do you want some company?" Nate pulled a chair up beside his son.

They sat quietly for several moments, the beeps and whirs and bustle of the hospital a symphony surrounding them.

"Want to talk about it?" Nate hesitated as he asked. He knew Decker had shared some of what he saw with his brother and cousins, but he'd not been able to get through the whole story with any of them. The police had been right behind him when he came upon the scene so they had needed very little from him to fill in the holes in the investigation.

Decker sat stoically for several minutes as if contemplating whether he wanted to speak the words. Closing his eyes, he finally spoke in a pained voice. "There was so much blood, Dad. I heard a scream, then a gun shot, and then nothing. When I opened the door to the locker room, Kate was on the ground and a pool...a pool of blood was all around her..." Stopping to breathe deeply, he looked at her face to reassure himself that she was still alive. "I ran to her and held her, but she wasn't talking, wasn't moving. I thought..." He pinched the bridge of his nose and took several deep breaths. "I thought she was dead, I thought the gun shot had been for her." He returned her hand to his mouth and kissed it while he stared reverently at her still form upon the bed. Tears streamed down his face as he replayed the events in his mind.

Aside from the bandage around her head for the large cut and resulting stitches from her falling and banging her head, there was very little on Kate that would outwardly indicate she was injured. She had a small red cut on her cheek from Angela cutting her, but it was a very superficial wound. No one could see the 5 inch gash along her side where Angela had slashed her with the knife, no one could see the excessive amount of blood she had lost from that wound and her head.

She looked like she was simply sleeping, like she would wake up from a restful nap at any moment.

But, she had been sleeping for three days. The doctors said her knife wound was healing well and would leave only a slight scar. The gash on her head had been stitched nicely and wouldn't require anything more. The blow to her head was caused by Angela charging her; when they both fell to the ground, Kate's head had sustained a concussion from hitting the locker room floor. The doctors said the concussion was something to keep an eye on, but it didn't appear to be anything terribly serious at the moment. They hypothesized that the trauma from being attacked and shooting Angela were keeping Kate in a very deep state of rest so that her body and mind could heal from the events. Medicines were keeping her comfortable while she rested. The medical staff had spoken to her parents and Decker at length, and it was decided they would lessen the medications at day five if she hadn't shown any stirrings before then.

Decker's mom, Libby, walked into the room soundlessly and stood behind her son; resting her hands on his shoulders, she spoke quietly. "Decker, I really feel like she's going to be fine. Dad and I are going to go grab some lunch with Katie's parents and give you some time alone with her. Talk to her, I know she can hear you; a long time ago when your Uncle Nicky was sick in the hospital, your dad and I talked to him all day long. When he finally woke up, he kept talking about the things we had told him while he was sleeping. So talk to her, Decker." Leaning down to kiss his head, Libby wished she could take away his fear and pain. "I know things had been rough between you two, but I feel in my heart that you two are meant to be together. If that's what you want, talk to her; maybe hearing you're here and loving her will be the boost she needs to start waking up." Taking Nate's hand, the couple left the room.

Decker knew that some other family members were out in the waiting room. Standing, he leaned down to kiss Kate's forehead, "I'm going to go say hey to the guys. I'll be right back, Bug. I love you."

Stretching his arms and legs from being hunched over her bed day and night, he worked a sore spot on his neck. Rounding the corner into the family waiting room, he found Kate's parents and his own preparing to grab lunch for the whole gang.

"Decker, sweetie, I know you want to be here for her, but promise me you'll get some sleep. She needs you strong and healthy, not dead on your feet from trying to stay awake for her. Have you slept at all?" Kate's mom ran a motherly hand down his cheek.

"Yeah, I'm sleeping a little. I just came out to say hey to the guys and then I'll go back in; maybe I'll take a little nap with her." He smiled half-heartedly.

"Well, don't go to sleep until we get back with some lunch for you; you need to eat." With a final pat to his cheek, she turned to join the others heading out for food.

Decker turned to find Sawyer by his side; his heart swelled knowing that his brother would always be there for him. He also felt proud knowing that his whole family was there because they loved Kate too. Kendrick and Zach stood from the chairs they'd been lounging in and came over to him; Zach grabbed Zoey's hand and pulled her into the group as well. Heart full, yet broken, Decker hung his head, not sure if the words he needed to speak would come.

When Zoey took a step back and nodded to Zach, the three men stepped forward and wrapped arms around Decker in a way that showed their unending love and support. Through it all, the arguments, the messing with each other, the tension that any family would have, Decker knew that these three men loved him and it gave him strength to say what he needed to say.

"I'm sorry; I was wrong." Decker choked out and buried his head in Sawyer's chest. As the tears flooded his eyes and emotion choked his throat, he continued, "I should have listened to all of you; you were right. If I hadn't pushed Kate away, she wouldn't be in that bed not waking up. I thought I was getting control of the situation, but I just made it spin out of control even more, and I lost the girl I love." For several moments, the only sound in the room was Zoey's sniffles; she cried for the emotion and hurt and heartache she saw surrounding Decker.

"Okay, BDSM, I hate to break up this party, but I think Decker needs to get his ass back in there and say his apologies to Katie." Turning to speak directly to Decker, Kendrick laid his hands on his shoulders. "Decker, that girl loves you, and you love her. You both made some mistakes. Angela's psycho behavior isn't your fault; she was determined to get to Katie, no matter what. I agree you need some food and sleep, but you also need to talk to your girl. Get on in there, we'll let you know when lunch is here; don't worry about us, we'll keep ourselves entertained out here."

Turning towards Zach, Decker clapped him on the shoulder, "Sorry about the busted lip man. If you ever want to talk about, well, you know...I'm here for you; I may not understand it completely right now, but I'm here for you. For you both." Zach nodded and Decker saw Zoey's sad smile from behind his cousin. He took a last look at his family gathered in the room; knowing they were there to support him and Kate was a comfort. He turned to return to her room.

As Decker approached the doorway, Kendrick called out, "Hey, see if you can get me the number of that hot ass nurse; the blond one with the huge rack." He yelped when Zoey smacked him in the chest. "What?! She's hot. I've spent way too much time being celibate while I was taking care of Decker's girl; I need to get laid."

Decker had to laugh as he left the waiting room. Kendrick was...well, he was just Kendrick.

He walked into Kate's room to find his favorite nurse finishing up taking her vitals. "Decker, hon, you look exhausted." She eyed the bed where Kate slept and then spoke in hushed tones, "Listen, I'll deny it if you tell anyone, but I won't be back in for a couple hours, why don't you crawl on up there in her bed and take a little nap with her." She winked before bustling out of the room.

Removing his shoes, Decker found an extra blanket and gently laid himself next to Kate. Drawing her gingerly into his arms, careful not to jostle her too much, he wrapped them in the blanket and breathed deeply at how right it felt to have her in his arms again.

"I'm going to fall asleep soon, Bug, but I wanted to talk to you before I do." Kissing her cheek, he gazed upon her face before speaking again.

"First, I love you. I love you more than I ever thought imaginable. I'm so very sorry for the way I handled this whole situation from beginning to end. I've had some time to reflect, along with every member of the family throwing their two cents in, and I think I realized quickly that I had messed up, but then I was too proud to admit it. In a series of more screw ups, I let anger and pride speak for me, and I managed to make an even bigger mess out of things. By then, I was afraid I had screwed things up too badly, and I didn't know how to fix it." Drawing his hand up her arm, stopping at her shoulder, he kissed her again. "When you started asking for promises and assurances, I freaked out and let my damn control issues get the best of me. I may not be able to promise exactly what you're asking for, but I can promise you a few things."

Lacing his hand with hers and fighting off the wave of exhaustion that threatened to pull him under, he spoke softly into her ear. "First, I can promise that I will spend the rest of my life loving you. I promise to treat you as an equal and never take you for granted. I promise to dance with you whenever you want to dance. I promise to take any shit your grandma wants to throw my way, even if it includes sexual innuendos and groping. And I promise to buy you every sex toy ever made, as long as I'm the only one ever using them on you." Turning her in his arms so that he could roll them to their sides; being careful to avoid her knife wound and bandages, he cuddled in close behind her. As sleep overtook him, he whispered, "I promise my love, my life; please wake up."

HE WOKE TO HUSHED WHISPERS.

"No, let him sleep, he can eat later; they look so peaceful.

Minutes or hours later, he woke again to another voice.

"Boy, you better not be doing anything untoward under those blankets. I want my granddaughter to wake up, but I don't think waking her up with your 'business' all pressed up behind her would be appropriate." He cracked an eye and spied Grandma standing at the edge of the bed, arms crossed, eyes narrowed.

Smiling, he spoke in a whisper, "Nothing improper,

Grandma; just sleeping."

"Well, they sent me in to tell you lunch is waiting. You've been asleep for about 3 hours. Now, before I kick you out, there's something I want to tell you." When Decker's eyes had cleared from sleep, he pushed up on one elbow to listen to what she had to say.

"Boy, I need you to know that Katie was wrong in demanding promises from you. She and I had a long talk, one she didn't like very much, right before the attack. I know you said she had texted you and asked to come over before that Angela got to her; I want you to know that I believe 100% she was coming over to apologize. Now, *if she would just WAKE UP*, she could apologize in person." Grandma spoke loudly in Katie's ear before speaking to Decker again. "My grand-daughter is a beautiful, smart, strong girl, but even women like us make mistakes, and she made one. Take comfort in knowing she was coming to make things right with you; let her know you want to make things right." Hooking a thumb over her shoulder, she demanded, "Now, get your package out of my Katie's bed and go eat, you look like shit."

SHE WASN'T sure how long she'd laid there in a half-asleep, half-awake dreamland, but she had to smile at the conversa-tions she heard going on around her. She heard heartfelt apologies and promises from Decker, a hilarious diatribe from

Grandma, and jokes and kinds words from the rest of the family. She wanted to open her eyes, but they felt like they were weighted down with sandbags. Maybe she'd keep them closed just a little longer.

SHE WOKE AGAIN, feeling a little less heavy and weighted down, to hear Decker singing to her. She curled into his body and listened to his sleepy voice sing song after song. "Thinking Out Loud" by Ed Sheeran and "You Decorated My Life" by Kenny Rogers were her two favorite; those where 'their' songs. She almost wanted to sleep longer just to hear him sing to her for a little longer.

"I LOVE YOU, TOO, DECKER." Her voice was scratchy, but he heard her as clear as day.

"Hey there, Bug." Kissing her on the mouth, he rested his forehead against hers with a relieved sigh. "You've been asleep for days; I was so worried you were never coming back to me. I love you, Kate. Forever." With assurances to be right back, he left to get a nurse and let the family know she was awake.

THREE WEEKS later

"How's my Katie-girl?" Kendrick asked Decker as they went over some final numbers on the reports in front of them.

"Well, as much as I hate to hear you call her *your* Katie-girl, she's fine. I really do appreciate you taking care of her while I had my head up my ass." Decker smiled at his cousin sheepishly.

"No worries, man. I have to tell you, you're lucky that I'm not her type and vice versa because spending time with her made me realize I sort of miss having a steady girl in my life. Don't get me wrong, I love the buffet of pussy I have going, but that easy, settled, comfortable feeling that Katie and I had while we were away was really nice." Kendrick spoke softly, vulnerably.

Decker watched him with speculative eyes. "It's been a long time since you had a relationship longer than it takes to pull your pants down and put on a condom." He was surprised to see Kendrick look almost embarrassed at those words.

"You deserve to be happy, man. There's a girl out there who can put up with your crass comments and crude words; once you find her, it will be true love." Decker clapped his cousin on the shoulder. "So, just to be sure here, Kate isn't your type at all, right? There's no secret crush going on here?"

Kendrick smiled ruefully, "Nah, man, Kate is a beautiful girl. Fabulous rack, perfect ass, great collection of underwear, but her eyes and heart are only for you." Kendrick gathered up the paperwork he needed to get his coaches hired, and headed out the door.

Decker heard him talking to Kate in the hallway, but he was busy replaying Kendrick's words. He noticed his cousin never denied having a secret crush, he only pointed out that Kate wasn't interested in him. Surely Decker was reading too much into Kendrick's comment. Right?

Decker caught laughter in the hallway and shook from his musings to hear Kate walk into her office from her final doctor's appointment, she laid her bag down and walked straight to his office.

"Hey, Bug. Everything go okay? I'm sorry I couldn't be there." He gingerly touched the back of her head to examine the freshly removed stitches.

"Decker, they snipped some thread from my head, I'm pretty sure I can handle that by myself. Plus, I needed you here to take that conference call; thanks for covering for me. Did anyone notice I was missing?" She wrapped her arms around his neck and breathed deeply at his neck.

"Nah, not really. Well, one person asked how you were doing and Kendrick told them you had diarrhea and wouldn't be joining us today." He chuckled at the look on her face.

"He did not! Oh, that man is going to get it." Forgetting her anger at Kendrick, she nuzzled her nose against his throat and trailed her lips across his jawline.

"Guess what? The doctor said I'm all clear for any activity I'd like to take part in." Smiling seductively at him, she ran her hands down his back and cupped his backside in her hands. "Do you know what activity I'd like to take part in?"

Unable to resist, he gathered her in his arms and kissed her passionately. They'd been able to do a few things in that department over the last few weeks, but the doctors had wanted her to wait until all of her stitches were out and her last CT scan was clear before clearing her for anything too strenuous. And Decker had plans for them to be very *strenuous*.

"Mmmm, I'm thinking your activity ideas are the same as my activity ideas." Running his tongue over her bottom lip, he pulled her bottom flush with him. Feeling the length and heat and solidness of him pressed into her midsection, Katie wasn't sure how they'd wait until tonight.

As if reading her mind, Decker spoke, "Want to eat lunch at home today?" He waggled his eyebrows at her and rubbed himself against her core.

"Decker, it's 10:30 a.m." She giggled.

"It's got to be lunchtime *somewhere*. Come on, let's get out of here. The guys can cover anything we've got planned today; I'll text my dad and Jeremiah too, they can help out if needed. I'm not wasting this whole day waiting to get you in my bed." Grabbing his keys, he walked them through her office to get her bag and then out the door.

"Decker, I've been in your bed for the last three weeks." Katie wasn't really protesting, she wanted to be with him just as much as he wanted her, but she was enjoying giving him a rough time.

"Fine, let me rephrase, I'm not wasting this whole day waiting to get inside of you. Now, let's go." He stopped by Sawyer's office and offered a quick explanation.

"We're heading home for lunch, won't be back in today. Tomorrow is questionable. You're in charge. Let the others know." Quickly closing the door behind him, he heard Sawyer laugh.

"You two have fun! Make him work for it Katie-girl."

DECKER RAN a hot bath and lowered himself down into the soothing water. Positioning herself between his legs, Katie leaned back and let the warmth of the water soak into her. The steam from the warm bath filled the room and she let her head fall back against his chest.

"I know the therapist says it's normal, but there are days I feel guilty and days I feel glad; guilty I took a life, but glad she's out of our life for good." She sighed into his touch and let his whispered words warm her soul.

"Kate, she didn't have a life. She was a sick, miserable person. At one time, she had everything going for her, but something happened to change all of that. If that gun going off hadn't killed her, she would have been locked up in a mental hospital or jail for the rest of her life, and that would have been no life at all. Honestly, even though you didn't intend to kill her, you did her and everyone else a favor. She's out of her misery and we can all breathe easy." He let his hands roam her body as he spoke. She took in the words and their meaning and felt a peace inside her heart.

All too quickly, her peacefulness was replaced by a neediness. Decker's hands continued to caress her body, causing every nerve ending to come to life.

Minutes later, her entire body thrummed with anticipation, and she could feel his arousal pressed against her bottom. Grabbing a towel, they dried off as quickly as possible. Gathering her hair to one side, he stood behind her and gazed at her in the mirror. Kissing her shoulder, he turned her to face him. "In a minute, I'm going to lay you down in my bed, whisper sweet words to you, and make love to you all day long." A long, slow kiss delivered delicious promises. "But right now, I'm going to sit you on this counter, spread your beautiful legs around me, and fuck you until you're screaming my name." Another kiss, this one harder and hotter, "If you're okay with that."

Lifting herself onto the counter, Katie opened her legs to accommodate him standing between them. She rubbed herself against his length and moaned, "Mmm, yeah, I'm more than okay with that." Three weeks without him inside her was three weeks too long; he positioned himself and drove into her with one thrust.

Stopping momentarily to let her adjust, he gripped her

bottom and continued his quick thrusts. Katie wrapped her legs around his waist, her arms around his neck, and held on for the ride. Several more thrusts and her body tightened around him; he drove into her once more and they both moaned through their release.

Cleaning themselves just enough to make it to the bed, Decker hovered above her as she positioned her body to accept his weight.

"Before we do that again, I need to say something." He propped himself on his elbows and stared intently into her eyes. "Kate Turner, you have completely rocked my world. I needed control; I feared I would be lost without it. But you gave me the courage to loosen my grip; instead of being lost, I was found. Letting loose allowed me to live; living allowed me to breathe; breathing allowed me to see. And when I could see, I saw you." Kissing her, lips clinging with emotion, he continued, "You saved me from my black and white existence with your bright colors, you brought light into my world. I promise to spend the rest of my life loving you."

Tears in her eyes, love swelling in her heart, she took his body in with hers and vowed to spend the rest of her life loving him as well.

BONUS CHAPTER

BECKETT AND KENJA

Beckett Jordan had been a precocious charmer for as long as the Deckers and Morgans had known him. He was one of the biggest reasons his father, Jeremiah, married Audrey Decker all those years ago. Beckett had faced many challenges growing up, but he also had practical wisdom and the ability to read a situation and face it head-on that surpassed that of many adults.

It was hard for Audrey and Jeremiah to let Beckett go when he left for college; they wanted to keep him home and sheltered and protected. "Mom, Dad, I'm legally an adult now. I know you want to protect me, but if I live at home forever, I'll never get to experience all that life has to offer, and I'll always wonder what I might be missing. What if there's someone out there that needs me or I need them? I don't plan on being gone forever, but I need to go out there and live." Beckett had chosen a college a couple hours away, partly because it offered the courses he wanted to study and partly because he knew it would ease his dad and Audrey's worries if he was within driving distance.

Within the first week of college, Beckett met Kenja. She was a beautiful, meek, Japanese girl who had escaped a life not worth living in Japan and come to America. The name Kenja meant "wise one, sage," and she was definitely that. Beckett and Kenja clicked as fast friends; they kept each other company, helped each other navigate the new world they were inhabiting, and challenged each other to philosophical debates late into the night.

Their friendship, strong from day one, grew stronger over the next two years. Beckett brought Kenja home for every holiday as she had no family to spend time with. During their third year in college, Beckett began to realize that his feelings for his friend were possibly more than just friendly.

"Dad, remember when I was little and you and Uncle Nate and Uncle Nicky, and even Uncle Kyle, would talk about things having to do with your wives and you'd not want me to hear because I was too little? And remember the really awkward talk you had with me about how babies are made and falling in love and all those life lessons?" Beckett, not usually one to hem-haw, chattered nervously in the garage with his dad over a break from school while Kenja was in the kitchen learning how to make the best darn chocolate sheet cake ever invented.

"Yeah, Beck, I remember all of that." Jeremiah Jordan replied with a smile and a questioning look. "Does this chatter that's so unlike you have a point, son?"

"Well, I think I feel all those love feelings for Kenja, but I don't know if she feels it for me. How do you know if a girl likes you the same way you like her? I've been wanting to kiss her, but what if she doesn't know about kissing or doesn't want me to kiss her? Uhhhh, this stuff is hard, I think I liked it better when I didn't know about any of the things that made all the grownups red in the face." Beckett put his hands on top of his head and paced the garage while his dad watched.

Jeremiah was overcome with memories of a time when

doctors weren't sure Beckett would speak or walk, and now he was asking how he could tell if a girl wanted to kiss him. True, he was about 5 years later on the girl stuff than most kids his age, but that was okay, Beckett had always been his own person.

"Well, son, first I'd say that Kenja must like you quite a bit if she comes home with you every single holiday and break." Jeremiah ticked his first point off on his finger.

"She doesn't have anyone else, what if she just hangs with me because I'm better than nothing?" Beckett, usually so confident, seemed to have a moment of self-doubt.

"Second, since she's always asking Audrey to help her learn how to cook your favorite foods, I'd say she plans on being around long enough to cook meals you like." Jeremiah's second point was harder for Beckett to counter.

"And third, your mom and I have watched the two of you together since the first time you brought her home. That girl is gaga for you; I bet she's wondering just how long it's going to take you to figure out you two are more than friends. I've seen her look at you; it's always with stars in her eyes and absolute adoration." Walking to his son, Jeremiah put a hand on his shoulder. "Beck, talk to her. Let her know how you're feeling. And then just let it go from there. You two are best friends, I'm sure you'll get something figured out. Now, let's go see if that kick-ass cake Kenja is baking is ready."

That evening, Beckett had stumbled around his words, trying to tell Kenja how he felt. Much to his surprise, his beautiful, quiet, wise best friend had placed a finger to his lips and told him to stop speaking. She had leaned in and kissed him, the first for both of them, and smiled as she pulled back. "I like you too, Beckett. I want to be your girlfriend. I've been waiting on you to ask me."

From that point on, Beckett and Kenja were even more inseparable than ever before. The two had gone to school to get their degrees in psychiatry; both had a passion for working with pediatric psychiatric patients. Both Beckett and Kenja had faced numerous struggles in life; both had overcome, but they wanted to help kids who weren't able to overcome as easily.

With their medical degrees, internships, and residencies firmly under their belts, Beckett and Kenja were more than ready to get married. The wedding was a small one compared to many weddings, but it had all the people who mattered the most. Beckett's family, now happily considered Kenja's family as well, and their friends were there to help them celebrate.

Notes

I started writing my first book (For Nicky) in October 2013; I had no clue if I could do it, and even less clue about what to do when I finished it. About halfway through that book, I realized that the mean, terrible sister, Audrey, had a story to tell; I started Because of Beckett as soon as I finished For Nicky.

I had no intention of continuing the Torey Hope Series. However, readers had fallen in love with the stories and they asked for more. I created a heartwarming Christmas novella to lead into the third full-length novel, Loving Josie.

One day, in the shower (where else do great ideas come from?), I realized that the younger generation of Torey Hope had some stories to tell. I ran the idea by readers, and they loved the prospect of continuing the Torey Hope Series. So, voila, Torey Hope: *The Later Years* was born!

One of these days, I'll let the other characters and stories out of my head and create some new books and series; until then, I continue to fall in love with the hearts of my Torey Hope characters in each and every story.

Decker's story is first; his twin brother's story, Sawyer, is already started. The third book I'm planning in this series is Zach's, and then Kendrick will round out the four book series.

Sawyer's story will obviously be a male/male romance, but it will continue in true Torey Hope fashion with real-life issues, contemporary romance, and the love of family and friends.

I want to acknowledge that not all families/friends are as open and accepting of someone's sexuality as Sawyer's friends/family were. If you are in need of help for yourself or a family member/friend, here are some resources:

http://www.glbtnearme.org/
http://www.glbtnationalhelpcenter.org/
http://www.itgetsbetter.org/
http://www.thetrevorproject.org/

If you're interested in where Katie and Decker stayed, here's the link to Cayo Espanto:

http://www.aprivateisland.com/index.html

THANK YOU FOR READING! I hope you enjoyed; please take a moment to leave a review.

A.D. Ellis

Excerpts from other Torey Hope Novels

(THESE BOOKS ARE *the beginning of the Torey Hope books. The parents and grandparents in* Decker *are the main characters in these earlier books.*)

A *Torey Hope Novel Series* starts with For Nicky. Meet and fall in love with Nate and Nicky Morgan, twin brothers. Find For Nicky here: http://bit.ly/NickyAmazon

"Hey, Audrey, what's up? Come in." Audrey smiles, which seems a little fake, and comes on in. She's dressed to the nines as usual. Heels, tight skirt, tighter shirt, hair styled much bigger than you'd think is possible. I can smell her perfume

and hairspray as she walks past me. Who dresses like this for a normal day? Audrey does, obviously. She looks me up and down. "Are you going somewhere, Beth?"

I tell her I have a date. She looks pissed for a moment, then gives me a smile that doesn't even begin to reach her eyes, and says, "Oh, that's nice. Who's the poor shmuck?"

Obviously, she's baiting me, but I don't think quickly enough and I just reply, "Nathaniel Morgan."

Audrey rolls her eyes. "Beth, sweetie, I'm going to try to say this in the nicest/sisterly love type of way. But, Nathan Morgan is way out of your league. You are dressed in a flannel shirt, you might as well wear a sign that says 'frumpy' on the front and 'won't ever get laid' on the back. Nate is an animal in bed, I should know. He needs sex. I doubt you're giving it to him yet. If you ever decide to try sex again, it will probably be as bad as it was with Austin. Not because Nate isn't good, because the good Lord knows that man is G.O.O.D in bed, but there's no way your 'basically a virgin' body can live up to what he's used to. Hell, the boy wore ME out and I have as much experience as he does, if not more. I'm not sure why he's hung around this long. Maybe he sees you as a challenge. Yeah, maybe he's decided to string you along long enough to get in your pants, but, Beth, he's not going to stick around. Nate needs hot sex, a variety of girls, no strings. I don't want you to get hurt when he fucks you and leaves you. Oh, God, Beth, seriously, stop with the teary puppy-dog eyes. I'm just telling you the truth." ~Libby {Beth} Decker in **For Nicky**

The sequel to For Nicky, Because of Beckett (this is Audrey's story and as much as you hate her in For Nicky, you will find yourself liking her in Because of Beckett and you will fall in love with Jeremiah Jordan!) Find Because of Beckett here: http://bit.ly/BeckettAmazon

The one girl he should stay as far away from as possible, the one girl who had made him feel more alive in one evening than he had in several years, the one girl who threatened his well-designed single-dad, good role model position in life was Audrey Decker. Instead of letting her off the hook and planning the party himself, he had practically begged her to stick with it and all but promised her there would be no problems. That was all well and good, he was truly glad she was going to take the party, except for one small problem, he hadn't been able to get her out of his mind; he couldn't stop thinking of those gorgeous blue eyes or her beautiful hair or luscious curves. His heart jumped into his throat when he saw her walking toward the shelter house; his breath hitched in his chest when her hand touched his knee; he wanted to hold her hand and start right back where they had left off the other night. But, they'd agreed that this was a business deal only, so he wouldn't complicate it. They'd get through the party and move on. They were living in the same town; they'd surely see each other. Jeremiah was determined to keep things cool between them so that the party would be a success and they could be friendly toward each other in social settings.

And then, he watched her eyes light up as she knelt down and opened her arms to Beckett. He was gone; hook, line, sinker. Audrey didn't strike him as the type to be particularly caring towards anyone, let alone a child with special needs. But, there she was, on her knees, hugging his son... How was it, the woman he had just promised he wouldn't pursue, was on the ground hugging his child like his real mother never had? Jeremiah's gut clenched at the thought. He wanted this woman in his life. But, she'd made it clear that she wasn't interested and Jeremiah wondered if he had lost his chance to indicate any interest. So, he decided he'd have to settle for having her in his life as a friend. ~Jeremiah Jordan in **Because of Beckett**

The families celebrate the holidays in <u>Christmas in Torey Hope, A Novella</u>. Love and family and friendship abounds and readers get to learn of the older couples' love stories. Find <u>Christmas   in   Torey   Hope</u>   here: http://bit.ly/ChristmasAmazon

"Libby-girl, you never cease to amaze me. That was amazing." He kissed her and they proceeded to clean up and redress. *"Now, we better get back to the house before everyone knows what I've been doing to you."* Nate winked.

Libby's cheeks blushed but she said, "Nate, I'm pretty sure this is exactly what your mom had in mind when she sent us away for a bit."

"Well then, I'll have to sincerely thank my momma!" Nate

kissed her lips as they headed back out the door, locking it soundly behind them.

"UH, Mom, I'm all for reminiscing and I know you and Dad love each other, but could we please keep it G-rated. For the love of all that is good, please don't make me listen to sex stories involving you two." Jeremiah shuddered but smiled good-naturedly at his mother.

"What? We all had to see you and Audrey and Nate and Libby come in here glowing after your little 45 minute romp; I think a little steamy romance story about your dad and I would serve you right." Judy laughed at her son's expression. "Don't worry, I'll keep it clean." The whole group laughed at Jeremiah's visible relief.

BEFORE THE STORY could get started, Nate cleared his throat and said, "Mom, Dad, let's keep in mind that I've walked in on the two of you in some compromising positions that are now burned into my delicate mind; please don't add anymore trauma to my already scarred psyche." Everyone laughed at Nate's statement. "You all think I'm joking but I'm really not.

You don't know the images that still float through my mind." Nate teased his parents and pulled Libby against him as they settled onto one of the couches.

Loving Josie is a story of second chance love for two lost souls. This is a standalone novel in *A Torey Hope Novel Series*, so you can read it without reading the first books. Find Loving Josie here: http://bit.ly/LovingJosieAmazon

"What the hell are you thinking, Josie Decker?" This from Audrey. She continued, "I just left my house after calling in my reinforcements here. Did you know Kyle's over at my house talking to Jeremiah? He's all dressed up, pierced up, tatted up, bleached up, and styled up. Do you know why? He's got a date. Oh, but that's right, you already knew he had a date, didn't you?!"

When I didn't respond, because I wasn't sure if this was a rhetorical question or not, she powered on. "It was bad enough when you bought a house with the man. But now you're going to 'pretend date' him?! This isn't a good thing, Josie. If he weren't so fucked up, I would be cheering you on. And, honestly, I think dating you would be truly good for him. But, he's so damn stubborn, I worry he'll never let go of the notion that he can't love you the way you deserve and, in the end, you're going to end up being hurt." ~Josie Decker in **Loving Josie**

Turning me around he tipped my chin up, "We need to

talk, Jo. Some things have changed. No more practice dating. No more stopping kisses and pretending they shouldn't happen. I want to see more than my ink on you; I want to see me on you." With that final comment he brought his mouth down on mine. This kiss was different than all of the others had been. This kiss was all Kyle, he was holding nothing back.

*~Josie Decker in **Loving Josie***

CHERRY PIE RECIPE

THIS RECIPE COMES from the 1971 Better Homes and Gardens cookbook and has been used by the author's mother for almost 40 years.

Pastry crust:

2 cups sifted all-purpose flour

1 tsp salt

2/3 cup shortening (author's mom uses lard instead and it's much better!)

5-7 tbsp ICE cold water

Sift flour and salt together; cut in shortening with pastry blender till pieces are the size of small peas.

Sprinkle 1 tbsp water over part of the mixture.

Gently toss with fork; push to side of bowl. Repeat until all is moistened.

Form into a ball for each pie

Flatten on lightly floured surface by pressing with edge of hand 3 times in both directions.

Roll from center to edge til 1/8 inch thick

Fit pastry into pie plate, trim ½ to 1 inch beyond edge

This is a lattice top pie, to make the lattice top:

Roll remaining dough out

Cut strips of pastry ½ to ¾ inch wide with knife

Lay strips on filled pie at 1-inch intervals

Fold back alternating strips as you weave cross strips

Trim lattice even with outer rim of pie plate, fold lower crust over lattice strips and

pinch/flute the edges

Cherry Pie Filling

¾ cup juice from cherries

1 cup sugar

2 TBSP quick-cooking tapioca

3 cups canned pitted tart red cherries (water pack)

3-4 drops almond extract

1 bottom pastry, 1 lattice top pastry

1 TBSP butter

BAKE at 400 degrees for 50-55 minutes.

ACKNOWLEDGMENTS

This is always one of the hardest parts of finishing a book, but quite possibly the most important part! It's so hard because I fear I'll miss someone who has helped me out, supported me, been a listening ear, or offered advice and encouragement. If I miss listing your name here, please know it wasn't on purpose and I love you dearly!

To my editor, Stephanne, thank you from the bottom of my heart for your sharp eyes and professionalism. You were a gift to me over 9 years ago, and you continue to be a blessing.

To my friend, fellow author, and cover designer, Andrea Michelle at Artistry in Design. Thank you for taking my vision and bringing it to life through your design. I love you!

To my dear beta readers. We've grown in numbers recently, but all of your input and feedback and encouragement has proven invaluable to me! I truly trust you all and value your opinions more than you'll probably ever understand.

To my street team/pimpers. Those of you who list me in contests and comments and shout outs all the time, you're amazing and I love you for always working to get my name out there! If I start naming people here, I'll be sure to miss some; just know if you've ever shared my name or my books, it means the world to me and I appreciate you more than you'll ever know!

To my READERS!! Without you, there would have never been a third book, let alone a fifth book! Thank you for loving Torey Hope and the characters as much as I do; knowing you are looking forward to another book is a lot of what keeps me writing some days. As long as these stories are in my head, I'll keep sharing them with you.

To the BLOGGERS who read and review and share my books!! You are beyond a shadow of a doubt some of the most dedicated and selfless people I've ever known! Thank you so much for being such a support to those of us who have stories to tell. I love BLOGGERS!

To my girls at The Indie Erogenous Zone. You are beyond fellow authors, you're my support, my heart, my friends. There have been days I wanted to give up, but I had you to turn to; days when a bad review breaks my heart, but I talk it out with you. I truly consider you all my close friends and I wouldn't want to be facing this crazy journey without you! IEZ4Life! T&F girls!

To my Juice Box ladies! Thank you so much for welcoming me into your crew and sharing your knowledge, experience, advice, and fun with me! Having some real-life authors/friends I can collaborate with is a great feeling. Dance parties, lunches, movies, videos, wine, pizza...the list goes on and on! Thank you for letting me a Juice Boxer!

To my fellow authors. Those of you who read my work, share your work with me, cross-promote with me, and offer advice and support, THANK YOU! You make this a little easier and enjoyable.

A new addition to my acknowledgments list on this book: Brett. Your momma is one of my favorite readers and I lucked out when she introduced me to you! Your input on this book was beyond valuable. Every time I logged on to chat with you I found myself with a huge smile on my face because you're such a great guy and so very fun to talk to! Thank you for answering my questions and reading my work.

To my family and friends. I know most of you don't understand my obsession with getting these stories out of my head and on paper, but you're proud of me either way. Some of you get to read my books, some of you get to see cover ideas, some of you have to watch me lose myself in a story, some of you have to hear me vent about the hard parts of all of this; all of you love me and support me and for that, I am truly lucky and grateful.

Songs

This is the song that Decker dedicated to Kate at the wedding. It's an old one and not everyone is a fan of Kenny Rogers, but the lyrics were just too perfect to pass it up. "You Decorated My Life" by Kenny Rogers.

You can find it here: https://www.youtube.com/watch?v=2W7gp47OT_Q

Here are the other songs they danced to at the wedding:

Ed Sheeran Thinking Out Loud https://youtu.be/lp-EO5I6oKA

Olly Murs Dance With Me Tonight https://youtu.be/F3EG4olrFjY

Walk the Moon Shut Up and Dance https://youtu.be/6JCLYoRlx6Q

You can find A.D. Ellis' playlists for all of her books on Spotify.

ABOUT THE AUTHOR

A.D. Ellis is the author of A Torey Hope Novel Series. Her 2014 debut novel, For Nicky, was voted #3 of the Top 50 Indie Books of 2014 by ReadFree.ly readers/voters. She is a member of the Romance Writers of America and the Indiana Romance Writers of America.

A.D. was born and raised in a small farming town in southern Indiana. An avid reader from the time she learned to read, A.D. could often be found curled up somewhere with her nose in a book. Most of her friends and family were not such book enthusiasts, so A.D. got used to dealing with snickers and joking comments about her constant reading habits.

A.D. always dreamed of being a teacher. Graduating from Indiana State University in 1999 and earning a Master's Degree from Indiana Wesleyan in 2003, she met her goal of entering the world of education. A.D. has been teaching in the inner city of Indianapolis, Indiana for 16 years; most of her years of experience have been in 3rd, 4th, or 5th grade. A.D. loves teaching fractions, variables, probability, and graphing in Math. She loves almost all aspects of English Language Arts. Figurative language, theme, making predictions, drawing conclusions, inference, context clues, making writing come to life, A.D. loves it all! Her students don't always share in that enthusiasm.

A.D. met her husband in college in 1996 and they married in June of 2000. She lives in a south side suburb of Indianapolis, Indiana with her husband and two school-aged children. When she's not reading or writing with music blaring, she can be found shopping at thrift stores, reading to her children, and sweating at the gym.

A.D. began her writing journey in October 2013; she is grateful for the friends and support she's found along the way.

Please connect with A.D. Ellis on Facebook. www.facebook.com/adellisauthor

Find A.D.'s author page on Amazon at www.amazon.com/author/adellis